Sue & Stu - A Diary of Two

STEPHEN PURCELL

pendletonpress.co.uk

In memory of Christina Sexton

Stuart (Saturday, February 14th)

It is now 7:40 am Sunday and I'm officially in love. Again! I first fell in love when I was 7 years old. Her name was Linda Lee, better known as Supergirl, or the actress Helen Slater to most. I bugged my parents to buy the home video version of *Supergirl* for quite some time. When they eventually caved in, I would watch that thing over and over, and to this day could probably recite it word for word.

Tonight, I encountered the most beautiful girl I have ever seen while having a few drinks at The Barge with Charlie, Maggie and her friend Cora. For the first hour, the table to my right had been empty, but in the time it took me to get another round of drinks and some cigarettes from the machine it became occupied by what I can only describe as a young Kim Gordon lookalike, sipping on an ice-cool cider with her friend.

Question... Does asking for a light (I should state, asking me directly, as opposed to the table at large) on three separate occasions constitute flirting? It's been so long I forget what the protocol is. Either way, Kim Gordon Jnr did just that and on the third occasion, I had to take some initiative so I handed her the lighter and said, 'Here, you can have it.' The blow-in beauty paused, smirked, held the lighter in her hand for a few seconds and replied, 'No, no, it's OK, but thank you. I appreciate it.' She handed back the lighter. 'Fair enough,' muttered Charlie under his breath. It sounded like Charlie was having a dig. I'm not sure if the girl heard him or not but she made a break back to her seat. While I tried my best not to make it too obvious, I couldn't help myself from looking her way for the next hour or so. That was of course

1

until this Kim Gordon-like stunner and her friend got up to leave. Many thoughts ran through my head…

Go over to her!

Get her number!

Ask her where she's headed.

Give her your lighter and don't take no for an answer.

Tell the lads that you'll meet them later and just walk with her.

After downing the remnants of the bottle and packing her belongings, Kim Gordon Jnr (that will be her name from here), accompanied by her friend, up and left. My heart sank. After several steps, she turned around, smiled at me and then disappeared into the night. Gone! Just like that. I'm an absolute idiot for not saying anything, but I didn't want to come across as creepy. On top of that, Charlie said that it looked like I was partnered with Maggie due to the unplanned seating arrangement at our table. 'We looked like two couples, man. It's no wonder she didn't take the lighter,' said Charlie in the cab home. That hadn't even crossed my mind. He was 100% right; Maggie and I laughing and joking on one side of the table, Cora and Charlie doing the same on the other… of course, we looked like two couples.

Suzanne (Saturday, February 14th)

Dear Diary, Dearest, my saving grace…

Too drnk to write… lost ny handbagg.

Stuart (Sunday, February 15th)

I got out of bed at 6 pm this evening. Shocking! My head was still pounding from last night and no matter how hard I've tried I can't get

Kim Gordon Jnr out of my head. I keep replaying those events at The Barge. I mean, why would she ask me for a light that many times? I'm beginning to think Charlie is wrong about the whole couple thing. Surely, she caught me looking at her all night. I felt she was looking at me too. I don't know what to think now, my mind is going crazy!

Tony and Rodge's band Satan's Arse got a spin on national radio tonight. Judging by the excitement in our group chat, the two lads are over the moon! I'm happy for them both, they certainly put in the work.

Dad called to say he has accumulated €1500 of the €2000 needed for his skydive. He also said Gummy has agreed to join him as he wants to celebrate his 95th birthday in style. Dad said Gummy has pulled in €4500. That's over twice the target fee. Fair play to Gummy! I'm over 50 years younger and I could never bring myself to jump out of a plane.

Suzanne (Sunday, February 15th)

Dear Diary,

That's it!!! I'm officially done with alcohol. This hangover is almost death-like (not that I know what death is like), but yeah, I am destroyed! The end of last night is a complete blur and I have no idea how I got home. From the mess that greeted me on the kitchen table this morning, it looks like we made a stop at Fabkebab. Ugghhhh, just the thought of it... To make matters worse, my new shoes are covered in vomit and my handbag is nowhere to be seen. I just searched the entire house. I texted Fi asking her what happened, but I haven't heard back. That was my favourite handbag! Grrrrrrrr! It's a good thing I kept my wallet and my phone in my pocket. The thoughts of cancelling cards on a day like today would be way too much. The last thing I can remember is an

American family asking me to take a picture of them by the fountain/statue thing outside the kebab shop. I have no idea where we ended up after that. What I do remember was enjoyable though. We started at Resolute (full of rugby knobs) and then went to The Barge, which was mobbed but very chill. There, I bumped into some of the girls from Uppercuts (the new men's hair salon run by the Reeves brothers), they were on a wild one. They're all flying out to Greece for a week tomorrow. God help the people of Santorini. From there we made our way to The Townhouse where we started on the shots. I'm not so sure what happened after that.

2:10 am – I'm getting a flashback of dancing on the tables in Club Vista. Good, God! Club Vista, of all the shitholes we could have ended up in, really, that would be at the top of the list. Those green shots did us in. I think the barman called them lightning bolts.

Stuart (Monday, February 16th)

It appears Trish has confirmed an in-store gig with The Pogo Stix for Thursday afternoon as they are also booked to play The Plex Thursday night. Hopefully, this in-store isn't as bad as the Stina Hordes album launch last year. I'm still scundered for mistakenly ordering twenty copies of Tina Horde the uilleann pipe players' record, as opposed to Stina Hordes the upcoming singer/songwriter's record. As soon as Stina arrived on set she got tore into Trish and me, yelling, 'How can I promote a fookin' album if ye don't have the bastarding thing in stock?' Fair point. Over on the makeshift stage, it all started to go downhill. Stina sparked up a cigarette, threw her hat down for tips and began her protest, 'I'm not playing anything from me bleedin' record because that dickhead over there forgot to stock the fookin' thing.' The small crowd that had gathered to see Stina perform started to boo. Stina continued, 'I'm gonna play you a few John Lennon songs instead, and if ye don't like it, ye can all fuck off!!' The crowd whistled and hollered, encouraging her teenage angst. When Stina got to the closing bars of her song 'Give Peace a Chance,' I aimed and fired what was left of my cigarettes into her tip-hat in an attempted truce. She didn't look too impressed. Great album though!

I bumped into Tony from Satan's Arse in that new smoothie cafe, Milky Moo's. He said they have a gig at The Plex Saturday week and that the head of some UK record company was flying over to see them. I congratulated him and told him we'd all be down to lend our support. As I was up that way, I popped in to see Maggie after work, but the burly butcher (whose name escapes me) informed me it was her day off. I still get the feeling that guy doesn't like me. Me! A regular customer! If anything, he should be grateful for his regulars, as I am with mine... most of them anyway. Weird vibes aside, I took a chance on his new Mexican wraps. Four for five quid. Burnt lip aside, they weren't half bad.

Suzanne (Monday, February 16th)

Dear Diary,

I have booked Mr Snuggles into the vet as I'm getting a little concerned about his weight. He lost his footing coming down the stairs again and ended up colliding with the hall window and cracking the glass in the process. That's the second collision in less than a week.

Mum popped into the salon on her lunch break today. She said that Davey Rocket (a regular client at the salon, and a black belt in bullshit) asked her out to dinner this coming Saturday. He claims to be an Event Promotion Manager, and I didn't have the heart to tell her otherwise. I'll never forget the time Fi knocked his briefcase over, spilling the contents (a bunch of old newspapers) all over the salon floor. I can't tell my mother that Rocket is a dickhead. Her teenage lust for him is infectious!

I want to stay up and watch this TV documentary *The Dusty Tunnel* about a section of the New York Underground that has remained unused for many years. I love everything and anything to do with New York and it is my duty and honour to the United States of America, one nation, under God, indivisible, with liberty and justice for all, to return there one day. The thought of Davey Rocket and my mother going at it just brought up a little bit of puke in my mouth.

Stuart (Tuesday, February 17th)

Good God, what a day! It was pissing rain when I finished work, so I decided to take the bus home. I was no sooner seated when out of the corner of my eye I spotted her outside. There she was, the girl from The Barge last weekend – Kim Gordon Jnr!!! She was wearing the same light black summer dress with the butterflies dotted all over. She was saturated wet and battling the onslaught of rain as she sprinted towards the pedestrian crossing at Loftus and James Street. I leapt out of my seat and ran down the aisle of the bus. 'I need to get off,' I said to the driver and he opened the door.

As the rain blasted against my skin, I took a look around to see if I could spot her. She had crossed the road, but I couldn't see where she went so, I made a break for the pedestrian crossing. The traffic from Lower Loftus Street was coming thick and fast and that bastard of a red man was in no hurry to turn green. Finally, after what seemed like an eternity, there was a break in traffic. I made a break towards Topshop.

At this stage, I had lost sight of where she had gone. I had two options, it was either into Topshop or the adjacent Bershka. I opted for Topshop. The security chap at the door gave me a smirk. He could see that I was flustered and out of breath. He made his way over, 'What does she look like, pal?' I stumbled, 'How? Ah.... right... blonde hair to about here,' I put my hand to my shoulder to signal Kim Gordon Jnr's hair length and continued, 'Black dress with a–' He cut me off... 'Bershka, mate, next door.' I responded, 'You're a lifesaver,' before bolting out the door and colliding with a chap in a wheelchair. Unfortunately, I knocked both him and his wheelchair over. After what seemed like 20 mins of being cursed out of it by everyone on the street, I made a break for Bershka.

Prowling through the ground floor of Bershka, the stench of perfume was overwhelming. I caught a glimpse of myself in one of the store mirrors. I looked like shit. There was sweat pouring down my face, my clothes were soaked, and my right arm was covered in blood after colliding with the chap in the wheelchair. I had to pull my sleeve down to hide the damage as I'm sure I looked like an absolute maniac. Maybe I am a maniac? Anyway, the store was wall-to-wall women and I felt like I was playing a real-life version of the classic board game Guess Who? I regained my focus, zeroing in on the blondes. There weren't many. 'Fuck,' I accidentally said out loud. 'Did you lose something?' said a young girl passing. I replied, 'No, no... I just forgot to grab something earlier.' The young girl replied, 'Put it in your phone, I do it all the time'. She smiled and walked away. Why can't all women be that nice? With no sign of Kim Gordon Jnr, I took the escalator to the first floor.

On the first floor, the scent of perfume had now been replaced by the scent of leather; jackets, bags, boots, you name it. Again, I scanned the floor. There she was! Kim Gordon Jnr! I couldn't believe my eyes. I made my way across the shop and stood behind her. Her right arm was on autopilot, skimming through a rack of reduced shirts. I tapped her on the shoulder and said, 'Need a light?' She hung up the shirt she was holding, turned around and said, 'I'm good, thanks.' She looked like she had gone 12 rounds with Muhammad Ali. She had even developed a boxer's nose since our epic encounter at The Barge. I must have been a lot drunker that night than I thought. Then it hit me, it wasn't her!

Moments later I was smoking a ciggy and gathering my thoughts on the street. 'Any luck, pal?' It was the security guy from Topshop. I replied, 'Wrong one.' He nodded, scrunching his features into a face that somehow expressed sympathy and called me an asshole all at the same time.

Suzanne (Tuesday, February 17th)

Dear Diary,

Mum, bless her heart, really is tough work. First, it was her choice of clothes for her date with Davey (nothing in the briefcase) Rocket, or 'Mr Rocket' as she refers to him. Fifty minutes later and she was back on the phone looking for advice on waxing. Yes, my mother wanted advice on waxing. But Diary, it gets worse. I was halfway through a bridal brigade when Fi walked over to me with the phone in her hand. 'It's your mum, it's an emergency.' Fi (unaware this was Mum's third call to the salon) looked like she had seen a ghost. 'Sue, your mum said she needs an ambulance and quick.' Fi wasn't one for pulling jokes. I grabbed the phone in a panic and asked Mum if she was OK? 'HONEY, I NEED AN AMBULANCE!!' shouted Mum. 'I'm stuck, I can't move,' she added. I was confused and asked her where she was stuck? 'It's the wax, Honey, I forgot to read the instructions before applying it. I'm stuck to the fucking bath,' replied Mum. With little deliberation, I made my way over to Mum's house. There, I tried everything from baby oil to hot water, but Mum wouldn't budge. After two hours of pulling my hair out (no pun intended), I was left with no choice but to call Mr Grimble from next door. By 8:30 pm, Mr and Mrs Grimble, two of the students who rent the house across the street and the delivery driver from Pizza Pizza & Pizza, had done everything they could to free my mother from the tub. If it wasn't for Mr Rocket and his shovel, she'd still be there. I hope Mum and Mr Rocket's date isn't as catastrophic tonight.

My head was melted with all the commotion, so, to cheer myself up, I ordered a new fridge! As you do. No longer will the sight of that pickle jar send me into a whirlwind of frustration. Yes, the same pickle jar that I've been writing about for almost three years. Multiple unscathed attempts at removing the jar have been unsuccessful. I feel sorry for it at times, sitting there encased in ice and frozen in time. I wouldn't feel so bad if it had frozen in the freezer section, but the fridge? What next? Frozen tomatoes? Frozen eggs? Frozen salsa? Life doesn't warrant such complications. Speaking of... I hope the size doesn't become an issue when installing this thing. I didn't do any sort of measuring or planning. Let's hope it's a one-size-fits-all type of situation. I did contemplate going next door to ask Mr Grimble if he had a measuring tape, and whether or not one size fits all. I am thankful for the procrastination station in retrospect.

Stuart (Wednesday, February 18th)

Being fascinated with a butcher and a girl that asked me for a light on three occasions is tough going. One minute I'm fantasising about undoing the pins from Maggie's hairnet, the next minute I'm fantasising about zipping down that black butterfly dress as worn by Kim (the girl from The Barge) Gordon Jnr. Today, these difficult times were softened by the sounds of Neil Young's - *Harvest*. Neil's take on love is spot on, 'Only love can break your heart.'

Both Charlie and Maggie called this afternoon. Charlie picked up a few records (including a copy of *'Adventure'* by Television; better than their *'Marquee Moon'* album in my opinion and some old soul jazz reissues) as I recalled yesterday's events to Maggie. Maggie said I need to be careful as these types of, 'cold approaches' could get me in a lot of trouble. I asked Maggie what the alternative to a 'cold approach' might be and she was stumped.

Suzanne (Wednesday, February 18th)

Dear Diary,

I had to take today off because the fridge was being delivered and Mr Snuggles had an appointment with the vet. The guy who delivered the fridge was very charming. I'll probably live to regret this but after a bit of flirty banter, I stupidly agreed to give him my number. 'Here, a little present for you,' he whispered, holding out two fridge magnets as thank you of sorts. One had a picture of an ice cube saying, "I used to be cool." The other was a picture of a fridge with a smiley face that said, "It's what's inside that counts." The world could do with more gentlemen.

The vet reckons Mr Snuggles is overweight and that I'm feeding him too much. I blame Mum and her selection of meat she brings to feed 'the poor Snuggle-Monster.' When Mum called, I told her what the vet had said. Mum said, 'That cat was a bag of bones, he needed a good feed. Take no notice of that vet. What did he suggest? Hold on, let me guess, a gluten-free/vegan diet? It's a cat, Sue.' Mum's disdain for the vet is at an all-time high since he administered the shot that put Bonzo down. That image of Mum strangling the vet in the veterinary clinic will always haunt me.

Speaking of, I spent the best part of the afternoon consoling Mum yet again. The poor thing never seems to get a break. She called me in tears to say that her date with Mr Rocket was, and I quote, 'the most embarrassing night of my life.' According to Mum, all four of Mr Rocket's credit cards were declined. Mum ended up covering the bill, €200 for 2 x four-course meals and 2 x bottles of wine. Mr Rocket, what a goof!! I wanted to tell Mum what I think of him, but it would probably break her heart. Instead, I decided to give him a second chance. If he messes up again, he's done!

11:14 pm

A text message from Mum:

"Sue, darling, I'm sorry I haven't been in touch. My sleeping patterns are all over the place because of the medication. I put my back out doing some tantric exercises with Mr Stewart. Do call over tomorrow, miss you loads xxx."

Stuart (Thursday, February 19th)

Browsing through a bunch of used records at work, I stumbled upon the Suzi Quatro album *If you knew Suzi...* in mint condition. I asked myself, 'How well should I know Suzi?' I'm familiar with *"Can the Can"*, but other than that I don't really know Suzi at all. Regardless, I couldn't help but fawn over the album sleeve. I wasn't sure if it was the look of innocence in her eyes or that striking pose; Suzi sitting comfortably, holding her hair back to reveal a coyote-tooth earring. I was trying to picture Maggie on the cover of the Suzi Quatro album. Instead, the album was called *If you knew Maggie.* I imagined her sitting there in her butchers' uniform, holding her hair back to reveal her sleeper earrings. I wouldn't even question the purchase if I stumbled upon it at Reality Records.

I met Charlie for lunch. He had been speaking with Maggie early this morning. Maggie had asked if I was still harping on about my 'future wife?' She also told Charlie that I was, 'doing her head in,' on Saturday night. Charlie reckons Maggie is jealous. I don't believe that for a second. Maggie just thinks of me as a good friend. I think she feels sorry for me at times. That was the only reason she gave me those lamb hearts on Valentine's Day. Me, on the other hand, I used to have genuine feelings for her, but Maggie never seemed interested. Every time we went for a drink, Cora had to tag along as a safety net. Every time I asked her to go for some dinner, she used Patryk as an excuse not to go. He's 16 for crying out loud! Surely, he is capable of cooking something? For what it's worth, I don't think Maggie will ever get used to being widowed. Getting over Ulrich is going to take a lot more time. And besides I have a new love interest and I am certain she is the one!!!

Suzanne (Thursday, February 19th)

Dear Diary,

It's official. I am going on a date! Reluctantly I might add.

I was in the market getting some meat and veg when someone came from behind and put their hands over my eyes. 'Guess who?' I couldn't quite grasp the voice. 'Ah Jesus, I replied.' 'Nope, I'm not Jesus,' said the voice. It sounded like Fi's ex, Paulie. I replied, 'Paulie, come on, stop playing around.' 'Oooooooh, Paulie eh? It sounds like I've got some competition,' said the voice. He removed his hands from my face, and I turned around. It was Eric Reeves, the owner of Uppercuts. 'Eric, what are you like?' I said. 'I never see you out,' he replied, 'I just had to seize the opportunity while you were there.' Without missing a beat Eric continued, 'I want to take you out to dinner. Will you join me?' I was speechless. Eric is pretty hot, and to be honest, way out of my league. I had to play it cool, 'I've got a lot on this week.' Eric replied, 'Like what?' I was stuck for an answer, 'I've got to pay the bills, return some books to the library...' He put his finger on my lips, 'Shhh, relax, you can do all of that shit in the afternoon.' I admired his confidence. Eric continued, 'I think you're trying to give me the cold shoulder?' I said nothing. 'Well? Are you?' he insisted. I was. I don't know why really? Why do us women always play hard to get? Eric looked me dead in the eyes and said,

'Saturday night, 8 pm, I'll meet you outside the bank on James St. You in?' He wasn't taking no for an answer. 'OK, thanks,' I replied; speaking before thinking like I always seem to do. He made me put his number in my phone and told me to ring him if something came up. This is happening!

11:10 pm

I just received a text message. It was unsigned, but for what it's worth, it reads:

"Karen, I can't stop thinking bout Fri nite. I still have a horn from ya. D'ya fancy another round dis wknd? Bumba, Bumba, samba, samba lolz ;)"

Stuart (Friday, February 20th)

I met Maggie for lunch, she looked great! I found it tough to concentrate on eating my chicken fillets as Maggie's low-cut top was showing an ample amount of cleavage for a Tuesday lunchtime. I have to admit; Maggie seemed a little off today. I think Patryk's behaviour at school is wreaking havoc with her wellbeing as he was sent home yesterday for a blackboard drawing of his Religion teacher fucking his principal up the arse. We had a good laugh at the picture they sent Maggie as evidence. Maggie then asked me if I fancied going for a bite tomorrow night, 'Nothing too fancy,' as she put it. I recommended the new Asian restaurant Po-Ho. The prices listed on the ad in the *Rockwood Chronicle* looked reasonable and those stock pictures had me foaming at the mouth. Tonight, much like most Friday nights, it's just me, Paul McCartney's *Ram* LP and a nice bottle of Chilean red. There's a lot to be said for the simple life.

The occupants of the apartment above me are making a racket again, the girl is screaming in what sounds like French – 'Blue fart! Blue fart'. God only knows what they're up to.

Suzanne (Friday, February 20th)

Dear Diary,

Both Mum and Mr Rocket arrived at the salon without notice this morning. Mum wanted to know if I would like to join them for lunch. I'm not quite sure what to make of Mr Rocket. I could tell Mum was aware of his wandering eyes, and I can 100% vouch for his obvious-as-day innuendos. You'd swear he's never seen somebody eating corn on the cob. As for the noise he makes whilst eating, even the people sitting beside us looked awkward. Oh, and I almost forgot, I am not a 'child,' so the next time he insists on referring to me as one, I will be sure to call him out. Credit where credit is due though, Mr Rocket did foot the bill. Thankfully (more so for Mum's sake) his credit was in order this time 'round.

I can't believe I'm going on a date with Eric Reeves of all people. The girls didn't believe when I told them this morning. Siobhan went as far as calling the number he gave me, just to see if it was him. He picked up and answered by name. I hope Siobhan blocked her number, I'm not so sure if I'd trust Eric just yet.

Poor Mr Snuggles nearly killed himself trying to greet me after work. He came scrambling down the stairs as usual but lost his footing and went headfirst into the hall window. I think I need to change his diet as he's not as fit as he used to be.

Stuart (Saturday, February 21st)

It's 10:40 am Sunday and I've just returned from spending the night in Maggie's place. Oh boy, what a night!

We met as planned at Po-Ho for 9 pm. Due to my lack of pre-booking, the waiter sat us by the door on the ground floor. I knew Maggie wasn't happy with the seats as she was giving me that pissed off/half-smile thing she does for a bit. A girl that works with Maggie had advised her to book seats on the top floor as the view is supposed to be, 'unreal.' The waiter seemed to confirm this by calling it, 'very magic', when we asked for (but were refused) a seat upstairs. For the record, is there anything more frightening than a hungry/pissed off woman? I don't know if there is. After we were done with the starters (Meat Sung Lettuce Cups for Maggie and Chi-Chi Chicken Skewers on my side) Maggie's pissed off smile had evolved into her natural smile; the wine, a blessing as always. We were both in agreement that Po-Ho was worthy of its reputation thus far and assured the waiter that we will book in advance next time 'round. I asked Maggie if she wanted to go upstairs for a look at the view, but she said she was, 'hanging for a smoke.'

Outside, Maggie suggested a drink at The Barge. I knew where this was going. She was putting me through the ultimate 'shit test.' Maggie knew how infatuated I had become with the girl (Kim Gordon Jnr) I met there last week. I also knew Maggie had been talking to Charlie, asking him if I was still talking about her. Now she was going to put me through the ultimate test. Would I accompany Maggie to The Barge or make some excuse to go somewhere else? I didn't get a chance to think about it. Maggie grabbed my arm, interlinked it with hers and ushered me away from the front of the restaurant.

As we wound through the streets, my bloodshot and blurry eyes were on overdrive. What if I did see the girl from The Barge? Would that be it? Would the one opportunity to make her my potential wife be squandered forever? I had no choice, I had to go with it. Onwards we went.

By the time we got to The Barge, my mouth had dried up and I was a nervous wreck. I looked over to where we were seated last weekend. Our table was empty. So, too, the table that had been occupied by my lighter-seeking beauty. Maggie pointed at the seats, 'Those seats were pretty comfy last week, we had the heaters and all.' Petrified of what could potentially happen, I had no choice but to agree. I took a seat and waited for Maggie to get the next round of drinks. My mind was racing as my hands fidgeted with the remaining coins I'd been too tight to tip with at Po-Ho. Making myself comfortable, I began emptying the contents of my pockets on the table, my phone, my wallet, my cigarettes and my yellow lighter. Yup, the same light that had been gripped by that warm and beautiful hand. The same light that could have spent the last week in her presence; joining her for breakfast, lunch, dinner, bath time… well, maybe not. As I scanned the surrounding area looking for any glimpse of my future wife, Maggie returned. 'Nippy isn't it?' she giggled, as she handed me two of the four bottles of cider she was holding. I was fucking freezing, but I had to show my manliness, 'You'll be fine,' I replied.

The night continued, and so too the alcohol. Maggie completely opened up about Ulrich and his untimely passing, the day they got married, and the difficulties of raising Patryk as a single mother. At that stage, I had forgotten about the girl from last week and was enjoying the honesty and openness of our conversation, even if the bar had stopped serving. It was probably for the better as we were both tanked. With a mutual case of the munchies, we decided to grab a burger.

Arm and arm, we made our way down Main St to flag down a taxi. We were happy as Larry, munching away like two brazen school kids, roaming the town on their own for the first time. Fortunately, we didn't have to wait too long as a black Mercedes E Class pulled in to pick us up. 'Sycamore Close, please. Just the one stop,' Maggie informed the driver. 'Sure thing,' he replied. I couldn't quite comprehend what was happening, Maggie was bringing me back to her house. Was I still being subject to the 'shit test,' or was this the moment? The moment I had dreamed of for quite some time.

Back at the house, Maggie arrived in the living room with two glasses of red wine. She bent down and put *Led Zeppelin IV* on the record player. In doing so I caught a glimpse of a Rolling Stones tongue logo tattooed on her back. I had never seen that before. I had to say it, 'You're pretty rock n' roll for a butcher.' As she sat on the floor, attempting without success to get the stylus to fall at the start of 'Misty Mountain Hop,' I decided to join her. 'Here, let me try it,' I said, landing on the song on my first attempt. As the sound of John Bonham's drums filled the room, Maggie turned to me and smiled. She took the glass out of my hand, and before I knew it, we were on the couch tangled in a passionate embrace. When the record reached the end of side A, the sound of silence seemed to be too much for Maggie. The exciting and carefree ways of Zeppelin had now been replaced by the cold silent room; a setting Maggie had become all too familiar with since Ulrich's untimely passing. 'I'm sorry, Stu,' Maggie made a break upstairs. I assumed she had gone to bed, but moments later she was back in the living room armed with a blanket. 'Shove over,' she said, joining me on the couch and covering us both with the blanket.

I woke up about an hour ago and decided to head home. Maggie was still sleeping, or at least she did a good job of pretending she was still sleeping. I'm not sure either of us is prepared for the awkwardness of it all.

Suzanne (Saturday, February 21st)

Dear Diary,

My styling skills will have to take a back seat come Monday; I reckon I've broken my finger. You can blame that asshole, Eric Reeves. Why, Diary? Why do men turn into such assholes after drinking too much? Am I stereotyping? Forgive me if so. I'm just pissed off with guys, in general, these days. So many lurking creeps with one thing on their mind. I wouldn't be as upset if the entire night was a disaster. If anything, I was having a great time; that was of course until Eric decided to walk me home.

We started the night in O'Shea's bar. In fairness to Eric, it was a good suggestion. It was easier to break the ice there and have 'one or two' (three and a shot in Eric's case) before hitting the restaurant at 7:30 pm.

As a dining experience, Po-Ho was OK, certainly nothing special. The food was a bit greasy and the wait between the starter and the main was just that… a wait. Regardless, the much-lauded view of the city did live up to the hype as we were fortunate enough to be seated by the full-size window. Yes, the same window that Fi has yet to shut up about. I had copped Eric's perviness at that point, scouring breasts like prey on the street below. I thought, "boys will be boys," and all that, and did well not to mention it.

After Po-Ho we hit Hooligans. As sports bars go, it wasn't that bad. I reckon the plethora of hot American guys watching some American football game tied me over. We managed to stay at Hooligans for the duration of the night as Eric seemed hell-bent on getting value for money with the pitchers on offer (pitchers for himself that is). Now, let me be the first to say, I am A-OK with flirting. Hell! I've been known to be a bit of a flirt myself (Jesus, that sounded very American…) but pinching my arse every two minutes can get a little bit annoying (and for what it's worth I just noticed a bruise on my arse in the mirror). By the time Hooligans shut up shop, Eric could barely stand up, not to mind string a sentence together. I'm not sure if he offered to, 'talk me home,' or 'walk me home,' but either way, he was successful to an extent.

Reaching my front gate, I knew getting rid of him wasn't going to be an easy task. I told Eric I was exhausted and gave him a peck on the cheek. I had hoped he would have done the same and made himself scarce. Unfortunately, not. Poor Eric thought he was home free and went in for the spin cycle with his tongue. I managed to fend him off for the most part, but he had a tight grip around my waist. When I managed to get free, he began serenading me with compliments, most of which were work-related. He was waffling on about my styling skills and how he wanted to poach me for Uppercuts. He then spoke about our salon and how most of the girls had a reputation for being sluts. The final straw came when he said, 'I hear you give a great blow,' before grabbing my breast. The cheeky bastard! I didn't even stop to think, I just swung. There was an almighty cracking sound.

The idiot finally stopped ringing the bell and shouting, 'my fucking nose!' about ten minutes ago and is now asleep on the wall. What a dope. He can stay there for the night – it might teach him a lesson!

Stuart (Sunday, February 22nd)

It's 10:42 pm and I've only got off the couch to make tea, use the toilet, and grab this diary. Over the past few hours I've come to realise a few things:

1 - Maggie is a bloody good kisser for a butcher.

2 - *Led Zeppelin IV* is better than *Led Zeppelin II*.

3 - *Bullseye* gave away some decent prizes back in the day and I would have gone for a few pints with Jim Bowman before he sadly passed away.

4 - *Strike it Lucky* was pretty funny, and I've no doubt Michael Barrymore got his fair share of it back in the day.

5 - I need to stop buying AA-size batteries that don't fit the TV remote.

Suzanne (Sunday, February 22nd)

Dear Diary,

Forgive my sloppy left-handed writing, I am reaping the consequences of last night. That said, I felt pretty bad about leaving Eric asleep on the wall with a broken face, so shortly after my last diary entry I decided to ring an ambulance. On arrival, it took three paramedics to get Eric strapped down and into the back of the ambulance after he became loud and aggressive. Having copped my swollen and bloodied hand, the female paramedic advised me to go to the hospital with them. Pointing at my hand and then the ambulance she said, 'Yiz mite as well get yer moonies worth.' I'm guessing the other paramedics administered some sort of tranquilliser to Eric as he wasn't long shutting up.

Luckily, the A&E dept was quiet; I was in and out within the hour. The official diagnosis: one finger broken and two sprained. Before I left the A&E, I went to see how Eric was holding up. He had two black eyes and a big lump in the middle of his nose. The Indian doctor attending to Eric spotted my tape-covered hand and asked me, 'Just the one punch then?' I bit my lip and nodded without saying a word. The doc said, 'A very strong hand, madam.' Because of the medication, Eric just sat there chewing his face. He did, however, manage to crack a smile. It went well with his nose.

8:35 pm - My invisible texting buddy is back:

"hey babz, wats wrong? did ya lose yer fingaz?"

Work is going to be a nightmare for the next bit!

Stuart (Monday, February 23rd)

The new traffic bollards outside the shop are causing havoc. Some of the delivery guys were flipping out as they now have to do multiple runs up and down the street. Not only that, but I managed to hear several arguments between traffic wardens, drivers on Main St, and people who managed to get locked into the street. For some reason, these bumbling morons that got stuck on the street think Trish and I have some sort of magic key that will retract the bollards. We don't!

Trish seemed concerned about the amount of Led Zeppelin had on earlier. She asked, 'What's with the Zeppelin buzz? I thought you said they were hippies.' I told her I was curious about a song I heard and was convinced it was them. Trish's memory spooks me out at times.

I heard nothing from Maggie. In saying, I couldn't quite bring myself to pop by her place either. I may attempt that tomorrow.

Suzanne (Monday, February 23rd)

Dear Diary,

Eric Reeves sent flowers and a 'Thank You' card to the salon. I'd probably be right in saying the usual hospital gift shop cards (congratulations, happy birthday, sorry, etc.) were out of stock – unless he is truly sorry and realised that he needed all of this to happen as some sort of wake-up call for being a total and utter sleazeball.

The card reads:

Sue,

I want to apologise for upsetting you. I was completely in the wrong with both my attitude and my actions. Please, let me make it up to you. I'm not the guy you think I am.

Eric x

The girls at work couldn't believe what went down Saturday night. They spent most of the morning ripping Eric to shreds, but once the flowers arrived, they were all about him. Sadly, work tasks have now been reduced to blow-drying and sweeping with my left hand.

Diary, we do take things for granted, don't we? Not being able to use my right hand is a pain in the arse!

Stuart (Tuesday, February 24th)

Everything is good again. Phew! Maggie took it upon herself to call into the shop early and asked if I wanted to do lunch. I accepted her offer and arranged to meet her at the Market Cafe for 1 pm. When I arrived at the cafe, Maggie was seated outside smoking a cigarette. She seemed to have more makeup on than before, and her hair was split into a side parting as opposed to a middle parting. I don't ever recall seeing it like that, but it made her more exotic looking, somehow? Once seated, I recognised the scent, the same scent that had washed all over my face and neck a few nights ago. 'Stu, are you mad at me?' asked Maggie. I asked her why I might be mad at her? 'For not sleeping with you. Please, Stu, be honest with me.' I did pause, and I did think about it. Was I mad at Maggie? Some guys would be mad if a girl invited them back, seduced them with wine and then told them to sleep on the couch. With Maggie it was different. I realise that she is still mourning Ulrich's passing, and although things got pretty steamy, it might have been too much too soon. Maggie was staring a hole through me now, I had to reply and quick. 'No, I'm not mad at you. I had a nice time.' Maggie put her hand on mine. 'Me too,' she said before proceeding to light another cigarette with the end of the one she had been smoking.

Suzanne (Tuesday, February 24th)

Dear Diary,

I'm lucky today was my day off! I arrived at Mum's to find both her and Mr Rocket making plans to attack Eric Reeves. Knowing Mr Rocket, he would have proceeded with his claim if I hadn't talked him out of it. If I hear Mum say the words, 'sexual assault,' one more time, I'm going to snap. I'm not an idiot, I know what happened. It's up to me to press charges if I want. Understandably, I can see why she's upset. I would be, too. I'm only giving out as Mum was roaring in the front garden and now the entire street knows my business. After they calmed down, Mr Rocket joined me for a smoke out on the back porch. He said, 'Listen, love, I know some people that can look after this Eric creep. Just say the word and it'll be a done deal.' I was grateful for the offer but told Mr Rocket that I'd be fine.

A couple of hours later I was back out on the porch, this time on my own. I caught a glimpse of Mr Rocket in the kitchen window. He was holding up an empty Rice Krispies box and pointing to Snap, Crackle and Pop while making the shape of a gun with his hand. Mr Rocket had written, '10k' on the flap of the box and was using his gun-shaped hand to point to it while brandishing a sinister smile. I gave him a thumbs up to acknowledge the info.

Stuart (Wednesday, February 25th)

Mam and Dad were up in the city today, so I decided to treat them to some dinner after work. Dad has accumulated the full amount for his skydive and spent most of the dinner trying to convince me to take part.

I can see the appeal, but again, I have no ambition to jump out of a plane. None!

4:40 am

I'm just back from the shop. Yup, you read the right. I got a call from Trish just after 3 am saying that the cops had called her to report a potential disturbance at the premises. Trish was advised to meet the cops at the shop. I told Trish not to worry about it and that I'd pop down to meet the cops.

When I arrived at the shop, I met the two coppers and opened the store for them. The male copper seemed like a useless fuck and advised me to go in front and lead them up the stairs to the cash office. I was a total goner if I bumped into an intruder, at least the copper could use his walkie-talkie to clock someone over the head. The same goes for the female cop, she could have used that torch to send someone into next week. All I had was the shop key, attached to a rubber Franz Ferdinand logo. After some deliberation, the male copper took the lead, dragging the female copper by her shirt for support. The first floor isn't a Steven Seagal type industrial zone or anything, but the way these two were approaching it, I was prepared for the worst! Once we got to the top of the stairs the male copper took the lead once again and turned onto the corridor that leads to a stock room on the right, a cash office on the left and a small kitchen at the end. 'Bastards!' he proclaimed. The door of the cash office looked like it had taken a good bashing, but thankfully the intruders didn't get in. There were sawdust and timber all over the kitchen. It was obvious they had gained access through the ceiling. The female copper said the intruders probably knew they had one shot to break through the ceiling that led to the cash office, but they were unlucky in their judgement. She said that the shop alarm would have panicked them into leaving straight away. I was going to ring Trish, but I'll wait until the morning.

Suzanne (Wednesday, February 25th)

Dear Diary,

Stupidly, I answered a call from a private number this evening. I had assumed for some reason it was the hospital. It wasn't. It was the guy who installed my fridge and he wanted to know why I wasn't replying to his messages. I played it stupid and told him I didn't know what he was talking about. The fridge guy claimed he wasn't stupid and could see that I had read his messages and, in some instances, my profile status changing from offline to online shortly after his messages were sent. Bloody apps! Long story short, he wants me to join him for a drink Friday night. I told I was feeling pretty sick this week and that I didn't want to mix the meds with alcohol. I also said that I had an early start Saturday and hate being hung-over at work. Why do I always volunteer too much information? Why did I even entertain his call? Why am I such a pushover? Diary? Why? I don't even know his name!

Stuart (Thursday, February 26th)

I was an hour late for work this morning. When I arrived at the shop, the cops from last night were talking to Trish about the break-in. Thankfully, they saved me a good two hours of my life explaining every little detail to Trish. The female cop looked a lot hotter today. She, much like myself, seemed to be enjoying a hat off/hair down day. Both of the coppers spent a good 30 mins or so asking us about any suspicious activity we might have witnessed over the last bit. Trish and I couldn't recall anything out of the ordinary. The male cop said that they are waiting for the CCTV footage to be downloaded and that they'd call back tomorrow.

1:40 am

I can't sleep! The French couple who live upstairs are in the midst of another marathon 'session' and are making one hell of a racket.

Suzanne (Thursday, February 26th)

Dear Diary,

I arrived home to find Mr Snuggles sitting on the window ledge with a dead bird in his mouth. It was my fault that he got out as I left the front window open this morning. Isn't it weird how something so cuddly and innocent can lead a double life as a murderer? I suppose all murderers live a double life when you think about it. I felt a bit weird washing out his mouth with soap, but these things have to be done. I can't afford to pick up the Zika virus on top of my bandy fingers.

Stuart (Friday, February 27th)

Maggie's kid cracks me up! He popped into the shop earlier wanting to know if I could mind 500 quid for him. When asked about the money he said that he, 'earned it doing a few jobs.' I told him I had no issue with minding it, but I was concerned that it could get mixed up with my money. Smartly, he advised, 'No matter how much it gets mixed up, 500 of it is still mine.' Kids today, they don't miss a beat! I told Patryk I'd mind the money, but to stick it in an envelope and post it through my home letterbox. Patryk said it was too much hassle and that he'd have to cycle over to get it. I only offered to help Patryk out as Grandad Mick, naively at the time, used to mind wads of cash that we stole from the old corner shop back in the day. I sound like I'm accusing Patryk of such behaviour. I'm sure he did a good day's work... somewhere.

I managed to make it to the butchers before Maggie finished her shift. I didn't open my mouth about the 500 quid. When asked, Maggie agreed to attend the Satan's Arse gig tomorrow night. She said that the weekends are a lot less stressful now that Patryk has gone all Zen with his aroma meditation plants. Patryk's been sleeping a lot and is now more inclined to poach Maggie's Pink Floyd CDs than his usual binge of 2 Chainz and Chance the Rapper.

It would seem Maggie's younger sister is planning a visit next weekend. I've never met her, but from what Maggie has told me, she sounds like a character. Her name is Zofia, an accountant by day and a dominatrix by night. Maggie said that she's loaded and has several properties in Krakow. Not bad if you can get it, I suppose...

Word on the street is that the record label boss who is flying in to see Satan's Arse was also responsible for signing both Flesh of the Rotting Corpse and Devilorium. That's pretty good company for the Arse lads.

Suzanne (Friday, February 27th)

Dear Diary,

I passed Andrea Chan in Cosmo earlier, she threw me the dirtiest of looks. From what I've heard, all of the girls working at Uppercuts can't stand her. The only reason she's still there is that (a) she's Mark Reeves' fuck buddy and (b) the two brothers are pretty shit at running a business, so they get Andrea to do all the dirty work. I have no idea what Mark sees in her?? His wife is stunning! Maybe the creepo gene runs in the family. Hopefully, Mark gets found out and ends up with a broken face, just like his brother, Eric. Judging by the dirty look Andrea Chan sent my way, I'm sure there are all sorts of rumours about me floating around their salon.

Diary, you won't believe it! Fridge guy has a name! It's Paul. I know this because he finally decided to sign off on a text message. He wanted to know if we were still good to meet up tonight. I told him that I still felt out of sorts due to the meds, but I wouldn't be opposed to a pint sometime soon. He replied, 'Don't let me down :)'

Mr Rocket also sent me a text. He has it in for Eric Reeves:

"I know a bloke who'll do it for 8k. Giz a shout if keen."

Stuart (Saturday, February 28th)

3:20 am

I'm plastered drunk and deaf as a coot. That's what happens when you mix your day off with the heaviest band around, Rockwood's finest, Satan's Arse. The band was on fire tonight, with the place going bananas from the opening bars of 'Crucifixable', a true classic, it has to be said.

After the set, we bumped into the record company guy who had flown in to see Satan's Arse. He was out in the smoking area necking whiskey and mingling with the locals. He was plastered drunk, too. We did our best to put in a good word for the Arse lads by buying even more drink for the record company guy. He looked like he was enjoying himself. If that wasn't enough, no trip to Rockwood is complete without a trip to Fabkebab; the finest kebab eatery in the country. We could barely hold the record company guy up, but between the lot of us, we managed to get him to Fabkebab to sample a Big Nasty. The poor guy looked like he was gonna drop dead from a heart attack about halfway through, so we didn't push him to finish it. Hopefully, he made it back to the hotel in one piece. He seemed to be latching on to a girl half his age when we parted with him about 30 mins ago.

Suzanne (Saturday, February 28th)

Dear Diary,

I met a lovely girl named Zia at work. She was in getting her hair coloured before taking off on her holidays. We spoke candidly about the difficulties and pressures of being single in your early 30s. She seemed to be encountering a lot of the same problems as me. Will I ever get married? Is it too late for me to have kids? How could anyone love me? Am I destined to be a cat lady for the rest of my life? Zia said she hasn't slept with a guy in over four years... and I thought I was doing badly! I advised her to let rip one of these nights. What's the worst that could happen? What I didn't expect was a pretty sad back-story about an abortion she had back in 2011. She claimed it was a one-night stand, and at the time was too committed to her career to even think about having a child. Diary, it has to be said, considering some of the stuff we hear at work, most all hairdressers could double as psychotherapists. Anyway, she sounded pretty paranoid about falling into a similar situation. I got the feeling that she had said more than she set out to. For what it's worth, I advised her to enjoy life. The last thing you want to do is look back with regret. Cliché, I know.

Several hours later, having transformed Zia's natural blackness into a luxuriant blonde, she up and left with a spring in her step and a smile on her face. She looked fantastic and the blonde hair looked superb.

Before we closed, Zia dropped back into the salon. 'A little thank you,' she said while handing me a box of chocolates and a card. As I was saying thanks, she turned and made a quick dash for the door, 'I'm double parked,' the clip-clopping of her high heels echoing through the salon floor as she made her exit. 'She's a dote,' Fi proclaimed.

I was hanging for a glass of wine when I got home but had to say no as I'm still on these bloody antibiotics! Instead, I made some microwave popcorn and put my feet up with some shit television. One of the adverts made me think of the box of chocolates Zia dropped in earlier. How sweet of her. The card she attached is adorable, too. It has a picture of a stick man making a heart shape with his thumbs and forefingers. Above that, it reads, 'Thank You'. I have to say; her handwriting is impeccable. It doesn't even look real. It reads:

Thank you so much for listening. It's a simple skill that many people seem to have forgotten. I have a +1 for the Victoria's Secret Fashion Show next Friday. Would you like to join me? Here is my number: 555-6357891.

PS - I will be sure to take your advice.

Zia xxx

What a sweety. The Victoria's Secret Fashion Show is the hottest ticket in town, and unless you're part of the "who's who," you can forget about getting a ticket. I might just take her up on that offer. I could do with letting my hair down.

Stuart (Sunday, March 1st)

1:10 am

I just woke up from the most realistic dream EVER! I was en-route to Boreth (an inhabited planet in the Klingon Empire from Star Trek) with Charlie and, of all people, Charlie's mother! I have no idea why she was with us, but I did see her in Tesco today. Anyway, all three of us were travelling to Boreth on the USS Enterprise. Onboard, one of the Klingon's was celebrating his birthday with a big disco in the upper observation dome. Who do I see when I walk in? THE GIRL FROM THE BARGE! Kim Gordon Jnr! I couldn't believe it! There she was, looking hot as hell in her black butterfly dress. One of the Klingon dudes seemed to be chatting her up, so I decided not to waste any time. I strolled over, cool as a cucumber and slid in between them. 'Come here often?' I said. She put her drink down, turned her back on the Klingon and began mauling me... the good kind of mauling of course. Before we knew it, we were tangling through the corridors trying to find the officers' quarters. Minutes later we ended up settling for the impulse thrust array, probably not the safest of areas in retrospect. I wonder if Kim Gordon Jnr is like that in real life?

Suzanne (Sunday, March 1st)

Dear Diary,

Today was Dad's anniversary. I can't believe how quick the last three years have passed. Both Mum and I spent a good hour out in the graveyard where we cleaned up the headstone and replaced the old flowers with Dad's favourite, a bunch of red carnations. Afterwards, I took Mum for a roast dinner at The Old Lodge. It was so cosy in there, what with the roasting fire and comfy couches, I opted to leave the car and order a bottle of wine. Unlike past anniversaries, the alcohol didn't leave Mum in a flood of tears at the end of the night. Instead, she was jovial about her current relationship with Mr Rocket. I used to think he was a bit of a goof! I still do weirdly. But, he's a lovable goof, and Mum could do a lot worse.

We're such gluttons, on the way home we got the taxi driver to stop at the chipper. We got him a bag of chips too. He was thrilled with himself.

I sent Zia a text and told her I'd take her up on her offer to attend the Victoria's Secret Fashion Show. She replied, "GREAT!"

Stuart (Monday, March 2nd)

It looks like the record company guy who flew in to see Satan's Arse is still in town. He was in the shop this morning, looking a little worse for wear. He was browsing through the used vinyl when I approached him, curious to know why he was still in Rockwood. 'Sorry mate?' He looked out of it. I told him I met him at the Satan's Arse gig Saturday night and that I was good friends with Tony and Rodge. His head fell backwards, and he rolled his eyes upwards, 'I haven't slept in three days, mate. I'm fucked.' He looked fucked. Suddenly, that chick who's always in asking about rare punk 7-inches pops her head in the door, 'Lawrence, are we going for a pint or what?' It was 9:45 am. Lawrence, the record company bloke turned around to me. 'Some things are worth losing your job for,' he said, as he put down a handful of records he had spent the past half an hour accumulating.

I met Charlie for lunch. He spent the entire hour convincing me to sign up for Love Quest, a dating site for singles. I said it sounds like a dating site for simpletons. My remark didn't faze him. Charlie claims that he's had 20 profile views since last night and that, 'some of the birds are alright.' I told him I'd think about signing up and would monitor his progress over the next bit.

The hot cop was back in the shop today. She said the CCTV footage from our break-in had been analysed. The report said that a youth, reported to be between the ages of 15 and 20 was spotted acting suspiciously around the store at the time of the break-in. The copper said she could give me a copy of the footage on Wednesday as I'm off tomorrow. I agreed to take a look.

10:30 pm

I've signed up for this Love Quest dating app. Charlie managed to convince me with a text just now.

The text reads:

"You might find your future wife, the one with the bird dress."

I assume he meant butterfly dress.

Suzanne (Monday, March 2nd)

Dear Diary,

Mr Snuggles and that white cat from up the street have been scrapping outside the house. They were making some racket! When I went out to see what all the commotion was about, Mr Grimble and two of the young students from No.30 were already out. I could see that little white shit running up the road. That white cat has Mr Snuggles tormented. Mr Grimble said they were fighting over some ham he had left out. It wouldn't be the first time the cats kicked off about food. That white cat is always stealing food from Mr Snuggles' food bowl. I must follow him up the road next time, I'm curious to know who his/her owner is.

Both Mum and Mr Rocket appeared in today's issue of *The Gazette*. They were quoted and pictured about the rumoured UFO sighting over St Michael's church this past weekend. The heading read "UFO Yourself..." Underneath, it read, "We took to the streets to ask the people of Rockwood if they've ever encountered a UFO." Although both Mum and Mr Rocket were pictured, only Mum was quoted. The other quotes were from business owners and random people on the street.

Mum's quote read:

"I've never seen a UFO, but I do believe aliens tried to contact me a couple of years back. My daughter and I had just gotten home from a wedding and were waiting for the kettle to boil. I have a habit of turning on the radio in the kitchen, but that particular night we heard a very disturbing voice over the airwaves. It was calling my late husband and me by name, it kept saying, 'Rod and Hel, Rod and Hel.' That's what our friends would call us when we first started dating. I fainted!"

Diary, I'm mortified!

Stuart (Tuesday, March 3rd)

Charlie was right, there are some very attractive girls on this Love Quest dating site. It's pretty addictive, too, I spent most of my day off scrolling through profile after profile. Here's a particular highlight:

Name - Ibizaliza

Headline - No boring cunts!

Bio - Looking for my prince charming. Must have a job, a car, own his place. Must be clean-shaven, no beard, nice bod, tall, be able to change a light bulb. Must not get a hard-on looking at Superman and Spiderman, drink gin, enjoy weirdo music.

I took an hour out from Love Quest to get some bits and pieces down in the Farmers' Market. There I bumped into Rodge from Satan's Arse who was on the hunt for Kumquats. Rodge asked me what I thought of the weekend gig. I told him they floored it and that my ears have been ringing ever since. Rodge said the Satan's Arse boys have heard, 'fuck all,' from Lawrence and are a little anxious about their future. Rodge and co probably think Lawrence is back in his record company in London, little do they know he's still doing the rounds about town. I kept schtum.

Got soaked walking home. Decided to pour me a bath and set up this Love Quest profile once and for all. It reads:

Name: disco-stew

Headline: A chilled guy looking to find a chill girl

Bio: Easy-going music fan looking to meet someone chill. I enjoy going to gigs, listening to music, reading music magazines, watching music documentaries and reading music books. You?

Suzanne (Tuesday, March 3rd)

Dear Diary,

My hand seems to be healing pretty well after fending off that creep Eric Reeves. The swelling has eased up and I'm OK with lifting things again. I wonder how 'Knobhead' Reeves is? I'm content knowing that his nose will never look the same again.

I had a strange case of deja vu during lunch. I spotted this guy in the Farmers' Market, but for the life of me couldn't place his face. Then it hit home, it was the gay guy who offered me his lighter in The Barge not so long ago. I was going to say hi, but he'd probably think I was some sort of crazy stalker.

I had a brief conversation with Mr Grimble while unloading the groceries. He claims that he, much like Mum, has also heard aliens speaking through the radio. Alcohol does have a lot to answer for.

Stuart (Wednesday, March 4th)

The hot cop arrived with the CCTV footage of the break-in this morning. I took a look but couldn't make out much. This might sound strange, but the kid in the footage kind of looks like Maggie's kid, Patryk. Surely not…

Speaking of, Maggie popped in shortly after the copper left. She'd had just spent 200 quid on new cutlery and wine glasses. I didn't ask, but I'm guessing she wants to impress her sister Zofia this weekend. I wonder what Zofia looks like.

It has to be said, this Love Quest malarkey is going considerably well. I have 3 profile views. The first comes from a girl named Amie. Amie is 23, has 3 kids, and works part-time in a newsagent. She seems easy going, bar the number of times she has written, "NO FUCKING BULLSHIT," on her page. The second girl is 31, she's just back from 8 years in Australia. She has a PhD and would favour a coffee as a first date. Her name is Blathnaid, pale skin, red hair. She seems to speak in riddles. I haven't solved any of them. My newest visitor is Denise, her headline reads, "Ah, lads…" She is 28 and from up the road. I pass her on the way to work every morning. I wonder if she recognises me from my picture. Her 'About Me' reads, "qwertyuiopasdfghjklzxcvbnm." She has written the same thing under the First Date box. She looks like trouble in her profile pictures.

Charlie's company is flying him to San Francisco for three weeks' work. Some people have all the luck!

Suzanne (Wednesday, March 4th)

Dear Diary,

Mum and I got into an argument with some lady while doing Mum's weekly shop this evening. Mum didn't realise she had dropped 20 euro near the till until the man queuing two places back informed us that the lady standing behind Mum picked up the note and put it into her purse. The man said, 'Love, you dropped some money and that lady is after putting it in her purse.' He pointed at the woman. Mum looked around at the accused woman, who promptly turned to the man and said, 'Finders keepers!' The man replied, 'But that's not your money, it belongs to that lady,' as he pointed at Mum. The accused lady replied, 'I saw the money on the ground. I found it, so I'll be keeping it.' Having heard enough, I decided to butt in. 'I think you will find that money belongs to my Mum. It must've fallen out of her hand as she was getting money to pay the cashier,' I said without hesitation. The accused lady just stood there with a smirk on her face. Mum, bless her, turned to me and referring to the accused lady said, 'she's not worth the effort.' Mum paid the cashier and we made our way towards the car park.

Out in the car park, Mum and I spotted the accused lady packing groceries into her jeep. Without missing a beat, Mum marched over and picked up a large ham that the lady had placed on the ground while attempting to make more room in her trunk. Mum began walking back towards me. The lady copped Mum's movements. 'Excuse me!' she shouted. Mum threw the ham into the back of our car, slammed the trunk and replied, 'Finders keepers, darling.' The lady looked like she had been sprayed with a freeze gun as Mum and I whizzed past her and headed home.

Stuart (Thursday, March 5th)

Maggie's kid Patryk called to the house tonight. He said it was a pain in the hole having to cycle over. He wanted to know if I was still up for minding his 500 quid. After one too many joints (my first in quite some time) I agreed but on one condition. I needed help finding Kim Gordon Jnr from The Barge. I asked Patryk if he might know someone who could get their hands on The Barge's CCTV footage; in particular, footage from Saturday, February 15th. I told him that finding this girl has been impossible and that I need all the help I can get. Patryk said, 'I thought you were crazy about my mother?' I told him that someday, he'll discover the difference between lust and love.

After a two-hour crash course on how to make the best triple-decker toasted sandwich, I had Patryk's attention once again. I confirmed our plan, 'I need someone who could get the footage.' Patryk replied, 'Man, I'm an expert. I'll be in and out in five minutes - down through the roof and yoink, see ya later.'

I forgot how good relish is.

Suzanne (Thursday, March 5th)

Dear Diary,

I met Mum for lunch. She asked if I had seen her in the paper. I told her I had but couldn't bring myself to tell her about the supposed aliens she'd heard through the radio. The truth is, it was a song on that Heavy Metal radio show that contained the lyrics, 'Rot in hell' and not 'Rod and Hel,' like Mum had thought!

Paul (the fridge guy) sent a text asking if I'd meet him tomorrow night, I told him I'd love to, but I can't. The Victoria's Secret Fashion Show is on tomorrow. He didn't reply :(

Stuart (Friday, March 6th)

I had a great idea for a film last night, but I can't remember much of it today. I just know it was based on a dystopian Ireland, where the cops were holograms, and everybody travelled using transporter portals. I was telling Trish about it earlier when Maggie and her sister Zofia arrived in from the airport. Holy shit! Zofia is a knockout! She looks even more like Mariska Veres than Maggie does. First, Zofia hugged Trish and then made her way over to me, as Maggie gave a brief (but good) synopsis of my life. After my hug, Zofia continued to hold my hand as Maggie continued my life story. I have to admit; I had a bit of a semi going on below. Her smoky eyes and radiant smile must have had me blushing like a school kid. I could feel my face burning up.

10:42 pm

I have two messages in my inbox. Both from Denise (Love Quest/up the road fame).

They read:

7:05 pm

Hey hun, did I offend ya, lol? You online? Could do with a laugh x

4:40 pm

In work, lol. You're old enough to be my dad ;)

Suzanne (Friday, March 6th)

Dear Diary,

The Victoria's Secret show was a great laugh, and Zia is a sweet girl. She is super-genuine and completely different from the morose vibes she gave off in the salon last weekend. In fact, she's a mad thing! She admitted that she felt a bit weird about giving me chocolates after our very open conversation, but I assured her that her kind gesture had been well received.

After the fashion show, we went for a few in The Cat & Mouse. Zia wasn't short of attention there. Guys were swarming around her all night. And why wouldn't they? She's stunning!

With enough sleazy chat-up lines to last us a lifetime, Zia and I up and left The Cat & Mouse, only to bump into Mum and Mr Rocket on their way down Main Street. Unexpectedly, Zia and I ended up joining them in Lynch's Bar for the rest of the night. Zia got a great kick out of Mr Rocket and his impressions, and it has to be said Mr Rocket certainly took a shine to Zia, too.

After the pub, we got some chips from the takeaway and made sure Zia was OK getting a taxi home. I almost broke my ankle coming up the stairs just now.

Note to self - take off your high heels before attempting to climb stairs after 6 x glasses of red wine.

Stuart (Saturday, March 7th)

No entry

Suzanne (Saturday, March 7th)

Dear Diary,

I spent the day wallowing in misery. A hung-over misery that is. I did have good intentions today. I wanted to check out a food festival they were advertising in the paper, but the couch was more appealing. I must have watched at least 10 episodes of *Friends*, before crumbling to temptation and ordering a ton of Thai-food takeaway.

Having stuffed myself like a baby elephant and falling asleep shortly after, I was woken by a text message from Zia: "Are you alive? I'm dying a slow death here."

At 7 pm, Mum called with even more takeaway (Diary, I did…). Mum, who for some unknown reason never gets a hangover, was in bits. She claimed to have alcohol and food poisoning. She can be very dramatic sometimes.

Stuart (Sunday, March 8th)

Fucking hell. I feel like I've just stumbled out of a plane crash! My entire body is aching, and my head feels like it's getting jackhammered into the ground. The funny thing is, I did make it home last night. Sadly, I could barely string a sentence together, never mind type a diary entry into my phone. If I were to put a theme on the events of last night, I'd probably go with, 'Risqué Business.' *Why? I hear whoever might be reading this (Dystopian hologram in 2163, etc.) ask?* Try three separate bathroom shags with your best friend/part-time love interest's younger *a*nd more attractive sister. Oh... and make that three shags at a dinner party with 12 guests.

The night was going fine until, 'Lil sis,' broke out the Polish vodka over dessert. When I say fine, I didn't think much of the red-wine-induced footsie that had been taking place between Zofia and me underneath the dinner table. It would appear vodka to Zofia is like spinach to Popeye, but in this case, the only thing bulging was my pants. You can blame Maggie's seating arrangements and one crafty handed younger sister. Talk about playing with fire! Seated to my left, with her right hand on my balls and her left hand holding a hefty shot of vodka, Zofia seemed unphased when talking to Maggie, whom I might add was seated to my right. I'd almost swear that Cora, who was sitting directly opposite me, had copped what was going on. Cora was burning a hole through me with those hawk eyes all night. Thank God Trish was sitting to the right of Maggie – her lambasting of Donald Trump served as the perfect distraction from Zofia, me, and our blatant flirting; not to mention sexual innuendos.

By 11 pm, everyone was tanked on Polish vodka and had spilt out to the back garden. As the smell of cigarette smoke filled the air, the familiar sound of Queen *(Greatest Hits: Vol 1 to 3)* was Maggie's first choice to soundtrack the post-dinner shenanigans. From the mass sing-along of 'Bohemian Rhapsody' to the bass-laden groove of 'Under Pressure' everyone seemed to be in flying form. Time kind of stood still for a while (I had taken a few rips from Zofia's hash pipe) and I got lost in a trance watching Zofia dancing. The way I remember it from here, I was getting some ice for a White Russian (the drink that is) when Zofia came up behind me. She was singing along to Queen and flailing about the place like something out of a Kate Bush video. However, unlike Freddie Mercury's flamboyant flow, Zofia's vocal was soft and seductive. She whispered in my ear, 'I want to ride my bicycle.' I nearly fucking choked on the ice cube. The next thing I know, we're in the bathroom and she's bent over the sink with her arse in the air. 'My bicycle needs your pump,' said Zofia. Of course, I had to oblige. My God, she was loud!! I had fully suspected that somebody would catch us, but, come one... if you were to die there and then, what a way to go. The second shag was even better, and by the third one (when most everyone had left, and her sister Maggie was asleep in the sunroom) we could barely stand up; not to mind keep it up. After the 3rd shag, we were both shagged. Zofia then asked me if I wanted to sleep in the spare room with her. I couldn't. It would be way too awkward having to face Maggie this morning.

Maggie sent me a text this afternoon asking if I'd like to join herself and Zofia for a bite to eat. I didn't reply.

Suzanne (Sunday, March 8th)

Dear Diary,

Mum and Mr Rocket popped over to sample my finest Sunday roast today. For the most part, the conversation over dinner revolved around Zia. Both Mum and Mr Rocket have taken a real shine to her since Friday night; I'm going to go on record and say that Zia's unfiltered nature is quite appealing. Mum was curious to know why I hadn't invited her over for dinner. I didn't have an answer but blurted out something about Sunday being a day of rest. If I'm being honest, the more Mum and Mr Rocket sang Zia's praises, the more I did think about asking her to call round. She does me make me laugh.

I had to turn my phone off as the girls from work won't take no for an answer. Fi called at about 5 pm asking if I wanted to join herself, Siobhan and Nicole for a night out. All three of them are at work tomorrow. I told Fi that I was shattered, but I'll look forward to some stories in the morning. Half an hour later Siobhan called. I could hear Nicole in the background, feeding her lines as to why I should join them. They'd make a great sales team, I almost gave in.

Stuart (Monday, March 9th)

Fuck my life!! Why do women have to tell each other everything in detail? Not only does Maggie know that I shagged Zofia, Zofia knows that I tried to shag Maggie now, too. I know this because I reluctantly joined them for lunch before Zofia's flight back to Poland.

Over lunch, there was a sense of anxiety in the air. I think they had planned this and wanted to shame me face to face. Maggie and Zofia seemed very quiet, so I was left to handle the small talk. When Zofia excused herself to the bathroom, Maggie unleashed a torrent of abuse my way, 'Are you for fucking real, Stu? I can't believe you did that to me. My flesh and blood.' I was stumped. I tried to reason with Maggie, waffling about how we were all tanked, and how one thing led to another. Lucky for me, Zofia didn't take long and I was back talking about the new Neil Young reissues before I knew it. Just when I thought I was home free; Maggie took her turn to visit the loo. What followed? Zofia's 5 minutes of fury, 'You disgust me! Stupid Irish pig. I thought you were the great lover, but you are just like rest, filthy fucker animal.

You fuck whole family, even dog if could.' I tried to tell Zofia that she had a 'heart of gold' (I did have those Neil Young reissues on the brain). Zofia wasn't having any of it, 'You say line like that to all women. I'm not stupid women.' When Maggie arrived back from the loo, all three of us sat in silence for a good 15 minutes. Before I got up to head back to work, Maggie pushed the lunch bill to Zofia, who subsequently pushed it to me. 75 quid for three salads, two glasses of wine and a glass of water. It'd be hard to keep 'Rockin' in the free world' with those prices.

Suzanne (Monday, March 9th)

Dear Diary,

It was a good thing work was quiet. Nicole (bless her) turned up looking like *The Bride of Frankenstein*, Fi called in sick, and Siobhan decided 12:45 pm was as good a time as any to start the day. I'm too easy-going with them. Most managers wouldn't put up with that sort of thing. Then again, we were all young and carefree at some stage. Diary! I sound like my mother!

I was just speaking to Mr Grimble. He makes an awful racket when bringing his bin to the front gate. He claims that the white cat from up the street got flattened by a passing car. He said that a woman (whom he suspected was the cat's owner) was in tears scraping the remains of the cat from the road. As much as I hate that little shit of a cat, that's very sad. The thought of that happening to Mr Snuggles has me in tears.

Stuart (Tuesday, March 10th)

Something is up with Love Quest. It says I have five messages, but they won't open for me.

My Mother rang earlier to tell me Dad's parachute jump is this Sunday. She gave me a warning not to miss it. Mam said Dad's pal Gummy has been advised not to jump. Gummy's doctor advised him that at 94 he would be at high risk of a heart attack. In fairness, Gummy still managed to raise almost 7k for the charity. My mother said, 'If there's one thing Paddy Hinchey isn't, even if he is 94, and that is a fool. He never had any intention of jumping out of a plane. He knew the parish would cough up because of his age.' I reckon my mother was spot on.

I bumped into Jimmy the Punk on my lunch break. I hadn't seen him since The Pogo Stix gig. His trademark two-foot mohawk has now been reduced to a head of stubble; he looks like a proper football hooligan now. Word on the street is that Lawrence is no longer with the record company. He's run off with some girl and left the Satan's Arse lads high and dry.

No word from Maggie. I wonder if I should attempt to break the ice.

Suzanne (Tuesday, March 10th)

Dear Diary,

I had the most enjoyable day off. This morning I treated Mum and myself to a facial and back massage. We then ventured out to the shopping mall for some much-needed retail therapy. After two hours of viewing bland dresses, I picked up a gorgeous V-neck lace dress in Unique Boutique. It was pricey but looked great on, even if I do say so myself. As it's Mum's birthday on Wednesday, I bought her a jacket she had been eyeing up for the past few weeks. She was over the moon.

Fi was on to me this afternoon. She said that Eric Reeves popped into the salon looking for me. Fi asked him if he was OK and Eric said that he wanted to put an end to all this shite with me and offer his apology in person. Eric also told Fi he was in the wrong and 'completely out of order.' The word is that Eric's nose is destroyed, and he looks like a heroin junkie.

Stuart (Wednesday, March 11th)

My brain is in overdrive all day. I can't stop thinking about M&M's (Maggie and Zofia). I've also been thinking a lot about the girl from The Barge. I missed thinking about her; what with all this unwanted commotion. I have yet to hear from Maggie and, to be honest, I don't know where I'd begin. I have to break the ice somehow. I was thinking about ordering some flowers and getting them sent to the butchers. Is that a weird place to send a bunch of flowers?

I had to pay 10 quid to read my messages on Love Quest as my trial period is up. The most recent message (10:20 pm) is a picture of two arse cheeks with "LOL" written below them. That message came from Denise (the girl from up the road who told me I was old enough to be her dad). The second message (5:25 pm) is a riddle from Ms PhD, Blathnaid. It reads, "Why are you, copper and tellurium similar?" What is she on about? The third message (3:25 am) is from a new face, her name is Sletva and it reads, "Hi, how are you?" Her profile says she's originally from Poland. The fourth message (11:55 pm, Tues) is from a bloke, his name is Mark, "Hey, are you game?" The final message (11:12 pm, Tues) is from Michael, the founder of Love Quest. He wanted to wish me luck on my, 'Quest for love.' That was nice of him.

Charlie sent a text from San Francisco:

"Fun times here, lad. I smoked some of the best weed ever last night. Will try to bring some home. Hope all is well, bud."

Suzanne (Wednesday, March 11th)

Dear Diary,

Mr Rocket and I surprised Mum with a birthday cake this evening. The cake maker put some pictures of Mum's favourite TV-show stars on top. There was Ken Barlow from *Coronation Street*, the judge from *Strictly Come Dancing* and Graham Norton (although this version looks more like Hannibal Lecter). Mum was bawling. Mr Rocket went all out on the birthday gifts and presented Mum with a gift hamper wrapped in a pink bow. The hamper included a dressing gown, a bottle of Champagne, two tickets to see Meat Loaf at the Telecast Arena, a 12-month gym membership, a selection of shampoos, a jar of Garnier Wrinkle Lift - Anti-ageing cream and a pair of dog slippers. Mum began bawling all over again.

Stuart (Thursday, March 12th)

I'm speaking to Maggie again; well for now at least, as Patryk has been arrested! He was caught trying to break into The Barge by a member of their staff. The events seemed all too familiar when Maggie recalled them, sort of like a weird dream.

Maggie was long gone when it all came flooding back. I was responsible! I promised Patryk that I'd give him 500 quid if he got the CCTV footage from Feb 15th – the night I met Kim Gordon Jnr. Even though I was pretty baked from all the weed, it seemed like a great idea at the time. From what I could gauge earlier, Maggie had no idea that I was behind all of this. Hopefully, it stays that way. Unfortunately, I don't have Patryk's number, so I can't call him and ask him to keep me out of it. I've been sitting here all-night praying that the phone doesn't ring. First, the Zofia situation, and now this. Maggie's going to have my head on the chopping board (literally).

Suzanne (Thursday, March 12th)

Dear Diary,

Well, there goes another one! I spotted the fridge guy eyeing up wedding rings with a leggy blonde earlier today. They looked very cosy with their arms around each other. I can't remember the name of that jewelers, but it's known to be expensive. Fridge guy caught my eye when I passed them but pretended like he didn't see me. I smiled at him, acknowledging his dickheadedness in the process. Why am I so vulnerable to these sociopathic vultures? How is it that most girls have no problem meeting guys? Maybe I'm too quiet. Am I too boring? After all, I don't lead the most exciting life. I cut hair for a living. I live with my cat, and if I was to sum myself up in one word it would probably be 'loner'. I'm a loner! There I've said it. I don't have any friends. The girls at work are kind of like default friends, acquaintances at best. Mum, well she is my mum and doesn't have much choice in the matter. After that the only person I can call a friend is Zia and that's why I am here, in a post-work slumber, crying my eyes out with Mr Snuggles and Adele.

11:11 pm

Now the cat is crying. He sounds somewhat in key with Adele. We should apply for *Britain's Got Talent*!

Stuart (Friday, March 13th)

Fair play to Patryk for not ratting me out and for taking the brunt of everything related to The Barge break-in. I feel terrible for the kid as all of this will go on his record.

In an attempt to cheer him up, I stopped by the McDonagh house and got Patryk some weed. If only Maggie knew…

When I got out to Maggie's I managed to get Patryk on his own for a few minutes. I gave him the weed and told him it would cheer him up. I also gave him the 500 quid I had promised for the CCTV footage; granted I didn't get the footage in the end. Patryk said it's likely he'll end up paying a fine and doing some community service, as it's his first offence. Maggie, on the other hand, was extremely pissed off and ended up grounding Patryk for a month and suspending his pocket money for the rest of the year.

A text from Charlie who is still working in San Francisco:

"I got stood up on a Tinder date... this would never happen back home."

Suzanne (Friday, March 13th)

Dear Diary,

One of the students from No.30 roared, 'NICE ARSE!' at me just now. I'm going to take that compliment; God knows I could do with it.

Work was insane. We had two bridal parties this morning and prepped for a fashion show this evening. The girls from the Morgan Agency are stunning though! I'm sure they have no problems when it comes to guys. Lucky buggers. I ended up having cold pizza and a glass of milk for dinner (11 pm), then fell asleep until now (2:10 am) I'd give anything to sleep in tomorrow :(

3:43 am

I can't shut off…

Diary, what is the perfect woman?

Stuart (Saturday, March 14th)

The big Rockwood match was on today; hence the extremely quiet day at work. I am grateful in a sense as I managed to clock in some quality time on Love Quest. In doing so I found some very interesting profiles including that cute girl who works in The Coffee Cup, Charlie's ex, Natalie (still hot as fuck) and a girl named Tanish, who's a dead ringer for Chaka Khan.

Unfortunately, I've had to end the ongoing contact I had with Sletva (Poland) for the following:

Friday, March 13th (2:40 am) - Why the no reply?

Friday, March 13th (2:55 am) - I am not the drunk, I just want to talk to nice man.

Friday, March 13th (4:55 am) - I am good woman, one divorce.

Friday, March 13th (8:15 am) - FAGGOTT!!

Suzanne (Saturday, March 14th)

Dear Diary,

Zia treated me to lunch at Avellino's Bar & Brasserie. I had never been, but my word, what a great experience. We were both in a food coma when we were done. The food was delicious, the staff were super-friendly, and their menu was more than reasonable. I couldn't get over it! Zia asked if I had any plans for St Patrick's Day. I had forgotten all about it, to be honest. Zia said we should make a day out of it; the parade, some dinner, a club, the works! I said count me in. I haven't been to the St Patrick's Day parade in about 10 years.

Stuart (Sunday, March 15th)

I nearly missed Dad's parachute jump! I was woken at 4 am by some lad brandishing a samurai sword outside the apartment. He was dressed in his jocks and an N.W.A. shirt and was shouting, 'Come out you cunt!' at Judge Michael O'Sullivan's house across the street. I haven't slept a wink since. How I even made it to Dad's parachute jump is anyone's guess.

I'm proud of Dad. The jump looks like a piece of cake from the ground, but 13,000ft is pretty fucking high. It hit home when the committee played back the GoPro footage from Dad's skydive helmet on the big screen in the bar. Dad looked to be in his element on the free-fall. His smile was so wide I thought he might be in fear of losing his false teeth. He didn't. Speaking of, Mr Hinchey (or Gummy as he is affectionately known) was there, too. Although he didn't jump, he too was awarded a certificate from the skydivers' association. The total sum raised amounted to 53k between the 10 participants. Fantastic!

I'm not sure if I'll take the lads up on their offer to hit the pub for the day on Tuesday. St Patrick's Day is too messy for my liking.

Ms PhD has sent me the answer to her Love Quest riddle – "Because you're CuTe."

I don't get it!?

Suzanne (Sunday, March 15th)

Dear Diary,

A message from the Fortune Cookie I got at lunch:

"An alien of some sort will be appearing to you shortly!"

Stuart (Monday, March 16th)

Love Quest is a weird auld place. Most of the 'Women Recommended for You' profiles look like 12-year-old choir boys with their short hair and glasses. Is this a new trend I don't know about?

Suzanne (Monday, March 16th)

Dear Diary,

Fi arrived to work with the worst thigh tattoo I've ever seen. She even has a name for it, 'love handles.' Apparently, it represents Fi's lower backside (the love handles) her legs (the scissor blades) and her love for cutting hair (the full scissors). Siobhan and I maintained our best straight face as Fi strutted around the salon modelling her leg in the mirrors.

I met Mum for lunch. She was walking with a limp on the way back to the salon. When I asked about the limp, she admitted to trying out new things with Mr Rocket. I didn't push for more information. Mr Rocket's new Porsche isn't real. He paid Greg Fitz (part-time mechanic and a 'full-time mad bastard' - according to his Facebook) a couple of grand to build an imitation version of the Porsche. Apparently, it's one of those kit cars. It looks the part in fairness. I'm sure only a select few would know it was a fake.

Stuart (Tuesday, March 17th)

Joined the lads in town for a few earlier as I had enough of Love Quest. They managed to entice me by sending on candid pictures of their surroundings in O'Driscoll's Bar. One of the pictures showed a girl (who looked VERY like the girl from The Barge) wearing a giant leprechaun hat. I didn't waste any time.

When I got down to the pub the place was rammed full of tourists drinking Guinness and talking like pirates to some of the locals. There was no sign of the girl from The Barge. Out in the smoking area (car park really), it was a sea of green jackets, t-shirts and hats. It was tough to piece together the photo I had seen earlier, but more specifically the details of how the girl from The Barge was dressed. Then I remembered, I had the photo on my phone. Alcohol is a bad thing! When I looked at the pic the second time, I realised it was her and the importance of this sighting hit home. Finally. A sign! A glimpse of hope among the hopeless. I knew time was of the essence, so I scanned the picture one last time. Accompanying her leprechaun head-dress was a black leather jacket. Underneath the jacket, she was wearing a dark green army shirt buttoned to her neck. I took a look around. All I could see was rugby-looking guys with fake leprechaun ears. I didn't see one leather jacket or a green army shirt. She wasn't inside either. I contemplated asking several groups of girls if they had seen, spoken to, or knew of the two girls in the picture the lads had sent earlier. I decided against that as it would probably come across as ultra-creepy and I'm bad enough!

The rest of the evening was a bit of a downer. I had dragged the lads to every pub in town (including a double espresso at The Barge) in the hope of finding my princess. Unfortunately, she was nowhere to be found.

I just spotted a text from Maggie. I must have missed it earlier.

8:41 pm

"Stu, I'm not mad at you for what happened with Zofia. I hope we can go back to being good friends. I miss our chats x."

11:45pm

I'll probably regret this, but I just quit Love Quest. I came to realise that my real quest is not some coked-up 22-year-old from up the road, but in fact, the girl from The Barge. I will find her, and I will marry her!

Text from Charlie in San Francisco:

"Asian threesome, say nothing."

Suzanne (Tuesday, March 17th)

No entry

Stuart (Wednesday, March 18th)

Work was absolute hell. The place was infested with tourists (mainly Spanish kids in leprechaun hats who seemed intent on raising the decibel level) Fortunately, Maggie popped in and wasn't long cheering me up. She had a tray of prime-cut steaks and asked if I fancied sharing them tonight? Maggie claimed her cooker blew up and asked if she could cook them here instead. I was happy to oblige, and even more happy that things have settled down since the Zofia escapade.

All in all, we had a very nice night. The steaks were delicious, Maggie's homemade sauce was exquisite. I told her about my idea to combine an egg yolk with Yorkshire Relish and sell it as a super sauce...

she said it sounded vile. And that cheap wine we picked up in the off-licence wasn't that bad. Maggie said she lifted Patryk's grounding as he is behaving himself – even hoovering, cutting the grass, washing the windows, etc. Maggie claimed, 'Once he has his headphones and his aroma plants, he's happy.' I didn't comment. Anyway, everything was going swimmingly until the French couple from upstairs decided to go at it like rabbits. Talk about bad timing. To avoid the awkwardness of it all, Maggie excused herself to the loo. As convincing as she set out to be, I'm not so sure Maggie is over the whole Zofia thing.

Suzanne (Wednesday, March 18th)

Dear Diary,

If there was ever a day when I needed a day off it was today. I'm still rattled from yesterday, and I don't mean rattled from alcohol! Zia picked me up from mine at 10 am and we drove down to the parade.

We left the car in her sister's place just at the fire station. Zia's sister looks like a mini version of her. So too, her sisters' kids. Very cute!

When we got into town, we were fortunate enough to get a nice spot to see the parade pass through. An old man who owned one of the Georgian houses where we had been standing let us sit on his wall. There was a great variety at this year's parade; though I must confess, we didn't see everything on the bill as we left early to avoid the queues at the pub (priorities and all that).

For lunch, we opted to hit The Barge as we knew it would be quiet until 2 pm or so. We were right. From there we made our way up to O'Driscoll's for some good music. That place was an absolute madhouse, and by 4 pm or so was getting a little too messy for us so we made a break for Hooli's Bar.

Strangely, Hooli's was pretty quiet. Out in the smoking area, some bloke had mentioned that 'an undesirable family,' from the Broadfield Estates (who normally drink there on Paddy's Day) were about; hence the lack of regulars. The bloke could have mentioned the McDonagh family by name, everybody knows who they are. Even more so when you mention Broadfield. Hooli's was lackluster so we decided to head to The Copacabana for some cocktails. That's when it all went pear-shaped!!

After one too many Mojitos, Zia had asked me to accompany her to the loo. She said she needed to fix her dress as it had been tormenting her all day. When we got down to the women's bathroom Zia fixed her makeup and attempted to get rid of the wine stains on her teeth. As I was fixing my hair, Zia occupied one of the cubicles. She seemed to be taking forever before she whispered my name urgently, 'Sue, Sue, come here. This fucking zip is a nightmare.' I didn't even stop to think. I just made my way over. When I stepped into the cubicle, Zia was standing there in her underwear. She pushed the door shut, put her hand on my face and began kissing my neck. I was in so much shock it took me a few seconds to stop her. I yelled her name, pushed her away and then asked her what the hell was she thinking? She replied, 'I thought you wanted me?' I didn't know what to say. Had I been leading her along? I don't think so. We were just friends getting to know each other, as friends do. Embarrassed by the mess I had gotten myself into, I told Zia I had to go. Zia replied, 'That's it? You're just gonna up and go leave me here half-dressed?' Diary, I had to, it was too awkward.

When I got home, I plugged in my phone. It had been dead for most of the day since I forgot to charge it last night. There were three missed calls from Zia. I must have dozed off because that's the last thing I can remember.

I'm still in shock today. What to do? I called Mum and told her what had happened. It wasn't long before she arrived over with some fish and chips and plenty of hugs. Mum said she had no idea that Zia was into me in that way. Mum assumed Zia had a bit of a thing for Mr Rocket; she based this on the way she was flirting with him the night we were all out together. Mum was still here when Zia called my phone a while ago. I didn't answer it. I need to think about how we ended up as we did. Have I been giving off the wrong signs? Was it something that I said? I don't want to lose her as a friend, but it's going to be very hard knowing how she feels about me.

I went for some food with Siobhan and Fi after work. They were raving about this dating app called Love Quest; certainly, the last thing I wanted to hear about. Fi said she's been inundated with guys contacting her and said I'd be a fool not to sign up. I'm not quite sure if I could trust it. You wouldn't know what you're getting yourself into there: married guys, creeps, all sorts of unwanted distractions. I told Fi I'd be monitoring her progress. I will make an informed decision on whether or not I should sign up from there.

Stuart (Thursday, March 19th)

I spotted Polish Sletva from Love Quest earlier. I'd know those eyes a mile away. I was out having a smoke in front of the shop, and Sletva was standing outside the newsagents, speaking aggressively to someone on the phone. When she was done, she swanned past me like a peacock, her arms weighed down with an array of fancy shopping bags. She looked me dead in the eye. It was a look of disgust. She smelled great though.

Patryk called in shortly after. He asked me would I mind 1,000 euro for him. He said that he can't keep it in the house in case his mam finds it. Yeah, I'd look after it on one condition, I wanted to know the truth. I went on the attack. 'Was it you that broke into the shop a few weeks back?' He smirked but didn't offer up any information. I gave him one last chance and asked again. He put his head down in shame. I thought I had him, then he replied, 'It wasn't me, man.' Regardless, I ended up taking his money. I hid it in an empty floor-wash bottle under the canteen sink.

Suzanne (Thursday, March 19th)

I felt weird about ignoring Zia's calls, so I called her on my lunch break. I assured her I wasn't angry and that I might have overreacted in The Copacabana the other night. She claimed that she was in the wrong due to being drunk and horny. I couldn't help but laugh and reminded Zia that we've all been there.

Mr Rocket has purchased a new car. A 2009 Porsche Convertible, nonetheless. I'm not so sure where he got the money for that. I highly doubt it was the fruits of his event manager position. Fi said that she spotted Mum and Mr Rocket stuck in traffic – Mum looking like the Queen of England waving at passers-by, while Mr Rocket used the stoppage to put the roof up, and then down again, before cranking up Bruce Springsteen.

Stuart (Friday, March 20th)

CRAZY DAY!!

I'm still in Maggie's place, it's 2:25 am.

Not long after opening the shop I got a phone call from Maggie, or so I thought. 'Hello, is this Stu?' It was Maggie's phone, but I didn't recognise the voice. 'Who's this?' I replied. It was a paramedic. She had called to say that Maggie had collapsed on the stairs of the Grand Central Shopping Centre and wanted to know if I could come down straight away. I didn't even stop to ask what had happened, I just asked Trish to cover me and ran.

When I got there, they were loading Maggie into the back of an ambulance on a stretcher. She was awake but looked to be out of it. I grabbed her hand and asked if she was OK? She smiled and replied, 'Now I am.' Her eyes closed over. A young girl tapped me on the shoulder and said she'd been standing behind Maggie on the escalator when Maggie started shaking like mad and then fell on top of her. An older woman elaborated, 'I think she had a heart attack.' The paramedic chimed in, 'We can't be certain, but she might have had an epileptic fit.' I didn't want to leave Maggie on her own, so I went with them to the hospital.

At the hospital, there was a considerable wait in the A&E. It must have been after 4 pm when Maggie was finally seen to, and subsequently dispatched. The doc confirmed it was an epileptic fit, that could have been brought on for several reasons.

When we got back to Maggie's, I made her a sandwich and a pot of tea and put her to bed early. I reckon she's still in shock.

I've been trying to get in contact with Patryk all day, but he's not answering his phone. He has now powered it off altogether. Knowing Patryk, and the likelihood of him mistaking me for an intruder and stabbing me to death, I left a note on the door explaining everything. Hopefully, he reads the fucking thing.

Suzanne (Friday, March 20th)

Dear Diary,

I got an awful fright this morning before work. I got into town early so I decided to run up to get some stationery in the GCSC. I was standing on the escalator on the way up to the 2nd floor when I heard a thud behind me. A woman, older than me, collapsed and fell down a few steps on top of some school kids. I ran to the top of the escalator and pushed the 'Stop' button, before walking back down the still steps. The woman was shaking like crazy; her eyes were in the back of her head. Anxious, I shouted for help, then took out my phone and dialed 999. One of the shopping centre security guards came running down from the 2nd floor. Thankfully he seemed to know what he was doing and placed the lady in a recovery position. I had gotten such a fright that I was still shaking when the ambulance arrived. The sweat was pouring out of me and I was beginning to feel like I was about to faint. Once I could see everything was under control, I ran to the bathroom to splash my face with some cold water. I called Fi and told her to open the salon as I was running late. I must have sat in the cubicle for another hour or so before coming around. I'm way too soft for anything like that... a drop of blood, a bone break, any sort of fit, I can't handle it.

I felt a bit out of it for the rest of the morning, so I decided to take two paracetamols to get me through the afternoon. Luckily, we had a quiet one.

Fi is going on a date with an Italian guy she met on this Love Quest dating app. His name is Ugolino.

Stuart (Saturday, March 21st)

I overheard a customer talking about a new dating app named FumbleFun, so I decided to check it out. In doing so I also downloaded two other apps that came up on my suggestions, namely Cupid Quest and Happy Ever After. FumbleFun is like a one-stop-shop for sexual encounters – as opposed to Love Quest and Cupid Quest where most are trying to find genuine relationships. The other one, Happy Ever After seems to be geared towards divorcees, so I didn't spend a whole lot of time there. Weirdly, the thought of looking beyond Love Quest hadn't even crossed my mind. There I am, day in day out, scouring that place like a man possessed in an attempt to find my Kim Gordon Jnr from The Barge when she might be chillin' over on Fumblefun waiting to be swept off her feet. Unfortunately, there's been no sign of her just yet.

I brought Maggie some women's magazines and a coffee cake this evening. I didn't stay too long as it was after 3 am when I left her place last night. She seems to be a lot better in herself. I think the realisation that she is epileptic has come as a bit of a shock to her.

Suzanne (Saturday, March 21st)

Dear Diary,

Mum popped in this afternoon. She said that Mr Rocket put a hole in her kitchen wall after finding the word "Fake" scraped across the side of his new car. Both Mum and Mr Rocket reckon Greg Fitz (the part-time mechanic) put some kids up to it. Mum reckons Fitz sees Mr Rocket as an easy target that he'll continue to milk money out of. I reckon she's right.

When I was closing up the salon, I noticed a rather handsome man standing outside. He was holding a white rose. I mentioned him to Siobhan, who didn't recognise him. Fi interrupted our investigation, 'OH MY GOD! I AM MORTIFIED!' Fi knocked on the window and said, 'What are you doing, you eejit?' The dark stranger stepped inside, 'Fi-Fi, my sweetie, a rosa for-a you.' Poor Fi went purple. 'Ugolino, how did you know where I worked? We only met last night,' said Fi, wiping a tear from her eye. Ugolino replied, 'I look on-a the Facebook, I see-a the workplace.' After returning to a healthy complexion, Fi did the rounds, introducing Ugolino to everyone. Let me be the first to say, he was far from Ugolino.

1:18 am

Diary, I was just thinking about Ugolino and how sweet he was today. I wonder if this Love Quest malarkey is worth a shot. I'd be thrilled if I met a guy like that.

Stuart (Sunday, March 22nd)

It has to be said, FumbleFun isn't all that fun. In fact, it's a complete pain in the arse as you can't even send a message without having to pay for it. No wonder people are getting their hole – they're paying for it! I'm not down with prostituting myself! Fumbleoff!

Suzanne (Sunday, March 22nd)

Dear Diary,

I know I'll regret this, but I have signed up for Love Quest, the dating site where Fi met the ultra-charming Ugolino. I have no idea what I'm doing. I was asked to upload a photo but decided not to, as I don't want everyone knowing my business. The site seems to have a lot of paid features, too, which makes me believe the whole thing is one big money-racket. My profile description reads:

Easy going, hard-working-girl, looking to meet a nice guy.

I didn't know what to put in for hobbies, but under interests, I wrote:

Eating, Drinking, Socialising.

It's tough to separate yourself from the pack.

Stuart (Monday, March 23rd)

I bumped into Maggie in the Farmers' Market this morning. She said she was feeling a lot better and had been resting up all weekend. After following her around and holding her bags for about three hours, we decided to go for a pint and a bite to eat in Hooli's. We ended up staying there until 7:30 pm this evening! I kind of like it when Maggie is a little sauced up. She gets quite flirty and touchy-feely and makes me feel good about myself. On top of that, there were a few moments when she kissed me on the edge of my lips, kind of a half cheek/half lips kiss and looked at me lustfully, waiting for me to kiss her back. I wanted to horse in but was fearful of a potential retaliation because of the situation with her sister a few weeks back.

Text from Charlie:

"Got off with a jailbird in Alcatraz, German foreign exchange student."

Suzanne (Monday, March 23rd)

Dear Diary,

I have given in and put two pictures on my Love Quest profile. The first one is a picture from last year's staff party. Fi said the ample amount of cleavage on display is sure to pull them in. The second picture is from Nicole's Halloween party back in 2011. I don't care if the picture is old, I like it and have made it my profile pic. It's the one where I dressed up as Mr Tea; complete with handle, spout, mohawk and gold chains. As of writing, I have 'No New Messages' in my inbox.

Stuart (Tuesday, March 24th)

Right, back to Love Quest. These other apps have been nothing short of a pain in the arse! FumbleFun is a money racket! Happy Ever After seems to be full of American housewives who are only interested in how much money I make, and Cupid Quest, don't even get me started! Every profile on this thing is fake. Am I to believe this Baywatch looking beauty from Ballygobricken?

Name - Tiffany Jones

Age - 24

Sex - F

Occupation - Digital Marketing Manager

Hobbies - Baseball, Nascar, MMA

Interests - Wine tasting in the Valley, long walks in the fall, Netflix.

I very much doubt she's talking about wine tasting in the Gap of Dunloe. I think it's time to quit some of these apps while I'm ahead.

Suzanne (Tuesday, March 24th)

Dear Diary,

Finally, I am getting somewhere on this bloody Love Quest thing. Fi advised me to get rid of the Mr Tea picture and make the cleavage picture my profile image. I have also updated two new pictures. Both were taken at work by Nicole and Siobhan. The girls spent a good hour doing my hair and makeup beforehand and the photos came out well... even if I do say so myself.

I passed Eric Reeves walking down the street after work. His face seems to have healed pretty well. He smiled and saluted me when passing. I nodded and saluted him in return. I don't want to hold a grudge against him forever, life is too short.

Stuart (Wednesday, March 25th)

Patryk was in today. He asked if I would be OK to mind an additional €1,000 in cash. Reluctantly, I agreed and stuffed it in the wash bottles with the rest of his money.

I discovered some bruises on my back after yesterday's run-in with that French wannabe Mr Universe. I might call down to their apartment tomorrow and apologise, even though I wasn't in the wrong. I would go down tonight but I'm too sore.

Suzanne (Wednesday, March 25th)

Dear Diary,

I seem to be getting a considerable number of messages on Love Quest. I'm guessing it has something to do with prioritising the cleavage profile pic. I showed Mum some of the messages I received. She was in shock! I also showed her some of the pics guys have sent, some of which were a little inappropriate. Mum got a great kick out of these and was falling around the place laughing. Seriously, Diary, there are so many messages, I don't know where to start? One thing I do know is this - if the rest of the messages read like the few I've read; Love Quest can take a hike! I'll happily settle for a life with Mr Snuggles and become a full-time lonely-cat-lady.

Stuart (Thursday, March 26th)

I have been gifted a black eye and my face is cut to bits thanks to that French oaf and his psychotic girlfriend! All I wanted to do was apologise, so I called down to their apartment after work. I was standing outside their door, contemplating what to say when the door swung open unexpectedly. 'See, I told you,' the French girl said. Her French boyfriend came storming out, 'Le fucking pervert!' He hit me a couple of times. Each blow was hard and to the face. When he stopped, his girlfriend stood out from behind the door and said, 'He was looking in the peephole, DIS-GUS-TING!' She was kicking me in the head with her slippers as she shouted the words. I have no luck with women!

Text from Charlie in San Francisco:

"I wrote off one of the company cars. Will fill you in tomorrow... if I make it back, lol."

Suzanne (Thursday, March 26th)

Dear Diary,

I've received two new messages on Love Quest;

simonstudly91 – "Nice tits" - 2:06 pm

4204lyfe – "Hello, I like your profile, which, if I can be brutally honest, reads just as awkward as mine. Strangely, your picture would suggest otherwise... don't ask me why. Anyway, I'm going to assume you're not here to find a pen pal, so how about a coffee or a drink? I'm free tomorrow evening from 5:30 pm - 8:50 pm."

Diary, I think I'm going to take a gamble and meet 4204lyfe.

Stuart (Friday, March 27th)

I arrived to work with my black eye only to be greeted by Trish and her menacing laugh. She agreed that it looked brutal and offered a quick fix which involved 30 minutes of applying makeup and blusher to my face.

It was only by chance that I took a look in the mirror during lunch, I looked like a haggard version of Conchita Worst; the Austrian Eurovision winner, notable for her beard. I was wondering why everybody was smiling at me all morning. As far as Trish pranks go, that one was up there, albeit revenge is sweet!

Suzanne (Friday, March 27th)

No entry

Stuart (Saturday, March 28th)

I had to be up at 5 am to pick Charlie up from the airport. He was buckled drunk when he got off the plane and was buggering me to go to

The Oval for early pints at 7 am. Stupidly I agreed. We got thrown out of the place shortly after 4 pm after Charlie tried to rob two packets of bacon fries from behind the bar. I'm sitting here with a 5 in 1 (curry, rice, chips, beef and onion) ... filthy, I know, watching a documentary about the guy who played Big Bird on Sesame Street. What a job! He seemed like an affable chap and certainly the right man for the role. I'm not sure how I'm still functioning, to be honest, I think I'm wired from all the Red Bull & vodka.

Sue (Saturday, March 28th)

Dear Diary,

My sincerest apologies for not making an entry last night, I ended up sleeping with 4204lyfe (real name, Barry) from Love Quest.

It's safe to say Barry is an absolute gent, a real dote of a guy. He had me laughing all night with his witty one-liners and stories; even if they went on forever and went nowhere. We left the pub just after midnight and I agreed to go back to his. While the lingering smell of cannabis would put any Amsterdam coffee shop to shame, his house was very mod, like something you would have seen in the 60s with the decor and colour scheme. Barry said his housemate is an interior decorator, hence the attention to detail and different themes throughout the house. Everything was going swimmingly until we got down to business. Sadly, after much effort on my behalf, poor Barry couldn't get it up. I thought it was me, maybe he didn't find me attractive, or maybe he was turned off by my body. I didn't know what to say or do. After about 20 minutes of foreplay, Barry came clean and told me he was diabetic. 'Sometimes it doesn't work.' I assumed he was talking about his manhood. He continued, 'I'm really sorry, Sue. Why do I always assume this time will be different?' My heart went out to him, it did. I told Barry it was OK, not to worry – after all, sex isn't everything. I had to lie of course. Barry seemed content and was happy to continue the foreplay before stopping to smoke a joint and subsequently fall asleep ten minutes later. I managed to creep out and get a taxi home shortly after.

I received a text message from Zia;

"Hey darling, miss you. Let's meet up during the week xxx."

I'm happy to hear from her. I kind of miss her bluntness. Kind of…

Stuart (Sunday, March 29th)

I woke up with a massive erection; why do I always feel horny when I'm hung-over?

By this evening I was still feeling frisky, so I decided to reactivate my Love Quest profile. I sent out a few messages, and although I've received the read receipts, I've received nothing back. There seems to be a lot of new, hot profiles on there, too, some of which I have now added to my favourites. It's going to take me a while to filter through matches within the 25km radius I have set. You never know unless you go, right?

My eye is still very tender and very sore after my run-in with that French oaf. I have no doubt my current appearance will dampen any chance of success on Love Quest.

Suzanne (Sunday, March 29th)

Dear Diary,

I spent the afternoon shopping with Mum. Our first stop? Ann Summers. Mum said she wanted to pick up some sexy knickers to impress Mr Rocket for his birthday. She ended up buying stockings, boots, a corset and a whip, 'for the craic,' as she put it.

A message from Barry;

"Hi Sue, I enjoyed spending time with you on Friday. Thanks for understanding my situation and not passing judgement. I was just thinking; did you ever consider that a particle of dust might contain an entire universe? I mean not just a planet like earth, but multiple planets with a host of species? Also, imagine that we are living in a particle, and inside that particle, there are multiple particles all of which contain even more particles. Multiple worlds inside each other. Anyway, I'm starving, off to make some pot noodles. Speak soon - 4204lyfe xxx."

Stuart (Monday, March 30th)

I received a message on Love Quest from an Asian girl named Effie who doesn't seem concerned with the pleasantries.

Her message reads:

"You want to meet?"

She looks nice, kind of nerdy but kind of hot at the same time.

I replied with:

"I would love to. I am free in the evenings and have Thursday off."

Let's see…

Suzanne (Monday, March 30th)

Dear Diary,

Ugolino proposed to Fi in the salon! It was quite the affair. Dressed from head to toe in the Italian soccer team's away kit, Ugolino, accompanied by two lads playing the, 'just one Cornetto' song on accordions, waltzed through the floor just after lunch. Fi's face was scarlet red, but that didn't stop Ugolino getting down on his knee to pop the question. 'Fiona-Lisa-Blossom-O'Rourke, my a-princess, the love of my life-a... will you make me a-real-a-man and be-a my wife?' Fi had her hand over her mouth. I think she wanted to burst her hole laughing but had to hold it in. In reply, she didn't move her hand. Instead, she just nodded as a tear rolled down her cheek. It was tough to tell if they were tears of laughter or tears of joy but most everybody took her nod as a yes. Ugolino swept Fi off her feet and laid her onto his knee. Swooping down like an eagle targeting its prey, the Italian stallion embraced Fi in a passionate kiss. While the kiss went on longer than it should have, it will probably save Fi getting her teeth polished on Thursday. Everyone in attendance clapped as Ugolino, his two mates and Fi posed for photos.

A message from Barry:

"Hi Sue, I just wanted to say thanks again for the other night. I enjoyed your company. If you're doing nothing Friday and would like to grab a drink, I'm free. No funny business. Btw, have you ever tried guacamole on popcorn? It's a winner!! - 4204lyfe."

Stuart (Tuesday, March 31st)

I spent the evening chatting with Effie, the Asian girl from Love Quest. Things got a bit lost in translation at one point. I had assumed she was asking me where she could by some bondage gear, but after a lot of over and backs it turned out she was looking for a bandage having burnt herself with the kettle.

Suzanne (Tuesday, March 31st)

Dear Diary,

Zia has invited me to the Annual Press Ball this Saturday night. I'm delighted, as I've always wanted to go, but was never connected to anyone working in the media industry. This year's theme is Film Fancy Dress with the tagline... Dress to Impress. I can but try. I might have to give Barry a miss on Friday, otherwise, I'll be exhausted Saturday and in no form for the ball.

Mum called tonight to say that a bunch of kids stripped Mr Rocket's body kit car down to the seat and steering wheel. They did a runner with the rest. Mr Rocket took a baseball bat to what was left of the car. In Mum's words, 'he beat the living shit out of it.' Poor Mr Rocket, he's going to give himself a heart attack someday.

Stuart (Wednesday, April 1st)

I arrived at work to find the usual junk mail slid under the front door. Among the array of pizza offers and bills was a letter addressed directly to me. I thought it strange as most everything is addressed to Reality Records. Imagine my surprise to find a letter from a researcher at the BBC. His name was Andy Smith and he was curious to know if Reality Records would like to participate in a two-part series detailing the longevity and importance of the independent record store... and... by the way... the interviews will be conducted by Ray Davies (The Kinks) in our store. I had to do a double take. Thee Ray Davies!! The singer with The Kinks, my favourite band of all time. What the actual fuck? I ran down the stairs shouting, 'Trish! Trish!' When I got to the ground floor, I could see Trish smoking a cigarette in the doorway. I made my way over, 'You.Are.Not.Going.To.Believe.This,' I said, I could barely get the words out I was so excited. 'What is it?' Trish replied. I handed her the letter from the BBC. She began to read the letter. As I stood there waiting for her response, she began to chuckle, before bursting out laughing. 'I can't… your poor face,' she said. I had copped it. I was the victim, once again, to Trish's April fool joke. How does she get me every year? 'Sorry, Stu… I know…' I had to cut her off, I told her that was it and she had taken it too far this year. Trish was wiping the tears from her face and was now in hysterics. I shook my head in disgust. I wasn't angry, but I did take a vow of silence as a form of banter for the remainder of the day.

Effie, the Asian girl from Love Quest, has agreed to meet me tomorrow night. Well… she replied "Yap," which I guess means yes. I sent her my number and told her to meet me at La Maison. Chances are I won't bump into any of the usual faces there.

I called over to Maggie's shop after work to pick up some fresh cod and say hello. I was reluctant to tell her about my date tomorrow night as she would have kept me there for another hour asking questions. However, she did ask if I was, 'still stalking that poor girl.' I knew she was referring to the girl from The Barge, so I gave Maggie a snappy reply. 'Always,' I said. It did sound a little creepy, I will admit. Maggie also said that Patryk has been acting very suspicious over the last bit. She said that he doesn't speak much but is eating an awful lot these days. She also said that Patryk has become, 'very into himself.'

Suzanne (Wednesday, April 1st)

Dear Diary,

Boy, it feels good to be cutting hair again. I was a bit all over the place for the past two days, but today I realised why I do what I do. I love it! I was a little unsure about doing a full day of cuts on Monday but let it be said, my fingers feel fine. Hopefully, I can refrain from punching people in the face for the foreseeable future.

Stuart (Thursday, April 2nd)

What a bitch! I just passed Mr Universe's French girlfriend in the hallway. While I'm not 100% certain, I could have sworn she said, 'Prick,' under her breath as I passed.

Nonetheless, my date with the Asian girl, Effie was nice. I have no fucking idea if she understood anything I was harping on about as, for the most part, she replied with, 'Nice!' while nodding and smiling. In saying, she did down seven pints of Guinness and beat me to the end of the glass every time.

PS - I will get over having to pay for EVERY round as she did point to the speakers and gave a subtle thumbs up when The Kinks 'Waterloo Sunset' came on the jukebox. We have arranged to meet again on Sunday afternoon.

Suzanne (Thursday, April 2nd)

Dear Diary,

Mum and Zia have been here all evening helping me finish my Catwoman costume for the Annual Press Ball. It looks pretty sweet. The only thing I'm missing is the gloves, which I hope I can source tomorrow. Zia has decided to go as Wonder Woman and has also made her costume from scratch. The only thing Zia was missing was Wonder

Woman's signature gold whip. Mum, bless her, offered up her bondage whip but after much explanation realised it wasn't that kind of whip. After disappearing for a bit, Mum popped back to the living room, soaked to the bone and holding the clothesline from the back garden. 'I'm sure Mr Rocket has some gold spray paint leftover from his car kit. We could spray paint the clothesline and turn it into a Wonder Woman whip.' It wasn't the worst of ideas in fairness. We took the rope, sprayed it up, and left it to dry for a bit. Later, we attached it to Zia's belt. It looked great! Zia was thrilled, as was Mum, and they both celebrated by downing the two bottles of Prosecco I had. They are both passed out, wrapped around each other on the couch downstairs.

11:50 pm

Shit, a message from Barry -

"I knew you wouldn't reply. Sorry for wasting your time. Why would a girl like you have any interest in a lame-ass, limp dick, like me? You deserve better - 4204lyfe."

Diary, I feel so bad. He is such a sweet guy.

6:30 am

I messaged Barry and told him I would meet him. I said I'll be taking it easy as I have the Annual Press Ball on Saturday. My guilty conscience got the better of me.

Stuart (Friday, April 3rd)

Earlier today, Rodge popped in to say he had two spare tickets to the Annual Press Ball. His flatmate was scheduled to go with her boyfriend but she's sick. Rodge had no interest and asked me if I wanted to take the tickets. I agreed. Now, who to bring?

Option 1 - My new Asian friend, Effie? I thought it might be too soon.

Option 2 - Trish? Not her thing.

Option 3 - Charlie? Would be too messy.

Option 4 - Maggie? What the hell. I decided to give her a call. Maggie was over the moon and arranged to meet at lunch to put some last-minute costume ideas together. I settled on an XL Spiderman costume from the kids' toy shop. It was a little tight, but I think I'll get away with it. Maggie, on the other hand, looks great as Princess Leia from *Star Wars*; the hair, the big toy-gun and the infamous long white dress that went perfectly with Maggie's white boots. I think she'll go down a storm!

After lunch, Patryk popped in. Regretfully, I took an additional €2,000 from him and hid it in the wash bottle at work. Patryk said his mother is, 'like a detective going about the place.' She's grilling him about everything. I know how Maggie can be so that's why I tend to help him out. Albeit, I need to find a better hiding place before Trish finds it.

Dad phoned this evening. He has some bad news. Paddy 'Gummy' Hinchey is in the hospital with pneumonia. Dad said he caught Gummy drinking a can of Guinness in the hospital bed. Gummy told Dad it was a gift from one of his fellow army retirees and to 'mind his own business.'

Suzanne (Friday, April 3rd)

5:10 am

Dear Diary,

I've just returned from Barry's but before I go there, I want you to know... my Catwoman outfit is complete! I found the perfect set of leather gloves in the charity shop and spent the afternoon doctoring them (and not working) so that they run the length of my arm.

Anyway, back to Barry. Diary, please forgive me. I ended up sleeping with him once again. Yes, he's a nice guy and sure, he's a great kisser, but I'm not sure I can hack another night of trying to make his penis stand up. Tonight, was in essence, a carbon copy of our first night together, but instead of lurking about after he smoked a joint and passed out, I ran out the door and flagged a taxi. I can't keep doing this. I'm soft, but not that soft... ahem!

Stuart (Saturday, April 4th)

I got into a scrap with Captain America outside the taxi rank – well, a bloke who was dressed as such – coming from the Annual Press Ball. He tried to hijack the taxi Maggie and I had called and went as far as to clock me with his shield after I argued that we were there first. If the scene of Captain America scrapping with Spiderman outside a taxi rank wasn't odd enough, the entire debacle was pulled apart by a bloke dressed as a Brokeback Mountain cowboy.

Assholes aside, the Press Ball was an absolute blast and the level of costume creativity needed to be seen to be believed. Maggie got a lot of attention, too, mainly from the nerdy comic book millennials who tried but failed miserably to get her number on several occasions.

Post dinner, we descended on the smoking area as the music wasn't so loud – and more importantly – as shit. I ended up chatting to Art Townsend (Culture section of *The Gazette*) for a good bit. Nice guy, but

I've heard the 'Morrissey is a genius,' fanboy comments, one too many times. We also bumped into a lively couple of girls, one dressed as Catwoman and the other dressed as Wonder Woman. They looked great! We spent the remainder of the night chatting with them before losing them to a bunch of lads dressed up as Chippendales.

I've been nursing my eye with a frozen bag of peas for the last hour. Maggie, bless her, is passed out on the couch clutching the remnants of her bag of chips. Trish is going to have a field day when she sees my face. And Effie? Well, she'll probably run for her life!

Suzanne (Saturday, April 4th)

6:40 am

Dear Diary,

Forgive me if I'm not making sense, it is very early Sunday morning and I'm very, very drunk!

I have just escaped from a house party full of mad bastards dressed as Chippendales. Zia, on the other hand, is still there, sitting on the countertop, wrapped around some rugby player. All nice guys in fairness, but I struggle in an environment where everyone is off their nut on drugs. I quit that scene many years ago.

The Annual Press Ball was A-MAZING! We started with a four-course meal; I had the chicken skewers for starters, duck with sage for the main, death by chocolate (incredible!) for dessert, and Irish coffee to finish me off. Our table (6 in total) managed to get through 5 bottles of red wine! Not a bad effort whatsoever. After the meal, Zia and I were a bit giddy and ended up dancing (and singing with the band in Zia's case) to a medley of Abba songs. That didn't last long as my Gucci heels were killing my feet.

With my shoes in my hands, Zia and I descended on the smoking area. We ended up cracking jokes with a lovely couple; a bloke dressed as Spiderman who spent the evening sipping whiskey through his mask, and his partner, a gorgeous Polish girl dressed as the princess from *Star Wars*. They were adorable, so funny! We were going to invite them back to ours, but we lost them in the madness.

All in all, it was a great night! I just hope Zia is OK with all those muscleheads back in the house.

Stuart (Sunday, April 5th)

So, I woke up to find myself sporting a 2nd black eye, just when I thought the first one was healing up. Thanks, Captain America! Neither Maggie nor I spotted the extent of the damage as I was still wearing my Spiderman costume at the time. Unfortunately, I got a bit of a rude awakening when I looked in the bathroom mirror first thing this morning. Knowing that I had a date with Effie this evening, I called Trish and begged her to call over and fix me up with her makeup skills. Trish said she'd help, but only if I covered her taxi fare and made her lunch. So, over she came and did a great job of hiding the damage inflicted by Captain America using a mixture of concealer, foundation and a light coat of makeup.

The date itself went well, although Effie did get a little heated when I couldn't remember her birth name (Jiālíng... she made me write it down). Tonight, once again, she stressed that she was looking for a 'friend,' to help her 'improve the English.' Weirdly, I'm OK with that as she is pretty funny and seems to have a unique take on the world. Effie believes movies are for children and books are for adults. She also believes music died in 1994. She is also obsessed with a lady named Kiyoko Takagi (she made me write it down) who is famous for eating large amounts of food in a single sitting. I'm watching her right now; two massive plates of sushi, a giant bowl of noodles, three giant bowls of rice, a giant bowl of seafood, two giant bowls of what looks like seaweed or cabbage and a massive platter of meat. This Kiyoko Takagi girl is unbelievable! She's as thin as a rake! Is this shit real? I'm not sure I should mention the wonders of video editing when I see Effie again, she'll probably have me on a platter.

Suzanne (Sunday, April 5th)

Dear Diary,

I'm having a lot of flashbacks from last night. I just remembered galloping through the bar on Spiderman's back. I am mortified!!

Mum and Mr Rocket invited Zia and me over for Sunday dinner. Unfortunately, I couldn't get in touch with Zia as her phone was off all morning. I made my way to Mum's, nonetheless.

Mr Rocket said he has given up on the body kits and is now in the market for a second-hand Mercedes. He said the kits were a waste of time and that the kids are hell-bent on showing you up. I guess he was referring whoever wrote "Fake" on his Porsche body kit. Mum reckons Mr Rocket is having a midlife crisis and has advised him to get something more appropriate for a man of his age. She also went on a rant about Geraldine's (Mum's neighbour) hatchback and the number of groceries she manages to squeeze into it. Mr Rocket made it through a full bottle of wine by the time Mum properly drew breath.

10:05 pm

Text from Zia

"I can't walk, but I'm OK! Xxx."

Stuart (Monday, April 6th)

I spent a good hour massaging my eye with the frozen peas this morning. It didn't make any difference. Again, I had to ask Trish to work her magic with some foundation and makeup. Much like yesterday, she did a great job as only a handful of the regulars copped the damage.

I took a further €2,000 from Patryk before close. He said, 'That's it for now.' I told him that it better be as it's not a fucking bank I'm running there.

1:19 am

A text message from Dad

"Gummy has passed."

It feels weird even writing that. Gummy was one of those people we'd always see about; birthdays, weddings, funerals, Christmas, you name it! Never in a million years do you think about a guy like that passing away. He seemed resilient to everything that was thrown at him. It's clichéd but true, all good things do come to an end.

Rest in peace, Paddy. I'll be sure to have one for you x

Suzanne (Monday, April 6th)

Dear Diary,

I ended up taking the bus to work as it was pissing rain. Who was seated behind me? Eric Reeves. I was no longer seated, when he tapped me on the shoulder and said, 'Hello, stranger.' I said hello and pretended like I hadn't seen him. He knew I had. Our small chat continued for what seemed like an eternity, but in chatting he did offer another apology for 'approaching me,' (assaulting me, asshole!) and seemed pretty content with the reshaping of his nose.

Barry (4204lyfe) has invited me to Amsterdam for the May Bank Holiday. He needs to get out of that fog (in every sense).

Stuart (Tuesday, April 7th)

Rolling Stone had an article about Kurt Cobain's passing today. Where does the time go? After discussing the who's, what's, where's, whys and how's of how we got into Nirvana, Trish and I ended up blasting out their much-lauded debut, 'Bleach,' for most of the afternoon. In doing so, we must've sold about 7 or 8 copies, with customers saying everything from, 'Is this the new Nirvana song?' to, 'I lost my virginity to this album.' Music is a beautiful thing.

2:12 am

I can't shut off. I'm lying here looking at my yellow lighter and thinking about the girl from The Barge. I wonder what she's doing now. Probably cuddling up to a hunky, gym-fit, multi-millionaire somewhere.

Suzanne (Tuesday, April 7th)

Dear Diary,

I woke up to this message from Barry;

"Got us tickets for the dam. Ready to blaze it up? - 4204lyfe."

If he thinks I'm going to Amsterdam to lurk about coffee shops he's got another thing coming. While the gesture is nice, at no point did I mention or agree to anything of the sort and if this is his way of locking me down, he can ball off.

I went for a bite to eat with Fi and Ugolino after work. It looks like Ugolino and Fi's brother, Rasher (Jason to his mother) have plans to open a chipper. Neither have experience in business or cheffing but Ugolino did say it best, 'Everybody loves-a the chip.' And who could argue?

Stuart (Wednesday, April 8th)

I left work an hour early so I could make it back to Summerdale for Gummy's removal.

When I got there the funeral home was mobbed, and almost everyone I met had the same question for me, 'What happened to your face?' I've had a few days of this, so I continued with the safe retort, 'I fell off my bike.' It would be safe to say the entire village had come out to pay their respects tonight. The embalmers, along with Gummy's daughters, Sheila and Bernie, did a wonderful job of making Gummy look like a million bucks. He always was a dapper cat, Gummy, and as he used to say, 'If I'm going out, I'm going out in style.' And that he certainly did.

Suzanne (Wednesday, April 8th)

Dear Diary,

This proposed trip to Amsterdam is no longer a concern. I messaged Barry and told him the truth – none of this is for me; the relationship, the stoner-talk, and the sense of guilt that comes with getting intimate and dealing with his inabilities. I know it's cruel, and yes, I do feel sorry for him, but I needed to be honest with myself. Did I see myself spending the rest of my life with this guy or was it best to part ways before it got too messy?

11:15 pm

I think I made the right decision. A reply from Barry:

"Duuuude, say whhhaaaaaaaaaat? - 4204lyfe."

Stuart (Thursday, April 9th)

What a day! I'm knackered!

Gummy's funeral passed without a hitch, bar Dad tripping over the mic cable and nearly breaking his neck after finishing his reading at the altar. Thankfully, some young lad caught Dad before he went headfirst into the casket.

Once the burial was over, I got a cab to the station and grabbed the first bus back to Rockwood for work.

Trish seemed a bit off when I got back. I assumed she had been flat out working on her own, but she claimed the shop had been dead. Trish gets like that sometimes and I always refrain from asking her why.

Despite being exhausted, I had to fulfil my commitments to Effie as she had booked us a table at a Korean restaurant called, Gimpo.

I could never get my head around chopsticks. I always wondered if people got lessons on how to use these things. I don't mean any offence to the Asian culture, but if you were born and raised to use a fork and knife (like we were) then why make life even more difficult by using two sticks? On top of that, I've always felt there was a sense of snobbery stemming from non-Asian chopstick users. It's like, '*look at us, peasant! It is us, and us alone, that is deserved of this otherworldly delicacy that we will now devour using two pieces of wood. You, peasant, should stick to greasy chips soaked in tomato ketchup, eaten with your filthy-as-fuck hands.*' Haha! Not anymore, as tonight I cracked the code! Maybe it's a case of most people having copped this, but anyway... when Effie first handed me the chopsticks, they were stuck together at the tail end. Instead of breaking them, as is the norm, I tried using them without detaching them and guess what? Huzzah! I could pick up the beef, most of the vegetables, and rice (with help from my other hand) You know what this means? I can also use chopsticks to eat popcorn, much like Trish's friend, Fiachra on our last cinema venture.

Effie seemed in good form. She was more confident in both herself and her English-speaking ability. By closing time, we had made it through three courses and two bottles of red wine. At this stage, Effie hasn't a notion what I was on about as I was talking a mile a minute. Most of her responses were either, 'Cool,' or 'Nice,' so I thought I had better wrap things up.

We both live in the same direction and on the walk home I couldn't help but ask, 'So, what's the story with us? Just friends?' Effie laughed, then grabbed my hand, holding it tight and saying, 'You like?' I did like it. Effie put her hand out to halt to our brisk walk, caught my hand and put it on her ass, 'You like?' I could feel a stir in my pants. 'Nothing wrong with that,' I replied. We continued walking hand in hand until we stopped at her place. She turned to me and with that irresistible smile said, 'You want me?' Before I knew it, we were going full throttle on her kitchen table and only made it to the bedroom about an hour ago. As I lay here typing away on my phone, Effie, bless her, is out for the count. I haven't slept a wink and need to be at work for 9 pm... not that I'm complaining.

Suzanne (Thursday, April 9th)

Dear Diary,

I have officially quit Love Quest. Done!

Mr Rocket was in the salon early this morning. He was asking if I had seen Mum anywhere. They had been out shopping and Mum went missing. As per usual, Mum thinks the battery on her phone is infinite and still brings the phone with her even when she knows it's dead; hence Mr Rocket's inability to track her down. I told Mr Rocket to go back to the department store and find the customer service dept. There were many a time when Mum and I became separated, and more often than not, she would have put a call out over the tannoy, much like you would do with a missing child. No doubt she is doing the same right now. Anyway, Mr Rocket said I looked very down and told me to cheer up. I told him it wasn't even 10 am and I had yet to have my morning coffee.

At around 4pm or so Mr Rocket returned holding a big paw print cat house. He placed it on the salon counter and said, 'A little pick me up. Now you can take that poor cat out of your bed.' I thanked Mr Rocket and told him it was a lovely gesture.

11:19 pm

Unfortunately, Mr Snuggles hasn't gone anywhere near the cat house and, as per usual, is now laying across my chest before I fall asleep.

Stuart (Friday, April 10th)

This money hoarding business with Patryk is getting out of control. Stupidly, I agreed to hide an additional €5,000. Patryk, knowing full well he was pushing it, managed to convince me by offering up 500 quid and an ounce of weed for my services. I was reluctant at first, but that copy of The Beatles' *Please Please Me* (one of 13 extremely rare copies) isn't going to buy itself. I've now amassed almost 10k for Patryk and desperately need to find a new hiding place for the cash. The wash bottle is full to the brim.

Suzanne (Friday, April 10th)

Dear Diary,

I cannot believe that I am writing this but here it goes...

Mr Rocket is on...

Love Quest - The dating app for young singles.

Diary, let me be clear, I quit the app, but it would seem my constant ramblings about it has somehow convinced Siobhan to sign up.

During lunch, Siobhan had asked if there was a way to hide your Read Notifications. In doing so I got a quick glimpse of her inbox and spotted a picture of Mr Rocket next to the message, "Fancy Blowing Me Dry." I nearly vomited there and then. Of course, I had to tell Siobhan who he was. When I did, she immediately recognised him and responded with, "Ooooh, gross!!!!" For the record, Siobhan is 22. I haven't mentioned this to anyone, especially Mum. It would break her heart. The question is... should I break it to Mum, or should I approach Mr Rocket first? If I was in Mum's position, I'd like to know what he's been up to.

Stuart (Saturday, April 11th)

No rest for the wicked! Instead of falling in the door to bed after sleeping a total of 2hrs in almost two days, I ended up going for last-minute drinks with Effie.

Man, can that girl drink! At one point she was three drinks ahead of me and by the end of the night, I had lost all count. She's an interesting girl, Effie. She seems to know quite a bit about quite a lot. By that I mean she is very knowledgeable, and no doubt a dab hand when it comes to the pub quiz. At one stage I was telling Effie about an old lad from Summerdale who used to work for my Dad. He had been in the papers this week after buying a life-size, glow-in-the-dark statue of Holy Mary. According to the papers, this old lad was half-blind, and now, since praying in front of the glowing statue has regained almost full sight. I asked Effie if she knew who the Holy Mary was. She said, 'He sell the fish? Holy Moly?' I tried but failed to keep a straight face. 'Holy Moly?' I replied. Effie knew she wasn't wrong, 'He the woman, sell the fish to the people on the street and then sell the body to the man at night. They have the statue of him in the city centre. (Effie has a habit of messing up her genders) He is very big,' she said; while pushing her boobs up to reference "Holy Moly". Then it hit home. I told Effie she must be thinking of Molly Malone (a fictional Irish character whose exploits were made famous in the song Molly Malone). 'Yes, yes!' Effie replied excitedly. 'She cure the blind man with the sex?' It took me another ten minutes to explain it all again; the Bible, fish, prostitutes, Molly Malone, The Virgin Mary, the whole shebang! I knew Effie had zoned out as she went back to replying with 'Cool' and 'Oh, nice.'

Suzanne (Saturday, April 11th)

Dear Diary,

I am evil, please forgive me!

I have reactivated Love Quest and set up a fake account with the intention of catfishing Mr Rocket. I want first-hand proof of his promiscuous, sleazy ways. As Mr Rocket is using a fake name (Barry Bond) on his profile I decided to do the same (Amy Grant) and used three random pictures of a random American girl I found on Facebook. The poor girl, if she only knew. Using my new profile, I took a look at Mr Rocket's Love Quest page to have a look at his profile. It was every bit as cringy as I had imagined.

Headline - The name's Bond, Barry Bond.

Bio - Single gentleman, looking to find a nice girl/woman to spoil. I'm young at heart with an appetite for life. Don't be shy, say hello... I don't bite... unless you want me to, lol.

My visit to Mr Rocket's page should activate the *People interested in you* notification on Mr Rocket's page, so hopefully, 'Barry' likes what he sees in 'Amy' and strikes up a conversation. Once I have enough detail, then I will decide what to do with it. For now, at least, Mum is none the wiser about this.

Stuart (Sunday, April 12th)

It's all over with Effie. She walked out on me this evening after spotting a pair of handcuffs in my sock drawer. I tried to explain how I ended up with them after Tony's stag, but she was having none of it. Effie called me everything under the sun, 'stupid, crazy man, murderer, the man from the horror film,' lectured me on quitting cigarettes for the umpteenth time, before punching me in the arm and chest and storming out. I didn't even begin to explain myself.

11.03 pm

I have a few nasty bruises on my arm from Effie's meltdown. I texted her a while ago asking if we were done. She replied, "Yap!"

Suzanne (Sunday, April 12th)

Dear Diary,

Mr Snuggles has discovered the cat house and is spending a considerable amount of time there. Reluctantly, I left a voice message with Mr Rocket to tell him the news, I'm sure he was too 'busy' to take my call.

This afternoon, Zia and I met up for a bite to eat and some retail therapy. Just when I thought I was about to leave town empty-handed, I stumbled upon a gorgeous leather jacket in Topshop, two tops in Bohemian Groove and this quirky vintage handbag in Catwalk. According to the guy in the store, there were only 50 of these bags made, all of which were lime green. While it might be a scary colour for some, I think it would work well with the leather jacket, my black jeans and a t-shirt. Zia thought it was hideous.

Stuart (Monday, April 13th)

I tried to call Effie several times today, but she refused to answer. This left me with no choice but to leave a voicemail explaining my actions. I came clean about the girl from The Barge and told Effie to think of it as her favourite movie, *PS I Love You* (the sole reason she moved to Ireland). I hope she can take me back.

Suzanne (Monday, April 13th)

Dear Diary,

What do we have here? It's only a Love Quest message from 'Barry Bond' aka Mum's partner and sleazeball of the year, Mr Rocket.

"Hello, Amy,

What a fantastic figure you have. You would put a young guy like me to shame. I see from your profile that you like sculpting. I can think of something big and stiff that your creative hands would love to get a hold of. I'm Barry by the way, very nice to meet you.

Baz xxx."

Uggggggghhhhhhhhh!!!! Gross!!!!

Stuart (Tuesday, April 14th)

Maggie invited me over for dinner after work. Patryk was there, too... well physically. He must have been starving as he ate three full servings of Lasagne with salad; even though Maggie told him it was to last the rest of the week. Patryk didn't say much, bar, 'Alright, man?' when I passed him the pepper. With Patryk buried in the lasagne, I caught Maggie's eye and motioned my head towards Patryk as if to say, what's up with him? Maggie shrugged, completely unaware of Patryk's dead, red eyes, the waft of weed and the five or so empty packets of crisps on the kitchen counter.

Suzanne (Tuesday, April 14th)

Dear Diary,

Bonkers day! I've been going non-stop since 7 am. In saying, I did find five minutes to reply to Mr Rocket's Love Quest alter-ego, Barry Bond.

"Hi, Barry,

Thanks for the message and the compliments, I'm flattered!

Sculpting, haha, yes indeed. At least you read my profile; unlike most of the idiots on this site. So, you'd like to sculpt something big and stiff, eh? How about a 16" dildo that you can stick up your arse, you sleazebag! Mum is going to have your head on a plate and as for Mr Snuggles, he hates that cat house, so I smashed the thing to pieces!

Oh yeah and before I forget... FUCK YOU!!!

Sincerely,

Amy (aka Sue)"

Stuart (Wednesday, April 15th)

Is there anything worse than a bad dose of the shits?

Suzanne (Wednesday, April 15th)

Dear Diary,

Mr Rocket has attempted to ring me several times today. He ended up leaving three voice messages; the second of which, I guess, was a pocket dial.

10:12 am

'Sue, honey… we need to talk… please don't tell your mother.'

10:14 am

Whistling 'Gold' by Spandau Ballet

1:03 pm

'Sue, I'm in Brentwich, can I call to the salon in the morning? I will explain everything. Please, Sue… don't tell your Mum. None of this was supposed to happen.'

Stuart (Thursday, April 16th)

I am back on good terms with Effie, or so I hope! She sent me a message earlier today saying she was disappointed but didn't want to be angry with me forever. We exchanged a few messages and before I knew it, she seemed to be back to her usual self, hammering out monkey emojis and LOL's while also sounding super-paranoid and passive-aggressive about my smoking habit. I told Effie I had a pretty busy day and that I was going to check out a band and unwind tonight. She replied, 'don't forget to eat something before you go to cancer.' I think she meant the concert.

Suzanne (Thursday, April 16th)

Dear Diary,

Please forgive me. I have used my fake Love Quest profile (Amy) to message a user who goes by the name Starman. The witty David Bowie reference on his profile sold it, '...got bored waiting in the sky.' While it's tough to make out his profile pic, I can see enough to know he's not a complete minger.

No word from Mr Rocket today. He must have gotten stuck in Brentwich. I did, however, speak to Mum, who spent two hours talking about potential holiday locations for her and Mr Rocket (both are hell-bent on Ibiza). I have yet to mention Mr Rocket's Love Quest exploits to Mum, reluctantly, I am waiting to hear his side of the story.

Stuart (Friday, April 17th)

I am a dead man walking! Trish has cleared out the contents of the canteen cupboard, including the two wash bottles with over 10k of Patryk's money. I asked Trish if she had seen them and she said the bottles were empty, so she chucked them out. Fearing for my life, I pulled the bin in the canteen apart but couldn't locate the wash bottles. After work, I made a break for the laneway behind the store and began rummaging through the collection bins. I soon realised that attempting to scoop shit out of the bin with my hands wasn't working so I said, 'fuck it!' and jumped in. Sadly, neither of the wash bottles containing over 10k were anywhere to be seen

Suzanne (Friday, April 17th)

Dear Diary,

I met Mr Rocket for lunch. I'm not sure if I believe his story or not, but for what it's worth he is off the hook for now at least. Mr Rocket explained how a journalist friend of his from the *Rockwood Chronicle* was doing a two-page spread covering online dating for divorcees. The journalist had approached Mr Rocket and asked him if he would be willing to go undercover and dish the dirt on potential Love Quest exploits. Mr Rocket said he was paid 300 euro for his part and swore he had no intention of going all the way with anyone he might have encountered. Unexpectedly, I believed his story. I promised not to say anything to Mum but did advise Mr Rocket to do so in his own time.

Stuart (Saturday, April 18th)

I met Tony and Rodge for lunch. They said that Lawrence – the ex-record-company guy –was found dead. Rodge claimed Lawrence overdosed after catching the Punk chick he was dating, sleeping with another Punk. The poor guy!

In keeping with the tragic news, I told the lads about Patryk's money and how Trish disposed of the two wash bottles I was hiding it in. Both of their jaws hit the floor when I told them just how much money I was dealing with. Rodge said he wouldn't want to be in my shoes right now.

I forgot to deactivate my Love Quest profile since meeting and subsequently breaking up with Effie. It's just as well as I've been chatting with a nice French girl this evening. Her name is Jeanne and she's from Nantes. Jeanne isn't pushed about having a pen pal and would rather meet in person. She has asked if I'm free next weekend. I said yes!

Suzanne (Saturday, April 18th)

Dear Diary,

I met Mum for lunch. She seemed very excited about Mr Rocket's undercover dating assignment. She seems rather chuffed that younger women would have an interest in Mr Rocket and went as far as to say, 'He's still got it.'

Things are going well with Starman on Love Quest, albeit I have yet to ask him his real name. He seems quite genuine compared to most other guys on there and seems to have a real life. It's infectious if I'm honest.

Stuart (Sunday, April 19th)

I contemplated visiting the city dump in an attempt to find the missing wash bottles earlier. Upon realising the mammoth task at hand, I succumbed to the fact I'm a dead man walking. Herman's Hermits couldn't cheer me up at this stage. I have no idea what to do about this. I gotta call Patryk but I don't want to get kneecapped and end up missing The Possum Fairies reunion gig on Tuesday!

Suzanne (Sunday, April 19th)

Dear Diary,

I had a nice chat with Mr Grimble over the wall today. He seemed pretty excited that his son, Royston would be finishing his college term soon and be back in the Grimble household for the summer. I don't think I've met Grimble Jnr as I'm only here since October. It'll be interesting to see how the offspring of Mr and Mrs Grimble turned out. Is that a bad thing to say?

Zia came over for some dinner this evening. We opted for homemade pizza and a few glasses of wine. I couldn't help but show her Starman's profile and messages on Love Quest. Zia said it was tough to see his face in his pics but that he looked able-bodied and lean. Zia took a real shine to another Love Quest user, one who I will admit not replying to and goes by the name, Bigdave. Zia asked me, 'Are you mad? Look at him!' Yes, he's a good-looking guy but the flags are there;

Headline - Two big guns and one loaded pistol.

About - A real man

Profession: Stripper

Kids - 4

Status - Divorced (x2)

Stuart (Monday, April 20th)

Both Maggie and Patryk called into the shop today. Maggie said the butchers she works in might be changing hands. The family who owns the business are looking to retire and are keen to sell up shop. Patryk didn't say much, only, 'Who's this, man?' while pointing towards the store speakers as Cluster's 'Zuckerzeit' wallowed through the shop floor. I gave him the only copy we had, even if it was one of the priciest imports in the store. I suppose I can't be any worse off at this stage. Fortunately, Patryk didn't mention money. I couldn't bring myself to update him on the current situation. I'm going to have to come up with a plan, and quick!!

Suzanne (Monday, April 20th)

Dear Diary,

I have somehow managed to put on a stone since January (I blame this bastard weather). All of my jeans have become a tight squeeze and I've even amassed a little pudge on my stomach. I'm not sure if all of this is down to old age or lack of exercise but either way, I need to get rid of it if I want any bloke to take me seriously.

Stuart (Tuesday, April 21st)

Patryk was in the shop today. He purchased a copy of N.W.A.'s 'Niggaz4Life'. I have yet to mention the missing 10k+ from the wash bottles. I also passed on The Possum Fairies reunion gig as I've been feeling out of sorts for the past few days. My anxiety levels are off the chart these past few days.

I had a good chat with French Jeanne from Love Quest. We have arranged to meet on Saturday night.

Suzanne (Tuesday, April 21st)

Dear Diary,

A client's water broke in the salon earlier, it was very exciting! Siobhan wanted to call an ambulance but Fi suggested bundling the lady into Fi's car in an attempt to get her to the hospital quicker. As Fi put it, 'If you're in my hands, you're my responsibility.' She has a heart of gold that girl.

Mr Rocket's undercover dating article, '50, Shady and Grey' was in today's *Gazette*. It was pretty funny actually.

Stuart (Wednesday, April 22nd)

I'm feeling battered, to say the least. I'm sitting here buried in the filthiest kebab known to man after an unplanned night of weekday madness with Charlie, Rodge, Tony, Maggie and Cora. We went to The Barge, and as per, I had hoped to bump into my luscious lighter-seeking lady, but as usual, she was nowhere to be seen. I think I've given up at this stage. On the bright side, tonight was very funny. Rodge could easily forge a career as a stand-up comedian as he had us all in hysterics from the get-go. I couldn't help but notice the sexual tension between Charlie and Maggie. They were very flirty with each other and there were many examples of exaggerated laughing, touchy-feely moments and eye contact. As I write, both Maggie and Charlie are drinking wine down in my living room. Am I jealous? I think lonely would be a better word.

Suzanne (Wednesday, April 22nd)

No entry

Stuart (Thursday, April 23rd)

Also, I came up with a good idea to get back Patryk's money – a sponsored parachute jump. I know it's a bad-minded scheme, but I don't have much choice at this stage. If I gather the 10k+ sponsorship money and pay for the parachute jump out of my own money, I don't think anyone will know, or care where the money goes. People are too busy with their shit.

Suzanne (Thursday, April 23rd)

Dear Diary,

Fi has opened up a can of worms after sending out a bunch of date invites on my Love Quest profile. It's my fault, I should know better than to leave my laptop open during lunch. I'm mortified! While I'm not complaining about the Cupid Award emailed to me for achieving a 100% date invite acceptance rate, I don't know where to begin!

Stuart (Friday, April 24th)

I spent my lunch break doctoring up a fake sponsored parachute card. It's passable in fairness; orange paper from the printers, dodgy, parachuting-related clipart on the front and inners and an account table to take note of who paid what on the inside.

11:10 pm

I've managed to collect 132.00 euro for my parachute jump.

NB - Do not call to the house of a known drug dealer at 10:30 pm on a Friday.

My date with French Jeanne is tomorrow night and I've got nothing to wear! I might wear my new Suicide band shirt. The white is kind of bright and cheerful and would go nice with some blue jeans.

Suzanne (Friday, April 24th)

Dear Diary,

Oh my god! I'm going on a date with Starman from Love Quest. He accepted my... well, Fi's frape invitation and we've agreed to meet at Clock Tower Square at 8 pm tomorrow. It's been ages since I've met somebody there. A lot of my misspent youth was spent hanging around that clock, drinking naggins of vodka, canoodling with long hair Eddie Vedder wannabes; all of whom only wanted to finger you so they could brag about it to their mates. It'll be nice to feel like a teenager again.

Stuart (Saturday, April 25th)

What a night!

I got home from work just after 6:30 pm and managed a shower, shit and shave by 6:45 pm. I pulled the house apart trying to find a shirt that didn't have a band name on it and was good to go. I told Charlie I'd meet him at Hooli's for a few quick ones before my date. Charlie said I'd be more fun and not so morose with a few pints in me. After three pints and three tequilas, I was well buzzed and made my way to the Clock Tower where I had arranged to meet my date.

When I got to the Clock Tower, I will a tad disoriented; a mix of what I can only describe as anxiety, excitement and utter confusion as to what the fuck my date looked like. I had looked at so many profiles that they all seemed to merge into a hybrid of right swipes. As I stood by the clock, attempting to remember the password to the Love Quest app, a well-spoken girl wearing a hat pulled down over her eyebrows and a scarf wrapped around her throat and chin approached me. She may as well have been looking at me through a letterbox. 'Love Quest, yeah?' she muttered, gesturing awkwardly towards me. 'That's me,' I replied as she pulled the umbrella back down over her face. You could tell she was nervous. 'Beer?' she said, before putting her arm out to link mine and pulling me under her umbrella.

On our way to the pub, the chat was lively and upbeat. I wondered if she had also been prone to a little pre-date potion or two. As we walked through town, I can remember waffling on about Love Quest, the quality of apple stuffing pork chops from Maggie's butchers, as well as my upcoming parachute jump. Even though I was well on it, everything was going swimmingly. As the banter continued, she took the reins for a bit, 'So, why Starman?' she asked. 'What's that?' I replied. She elaborated, 'Your Love Quest handle, Starman, why did you pick that as your username?' I was confused. I assumed she was confused. My brain was going as fast as it could... well, more along the lines of 'Sssssstttttttttttaaaaaaaaaaaaarrrrrrrrrrrrrmmmmmmmmmmmaaaaaaaaaannnnnnnnn nn, hmmm?!?' I was stumped. We continued walking, neither of us spoke for at least a minute or two. Then it all came flooding back, my Love Quest profile picture, my cheesy headline and more importantly my username. 'Disco stew,' I blurted, without much hesitation. 'That's S-T-E-W,' I continued. The words were enough to stop both of us on our tracks. She took two steps back and was now sheltering just herself with the umbrella. Once again, she pulled it down over her face to stop her from getting wet. Quietly, she asked, 'You're not Starman then? The guy with the "Waiting in the sky for you" headline?' I couldn't remember what my date looked like, not to mind my headline but I knew she had the wrong guy. 'I'm sorry,' I said; before explaining what, I assumed had happened. 'I think we picked up the wrong dates,' I confessed. Unexpectedly, she began to laugh, 'I think you're right,' she said, as we both tried but failed to contain the laughter. 'What now?' she continued. I hesitated for all of a split-second, 'Fancy a drink?' She put her umbrella down, smiled and said, 'Well, we've come this far.'

Before I knew it, we were back on track as we walked arm in arm towards the pub. We were laughing hard and wondering what our actual dates were doing. We ran through a host of fictional scenarios including: a Starman music video where he serenades my original date on his bed, a moving soundtrack that emphasised the lonely walk home for each of our dates after being stood up, and a porn video detailing a massive gangbang for all the people that get stood up by the Clock Tower. Yes, we are evil, but it was a nice icebreaker.

When we got to the pub, she asked me to get her a pint of beer before disappearing into the toilet. Maggie does this all the time, so I know the deal; hair = check, makeup = check, lipstick = check, teeth = check, cleavage = check, head-to-toe outfit scan = check. As I waited for the order, I couldn't help but feel sorry for both of our original dates, but with my adrenaline pumping and a fear of the unknown, I stopped to embrace the moment. Standing there lost in thought, I felt a tap on the shoulder. I turned but there was no one there, then realised I had fallen for an old classic. However, little did I know where it would go from here. There she was, standing in front of me, hat off, umbrella down and brandishing a smile that would knock an army; the girl from The Barge, Kim Gordon JNR!!! I was completely and utterly speechless. Did she remember me? I doubt it. Did I remember her? Of course!! She'd probably run for her life if she knew how much effort I put into tracking her down. She took off her coat and placed it on a stool by the bar. She looked incredible. I think she said something along the lines of, 'Is this seat OK?' I just nodded, still stuck for words.

Isn't it funny when your perception of someone you know nothing about is way off the mark? For some reason, I had assumed she (let me start referring to her as Suzanne from here on in) was some sort of high-rolling CEO. Don't ask me why. It turns out that she works in a hair salon, not too far from our store. She lives alone with her cat (name escapes me), has no kids and never married. Happy days!

Throughout the night we laughed and joked, mainly about all things Love Quest, our rejected dates, food, and dealing with the public in a working environment. Suzanne is very chill and very quick-witted and by the end of the night, I wanted nothing more than to spend the night with her but agreed to walk her to a taxi after she requested that we ease into things. Apparently, she had some sort of kerfuffle with another hairdresser that resulted in her breaking his nose.

NB - Ignoring the warning signs, that long-awaited kiss will have to wait.

3:45 am

I'm still in complete and utter shock. It's like some sort of weird dream where I constantly feel the need to pinch myself. Tony and Rodge aren't going to believe this, and as for Maggie, well, that's going to be a tough one.

5:50 am

Final thought;

FUCK YEAH!!!!

Suzanne (Saturday, April 25th)

Dear Diary,

I can't stop laughing. I'm not sure if it's my bad luck, the booze or the fact that I picked up the wrong bloody guy on my date! Yes, Diary, hahaha, I picked up the wrong date. Of course, this would only happen to yours truly. Not only was he the wrong guy, but he was also the lad I had assumed was gay when I met him in the pub a few weeks back. Well, I can confirm he is straight, and in fact, very cute! His name is Stu and I had an absolute ball with him tonight. As we sat chatting, there was a weird sense of familiarity between us, though I'm not sure whether or not he remembered meeting me in The Barge. If he did, he certainly did a great job of playing it down. We were never stuck for conversation, be it washing machine cycles, the benefits of paprika or people who skip ahead of you at the bar. I kind of felt like I'd known Stu for years. We have arranged to meet this coming Wednesday. Diary, I'm looking forward to it already.

Stuart (Sunday, April 26th)

I still can't get my head around last night. When I woke, I imagined it was all a dream. A very surreal dream where it seems all too real. As I lay on the bed gathering my thoughts and piecing the night together I soon realised that I hadn't been dreaming and everything I imagined to be a dream happened. This was established by the collective response in the lads' group chat after I sent them a pic of Suzanne and me.

I titled the pic:

"Look who I'm drinking with at The Barge."

12:05 am - Charlie – "WTF!"

12:05 am - Rodge – "What the actual fuck…"

2:40 am - Tony – "Is that the girl from Hollyoaks?"

I texted Suzanne after lunch asking her how she was holding up. She replied within ten minutes (a good thing) and said she was feeling rough but hoping lunch with her Mam might sort her out. I'm glad I wasn't the only one hanging. She said she had enjoyed last night and suggested that we take it handy when we meet on Wednesday.

I had every intention of getting out and about to raise more money for my parachute jump, but I couldn't get off the couch. Will have to pull my socks up this week.

11:10 pm

Just received a message from the Love Quest girl, Jeanne, that I was supposed to meet at The Clock Tower the other night:

"I knew you wouldn't show up. Duckhead!!!"

I don't think I look like a duck.

Suzanne (Sunday, April 26th)

Dear Diary,

For the life of me, I could not get out of bed this morning. I was in absolute tatters after all that whiskey last night. What were we like? I'm mortified for myself. First, I run away with someone else's date because I was too lazy to walk back to the Clock Tower. Then I spend the evening necking whiskey like it was going out of fashion, and to top it off, I just had a flashback of me dancing on the table to AC/DC's 'Hells Bells'. I'm almost sure we got a warning from the security. Then again, I could have dreamed that.

Somehow, after the night that was, I mustered up the energy to meet Mum for brunch today. I have no recollection of what we spoke about as I nodded off a few times. Mum, bless her, didn't know any different as I had my sunglasses on.

I spent most of the evening on the couch messaging Stu. His replies were very funny. I did my best not to be too flirty, but it was tough going.

Stuart (Monday, April 27th)

I went for a few pints with Maggie after work. I didn't plan on spilling the beans about Suzanne and our chance meeting, but I did. I had guessed Maggie would respond rather awkwardly and I wasn't wrong. Instead of congratulating me on finding Suzanne, Maggie became very insular. She clammed up for the rest of the night, bar referring to Suzanne as 'Jezebel' a few times and claiming, 'Every AC/DC song sounds the same, and if this Jezebel is a fan of them, then I'm certainly not a fan of her.' I love it when girls get heated about music, I find it a real turn-on.

Suzanne (Monday, April 27th)

Dear Diary,

Uggghhhh! What a day!

I woke up to a power-out, which meant no shower and no coffee for Suzanne. Not good! The day became increasingly frustrating when I got to work as both Fi and Siobhan decided to call in sick, leaving myself, Joanna the intern, and Mum (who I had no choice but to call for help) to cater for a bridal party of eight. As you can imagine, a lot of our regular clients weren't too happy.

On the bright, I've been easing through a bottle of wine and watching Blue Planet this evening. Stu is out with some friends and judging by the obscure music videos he's been sending for the past two hours, probably well on it.

Stuart (Tuesday, April 28th)

I died a slow death in work today; I blame Maggie and her fondness for top-shelf liquor. I can't remember what we were drinking but I do remember (a) it was from Mexico and (b) it was bloody expensive.

Regardless, I found the energy to go shopping for some new clothes for my date with Suzanne tomorrow night. I also managed to squeeze in a bit of door-to-door fundraising for my parachute jump. After tonight's run, I have a total of €855.50, a scratch card and a pair of rosary beads.

Suzanne (Tuesday, April 28th)

Dear Diary,

This morning I braved Love Quest for the first time in days. In a way, I felt sorry for my original date, (Starman) and was curious to know if he had been in touch. As expected, there were no messages from Starman. There was, however, a barrage of messages from a girl with the username 'Psychobitch.' Her messages were very detailed and very graphic; she wasn't asking but was telling me what she would do with me. I had no choice but to block her and delete my account for my safety.

Date No.2 with Stu tomorrow night, I'm excited!!

4:10 am

I just woke up in a panic, having experienced a traumatic nightmare. Psychobitch from Love Quest was trying to roast me in a giant oven and serve me to her family, carvery style. I'm traumatised.

Stuart (Wednesday, April 29th)

Some dude dropped in a bunch of old 90s cassette tapes to work today. Trish and I had a good laugh filtering through the stock, which included everything from Black Grape to B Witched. Hilarious! We threw the dude 50 quid as there were some real gems in there.

My date with Suzanne (or Sue as she prefers to be called) went swimmingly. We went for tapas and wine in a new restaurant just off Smith St. Sue looked smoking hot. She was wearing a black leather jacket, high-waist blue jeans, a red jumper and what looked to be a vintage navy scarf. She reminded me of the chick from *Scooby-Doo*.

Thankfully, we were never stuck for words and the conversation flowed naturally throughout the night. We spoke about our families, past relationships and our chance meeting at The Barge; the same night she assumed I was gay yet still asked me for a light (3 times, I did remind her). We also spoke about school and how much we both hated it growing up. Sue said she never bothered with college. I believe her exact words were, 'I couldn't be arsed.' I told her I felt the same and pretty much ran for my life when school ended. We both agreed that we were happy with our current situations and thankful we didn't have to put up with a bunch of college jabronis harping on about their five-year plans.

When the pub closed, I suggested a coffee at my place. Sue said, 'definitely next time.' I didn't push it.

I still can't believe my luck. Dating Sue feels like some sort of weird dream.

Suzanne (Wednesday, April 29th)

Dear Diary,

I'm a bit drunk but I just want to say two things:

I had a great night and Stu is a sweetheart!

Dipping crisps into Nutella is not a crime.

Stuart (Thursday, April 30th)

I can't stop thinking about Sue. I truly believe she is the one, my future wife, the girl I want to grow old with. I don't think she will age badly either, considering that mid-noughties fake ID she gave me a glimpse of last night. She looks the same now as she did 15 years ago.

Suzanne (Thursday, April 30th)

The students over in No.30 are having another one of their mammoth house parties. I was going to call the cops as the noise is a bit much, but I decided not to be the party pooper.

Mum texted asking me if I wanted to meet her after work tomorrow. She said she has a surprise for me!? I hope to God she's not pregnant.

Stuart (Friday, May 1st)

I had a close call with Patryk earlier. He came into the shop looking to take 500 quid out of the money I had amassed for him. I could feel my heart pumping and my vocal cords tightening, knowing full well his 10k+ was gone. In an attempt to swerve Patryk, I told him we were laying down new tiles in the canteen and the workers had restricted us from using the area. Patryk wasn't impressed and said he needed the money there and then. He continued to explain why it was so urgent, but I had zoned out in a state of panic. I do remember Patryk saying something about a lad with a machete who wasn't happy, and some girl called Martina who was a 'dirty rat.' I managed to muster up 450 quid between the two tills and had to cover my ass by telling Trish that the lads working on the canteen floor needed it for supplies. Trish was talking about *Neu! - 2* to some German customers and didn't bat an eyelid. I gave Patryk the 450 quid and apologised for not having the full whack. Patryk took the money and left without saying a thing.

I am up to my neck in it right now. 10k is a lot of money, and the way my parachute-jump fundraising is going, I might just leave the parachute.

Suzanne (Friday, May 1st)

Dear Diary,

I met Mum and Mr Rocket for a bite to eat after work. Mum has booked us a 'man-free' shopping trip to Amsterdam. We are heading away in two weeks and staying for two nights. I'm looking forward to it as I've never been, and it's been ages since I've travelled anywhere with Mum.

Mr Rocket was very inquisitive about Stu and asked me everything from, 'What does he do for a living?' to 'What does he drink?' Mr Rocket said you can tell a lot about a man from what he drinks. I'd never thought about it to be honest. I told Mr Rocket that Stu drank beer and whiskey on both dates. I also stressed that it wasn't crafted beer. Mr Rocket claimed, 'This Stu fella is a keeper.' Mum, as always, agreed with him.

Stuart (Saturday, May 2nd)

I'm officially up shit creek without a paddle! Patryk was back in the shop earlier, looking for €1,000 from the money I was minding for him. I had to come clean about the wash bottles and how Trish had chucked 'em all in the bin. To say his jaw dropped would be an understatement. As I stood there, elaborating on how Trish might have disposed of the bottles, and how my parachute-jump fundraiser was a quick-fix-way to recuperate all monies lost, Patryk didn't utter a word. Instead, he stood there biting his lip, his eyes transfixed on mine, nodding his head in a, *sure I don't believe a word you're saying,* type manner. He left without saying a word.

Thankfully, this evening wasn't as bad. I had sex with Sue!! It was everything I hoped for and more. Man is she hot! You could tell she had a good body but it's only when you get under the hood you realise just how good. Sleeping with the one I had labelled, 'The girl from The Barge' or 'Kim Gordon Jnr' had been a fantasy for quite some time, and not to sound derogatory or anything, but I reckon Sue has been around the block a few times. Sue did some stuff tonight that would make any man weak at the knees and I was no different. We ended up doing it twice and now she's awake and resting on the bed while I'm here taking a shit. I'm hoping for a 3rd round when I get back.

Suzanne (Saturday, May 2nd)

Dear Diary,

Why do men take so long in the bathroom? I'm here in Stu's bed waiting for him to come back from the loo. He must be in there for at least 30 minutes at this stage. Anyway, boredom struck so I start writing.

It was nice to sleep with Stu, although I struggled not to laugh at his sex face. It looked like he was concentrating on every thrust; his eyes squinted, his head back, thrusting in and out as if his life depended on it. He does make me laugh sometimes but in a very cute and harmless way. Uh oh, speak of the devil, there goes the flusher.

Stuart (Sunday, May 3rd)

Sue and I had a lazy start to the day. I woke early so decided to make her breakfast in bed; two poached eggs, avocado and toast, two slices of bacon, some fruit, a croissant and a pot of coffee. She rewarded me (I guess...) with some morning sex. My favourite!!

After lunch, we headed to the Commercial Mall for a spot of shopping. We spent about 15 minutes there before deciding it was too nice a day to be stuck in a retail environment. Instead, we opted to take a trip to Dernlock Lake for an impromptu picnic (sandwiches and a few cans of cider). I was tempted to tell Sue about the money conundrum with Patryk but decided against it. I guess she might think (a) I'm a fucking idiot and (b) I might be hinting at asking her for a loan.

10:45 pm

My balls are killing me!

Suzanne (Sunday, May 3rd)

Dear Diary,

I had the most wonderful day with Stu, he truly is a great guy with a heart of gold.

We had a late start to the day and ended up hitting the Commercial Mall after lunch. Stu did not want to spend the day shopping, so we dropped the pots and pans for chips and cans and took a spin out to Dernlock Lake. Diary, we were like two teenagers without a care in the world. Maybe deep down we are.

Stuart (Monday, May 4th)

No entry

Suzanne (Monday, May 4th)

Dear Diary,

I'm just back from the hospital (of all places) after checking in on Stu. He was attacked by a group of youths outside the record store and was left lying on the pavement in a bloody mess. Thankfully, he is OK. If it wasn't for the two students who found him and rang the ambulance, who knows what could have happened?

When I got to the hospital, two of Stu's friends, Charlie and Maggie were already there. While he had no broken bones, his face was a complete mess with some nasty bruising, two black eyes and some vicious cuts to his forehead and cheekbones.

When recalling the events, Stu said, 'It's a bit of a blur.' Charlie was quick off the mark, 'I thought you hated Blur?' 'I still do,' Stu replied.

At least he was in good spirits. While Charlie was very warm with me, the other girl, Maggie didn't say much. I did catch her eyeing me up and down, but other than that she kept her mouth shut. I wonder if Stu and Maggie were a thing? I got that vibe.

Some police officers arrived and were quizzing Stu about the events. They're going to obtain the CCTV footage, so there's a good chance of identifying the culprits. Poor Stu, of all the innocent guys in the world to get jumped. Either the culprits thought he had the day's takings from the record store on him or Stu probably booted them from the store, and this was their revenge.

Stuart (Tuesday, May 5th)

For fuck sake! I'm in the hospital.

I got jumped by a bunch of Patryk's cronies after work last night. The little shits! While I made a good attempt to fend them off, one of em hit me with a padlock and knocked me for six. I remember seeing it fall out of his hand as I hit the ground and the blood began to spill.

I'm so embarrassed I don't even know where to start. I've had visits from Sue, Maggie, Charlie, Cora, Trish, Tony and Rodge, not to mention a priest who brought me some communion. While I didn't volunteer much info, I've been subject to a serious grilling by all parties. What could I say? At this stage, I've lost count of how much money I owe Patryk, though I take full responsibility for the situation. I should have never taken his money in the first place.

The doc said I should postpone my parachute jump for now. He reckons I am showing signs of PTSD. I was reluctant to tell him it was probably post-traumatic-shit-disorder; knowing the colour of my face after eating and subsequently shitting out that hospital food.

Suzanne (Tuesday, May 5th)

Dear Diary,

I can't believe it! The salon is up for an award at Hairs to You, the annual hair industry awards show. I screamed when I read the nominations out at work. To celebrate, Siobhan, Fi, two random clients and I necked two bottles of Prosecco. The awards take place on a Saturday in August so we can all get pissed drunk. Woohoo!!

I didn't get to Stu this evening as I was a little wobbly on my feet come close. I did, however, have a brief conversation with him over the phone. I reckon the morphine had kicked in as he was talking some awful shite. Stu reckons he'll be out Thursday or Friday depending. The only reason he is being kept in is for some potential internal bleeding. Best be safe, I guess.

Stuart (Wednesday, May 6th)

A new nurse was lurking about the ward today. Not only is she smoking hot, but she's very generous with the morphine. Although I wasn't in any sort of pain, my morphine request worked as the perfect opportunity to strike up a conversation. When she asked, 'What hurts?' I replied with, 'Everything! Even the important parts.' With a blush, her eyes did glance over my midsection before giggling and commenting, 'I could do with a laugh. This place is fucking depressing.'

Both Sue and Trish paid a visit this evening. Not together of course. Sue said she won some award for cutting hair. She was well chuffed. I congratulated her and hinted towards doing something with my hair. Sue said that she would probably win 'Woman of the Year' if she managed to sort out my mop.

Trish, on the other hand, was in rare form. She has drafted in her brother Lenny to give her a hand in work. I can trust Lenny, he's a good guy with good taste. And he's a Felt fan, so he gets the thumbs up.

Suzanne (Wednesday, May 6th)

Dear Diary,

I think they've upped Stu's medicine as he was talking some utter bollox this evening. When I asked if he was still feeling sore, he told me he had, 'no pain whatsoever.' Let me stress that his eyes were in the back of his head and he was drooling pretty badly.

Mum is adamant about paying a visit to Stu. I'm reluctant to introduce them right now, especially considering Stu's state. Mum, as usual, did not want to take no for an answer and made me feel guilty for not inviting her this evening. I told her we might pay a visit to Stu later this week. Mum seemed happy enough with that.

Stuart (Thursday, May 7th)

Talk about rude awakenings... this morning, after my shower, I arrived back to the ward to be greeted by who else but Patryk. He shook his head in disgust and told me I had two weeks to pay back every penny in full and if I fucked up again, he was going to fuck me up. What could I say? I was telling him not to worry but Patryk cut me off and said the only thing I should be worried about is staying out of the hospital, before furiously slapping a bottle of Lucozade from my bed table to the floor. It was like a scene from a movie; albeit a low-budget one.

I have no idea how or where I'm going to get this money from. Doctor Lyons has advised that I will probably be here until Sunday. That gives me 11 days before Patryk comes knocking on my door.

Suzanne (Thursday, May 7th)

Dear Diary,

I spoke to Stu on the phone, he seemed a bit down. He reckons they might let him out this weekend. I get the feeling that he misses work terribly.

Stuart (Friday, May 8th)

8:53 am

The swelling in my knee has reduced considerably; albeit it is still tough to walk on. Doctor Lyons has said that I should be discharged Saturday morning, which means I need to make a serious plan of action if I'm ever going to recoup this money.

11:01 pm

God bless morphine! I had the brainwave of all brainwaves just now. Using the public internet in reception, I drafted up a second sponsor card for my parachute jump. I used a few of the hospital logos, cheekily added "In aid of Regional Hospital" and managed to get it printed at the reception without question.

12:33 pm

After lunch, I hobbled from ward to ward on my crutches and, believe it or not, managed to gather €1421.20, another set of rosary beads and two copies of the Bible. There is a God!! Unfortunately, I fell asleep in the garden for two hours after that.

3:10 pm

When I woke, I thought it might be a good idea to hit up the A&E. I figured most people would be either (a) in a state of shock and not worried about their finances or (b) happy to help somebody who (on paper at least) is helping them. I managed to pull in about 300 quid here (even if quite a few patients told me to, 'fuck off').

6:27 pm

Will do some more fundraising at the 7 pm mass down in the hospital chapel.

6:56 pm

I grabbed a collection basket and my sponsor card and made my way through the aisles of the chapel offering a brief synopsis of the pre-mass collection. As the church was filled with coffin dodgers, most were only too happy to part with their money.

Sue and her mam called tonight. Sue's mam bought me a copy of the *Sun* a packet of Penguin bars and a 2 litre of 7-UP and was adamant that the 7-UP would, 'cure my leg in no time.' Sue's mam seems like a nice lady and she's aged well, in fact, it's only now that I've realised who she reminds me of... Jane Fonda!

Suzanne (Friday, May 8th)

Dear Diary,

Mr Rocket popped by the salon this afternoon. He said that a chap from the community radio station was very impressed with Mr Rocket's undercover dating antics ('50, Shady and Grey') in the local paper and had asked him if he would be interested in presenting a weekly talk show for people struggling with relationships. Mr Rocket said he accepted the offer there and then. The chap from the radio station told Mr Rocket to come up with a name that would entice the casual listener, so Mr Rocket popped in to ask my opinion on some possible names, including:

The Hour of Love (Mr Rocket was wondering if he could find an instrumental version of The Power of Love that he could re-work as the show's theme tune).

Love is in the Air

Heartbreak Hotel

Love is all you need with Dr Davey Rocket (When I asked him what his doctorate was in, Mr Rocket replied… 'Luuuurrrrvveeee!').

I told Mr Rocket to leave the suggestions with me for now.

Mum and I went to visit Stu tonight. I was a bit nervous about introducing them as Mum had already necked two glasses of wine during dinner and Stu is still on morphine for his knee. That said, I do think they got on quite well. Stu, in particular, seemed very happy tonight, I wonder if they've upped his morphine intake? Although, maybe not as he is due out tomorrow. Maybe he's just happy to be going home.

Stuart (Saturday, May 9th)

I ended up getting discharged after lunch. First stop, Ferrari's, for a large bag of chips, drenched in salt and vinegar. I've been subject to what I can only describe as baby food for the past few days; mashed potatoes, soggy vegetables, even the smell of those dinners would make you want to puke.

I spent most of the evening cuddled up to Sue on the couch, and although my leg is still in agony, it was nice to see her again.

I'd feel a bit strange telling Sue about my daily diary. Little does she know I've been doing this in both manual and digital form for over 20 years. I'd feel like a bit of a nerd if she found out so that's why I always spend ages in the bathroom any time she is over.

Suzanne (Saturday, May 9th)

Dear Diary,

After lunch, Mum and Mr Rocket were kind enough to help me pick Stu up from the hospital. Stu's very funny sometimes, the only thing he wanted (and he had been on about this all week) was a bag of chips from the chipper, so who were we to deny him?

On the way, Mr Rocket was telling Stu about his new radio show, which led to Mum getting very excited. She said that it would be great to have a celebrity husband; even though Mr Rocket said community radio is far from celebrity status. Mr Rocket wanted to run with 'What's Love Got to Do with It? ...with Dr David Rocket' as a show title but the station manager wanted something simple that rolls off the tongue and didn't want to limit the show to relationship advice only, hence the new name 'Heartbroken with Dr David E. Rocket.' When asked, he said the "E" stood for the expert.

When we got back to Stu's place, we put our feet up (well, I helped him with his) and attempted to watch a couple of movies. Unfortunately, poor Stu fell asleep on my chest. I blame the medication and the red wine; I did advise against this. On the bright side, Stu is awake now and judging by my watch, taking one of his infamously long shits.

Diary, how much shit can one shit?

Stuart (Sunday, May 10th)

It feels great to have real food again. Being subject to that hospital shit is not something I want to return to in a hurry. Sue laid it on today; the full Irish breakfast, an amazing salad and soup lunch, and to top it off... the juiciest steak in the world. As I lay here in a food coma, I have to reflect on how grateful I am to have met this girl. She is the most beautiful, genuine and caring person I have ever met.

Tomorrow should be interesting. While I'm looking forward to returning to work, I don't think I can limit myself to a highchair for the day. I enjoy walking about and talking to the punters. I enjoy putting the new stock on the shelves – don't know how these office people sit there all day long. It must be very boring.

Suzanne (Sunday, May 10th)

Dear Diary,

Stu seems a lot better in himself; although I do think it's too early for him to return to work in the morning. We had a relaxing day... food, food and more food. I burned my finger while putting a pan in the sink, and as much as I wanted to scream, I managed to avoid it. The last thing I needed was Stu hobbling about the place in a panic. Anyway, I put some cream and a band-aid on it and the pain has eased off. As expected, Stu didn't seem to notice... even when I was rubbing his forehead later tonight. Men are so bad at paying attention sometimes.

Yesterday was another example; I spent about two hours doing my hair and makeup before collecting Stu at the hospital and what did he greet me with? 'Have you ever tried a 7-UP and ice cream float?'

Stuart (Monday, May 11th)

I made a bloody mess (literally) at work today after slipping on a Kinder Eggshell and cracking my head off the corner of the Ska section. Trish said it was my fault, I should have listened to the doc and stayed behind the counter. My head was splitting (in every sense) for the rest of the day, so I ended up taking quite a few paracetamols to ease the pain. Sue reckons I should get my head checked (she's starting to sound like my mother now) as I may have a concussion. I told her that I'd make an evaluation tomorrow, the last thing I need is another stay in that hospital.

Suzanne (Monday, May 11th)

Dear Diary,

I'm beginning to think Stu is cursed! He ended up injuring himself at work trying to do too much. Now he has a gash on his head and is monged out on medication again. Luckily Trish was in the shop and not on lunch, God only knows what could have happened if he had passed out on the floor. I told him to take tomorrow off, but he won't listen to me.

Stuart (Tuesday, May 12th)

What I assumed to be some sort of psychotic practical joke is only now sinking in as a harsh reality. I was holding the fort at work as Trish went uptown for something. This morning was like every other Tuesday morning, the same delivery drivers, the same heads passing the shop window, the same customers coming in for a browse before work, except this morning, around 10:30 am the shop phone rang. I answered; 'Good morning, Reality Records, Stu speaking…' there was no reply. 'Hello?' I said again, keeping with the polite tone. 'I'm pregnant.' I knew the voice, but I couldn't quite place it. It wasn't Sue and it was too harsh to be Maggie. Then I copped it, it was Zofia; Maggie's mad-as-a-brush sister whom I had that one-night stand with a few months ago. I thought she was taking the piss. 'You are taking the piss, right?' I replied. Zofia's response was sharp, almost venom like, 'No, I'm not taking the piss, you stupid man. I am having your baby. You, of all the fuckers in the world.' 'Woah!' I replied. 'It wasn't like you were complaining about me that night.' Quick off the mark in her strong Polish accent, Zofia said, 'It doesn't fucking matter. For record, I will keep baby and you will pay me for cost of living. Now, this is your problem with me. I want you to come to Poland so we can make the plan for the baby. I don't want you to be the married man to me, but I want you to be baby's father and give the shit.' She hung up. I was speechless. To be honest, I'm still fucking speechless. Nobody would be as cruel to do this as a joke. How the fuck am I going to tell Maggie? And Sue? Just when things couldn't be any better, now this!

On the bright side, I will be debt-free come Saturday lunchtime. I have arranged to meet Patryk in the Black Ball pool hall over by the market. He advised me to hand over the money alone. 'No funny business,' as he put it.

Suzanne (Tuesday, May 12th)

Dear Diary,

I picked up a few bits for the trip Mum and I are going on to Amsterdam this Friday, including a beautiful orange summer dress; although Mum believes it's red. Not one for filtering her thoughts, Mum had a pop at me and said she always suspected I was colour blind. You wouldn't want to be sensitive, that's for sure. I told Mum she needs to buy a small suitcase as she is hell-bent on bringing the 20kg case packed with half of her wardrobe. When I called this evening, she had three full-length jackets laid out on the bed! It's May, for God's sake! I lost track of the number of times I told her we hadn't paid for the extra case. All she kept saying was, 'I'll pay the extra, whatever it is.' Sometimes I just don't have the patience for her.

Stuart (Wednesday, May 13th)

I can't believe I'm going to be a father! I have no savings or any sort of financially secure plan for the future, but I guess it's good to know that (1) this kid might be there for me in my hour of need and (2) someone might take a gamble on my Yorkshire Relish/egg yolk super-sauce and make me a millionaire.

I have all of Patryk's money in one place now (my Doc boots). I'm afraid to leave it around the house in case the house gets robbed, so I just put the money into the bottom of my sock and then put my boot on over it. There's no fear of me losing it as these boots are very tight.

Sue was over for dinner this evening. She looked fantastic, like a 'Goo' era Kim Gordon but better. Sue copped that I was a little off and asked if I was OK several times, but I couldn't bring myself to tell her about Zofia and the pregnancy. I just can't do it!

Suzanne (Wednesday, May 13th)

Mum and Mr Rocket are excited about Mr Rocket's debut on community radio tomorrow. Mum has arranged a listening party at her place for the occasion. I thought it was a bit much... but what can you do?

I had a very enjoyable evening relaxing here at Stu's place. I think he's struggling to get over the assault, and that slip on the Kinder Egg hasn't done him any favours. The poor fella. He wasn't himself tonight. Fingers crossed he comes around sooner rather than later.

Stuart (Thursday, May 14th)

I called Zofia after finding the number had been logged on the work phone. She didn't seem very happy. I asked her if she was sure about me being the father of her unborn. She said she was, 'pretty sure.' I asked her how she knew, and she admitted to having no sex over the last bit. Instead of beating around the bush (actually, let me rephrase that) – Instead of wasting time, I told Zofia I wanted a paternity test. She flipped and hung up the phone on me once again.

I'm not sure what Zofia's problem is. I have every right to a paternity test, and she knows it. I'm going to take a wild guess here and say that I'm not the father, but this psychotic bitch thinks she can pull a fast one and milk me for everything I have. I think I should talk to Maggie; I believe she would be the best person to speak to. After all,

Zofia is Maggie's flesh and blood, and if anyone knows her, you can be sure it's Maggie.

Good news – I'm off the hook for the weekend as Sue is off to Amsterdam with her mother. It's probably just as well. There is a chance that something could go wrong when handing over Patryk's money on Saturday. Best if Sue isn't about.

Suzanne (Thursday, May 14th)

Dear Diary,

Mr Snuggles is pregnant! And more importantly, he is a she! WTF?? For the longest time, I thought Mr Snuggles was male but after our first visit to the vet, due to Mr Snuggles' refusal to eat over the past few days, the young veterinarian assured me Mr Snuggles is female. I'm such an idiot! Now, what am I supposed to do – call her Ms Snuggles? Maybe I'll use Mum's name for her, Snuggleflakes.

Zia and I attended Mum's 'Listening Party' for Mr Rocket's new show on community radio. Mum's house was thronged, what with half the street, the staff from the credit union, some of the walkers from Mum's club and a few random young fellas who thought it was a house party (they weren't long getting the boot) downing Prosecco like there was no tomorrow.

Unfortunately, there is a tomorrow and it's an early flight to Amsterdam. I told Mum not to drink too much this evening, but after Mr Rocket referred to Mum by her first name and called her, 'the love of his life,' on-air, Mum went into party mode. She was still going when I left. The last thing she said to me was, 'Honey, I don't think I can handle fame.'

Stuart (Friday, May 15th)

I met Maggie for lunch and came clean about knocking up her sister. She was thoroughly disappointed. Maggie said, 'I wouldn't mind if it was this Jezebel you're fooling around with, but not Zofia. Zofia's a vampire who is only good for sucking people dry.' I lost my train of thought and remembered Zofia and me in our risqué encounter in Maggie's house. God, it was fun! Maggie shook me, 'Are you listening to me? Are you sure you're the father?' I wasn't long snapping out of playback mode. I apologised to Maggie and told her it was a lot to take in. I also said I was looking at doing a paternity test just to be sure. Maggie thought it was a great idea. 'What about Jezebel?' Maggie asked. I wish she wouldn't refer to Sue as such. I told Maggie to keep this information about Zofia quiet as I didn't want to upset or lose Sue for that matter. Maggie responded by clenching her teeth, much like she always does when she wants to shout at me.

Suzanne (Friday, May 15th)

Dear Diary,

I am totally and utterly beat!!

Mum is still in her clothes and lying unconscious on the bed next to me and I'm not far behind as I sit here watching a German version of *Alf* on the hotel TV.

Getting to the airport was an absolute nightmare this morning. When I arrived to pick up Mum (4:30 am) she was still asleep and had only half packed. I found an empty bottle of wine and a half-empty glass on her bed locker. She was in another world. I had no choice but to wake her and throw her into the shower. All she kept saying was, 'Honey, I can't...' I just kept replying, 'You can, and you will.'

After all the commotion, we just about made it to the gate at the airport. Mum, bless her, looked like Grotbag from that 80s TV show. She was that green.

We were no sooner in the air and Mum was back on the wine. A 'cure' I believe Mum called it. She didn't say anything else for the duration of the flight; very unlike Mum on any journey.

When we arrived at the hotel, Mum spent the first hour vomiting up purple puke. I think she exceeded her wine limit over the past two days. Reluctantly, she joined me for lunch and seemed content picking bits of lettuce and the occasional cherry tomato from my plate. She couldn't bring herself to order anything.

After a bit of sightseeing and retail therapy on my end, we went back to the hotel for dinner. Fortunately, Mum had mustered up quite an appetite and devoured her steak in no time. We decided to have an early night and recharge the batteries. As I type, Mum is fast asleep. The poor thing is shattered!

I sent a text to Stu but heard nothing back, he must have had an early night.

Stuart (Saturday, May 16th)

I'm just back from the pub after a heavy session with Tony, Rodge and Charlie. What started as a way of celebrating my debt-free beginnings after handing over the money to Patryk earlier today, has resulted in me spilling the beans about Zofia's pregnancy. The lads were in shock. To be honest, most of em didn't even know that Zofia and I had gotten it on. Everyone wanted to know if I had told Sue; I assured them I hadn't and advised them to keep their big mouths shut. Rodge asked if my encounter with Zofia was worth it? It was a good question in fairness. I told Rodge that sex with Zofia was the most intense and passionate sex that I've had or will ever have. Was it worth it? It's tough to answer that as who knows what the future holds? Knowing my current status with Sue, I would say no, it wasn't worth it.

Man, I am so glad that the whole situation with Patryk is over. What I imagined to be a hostile environment where I'd be surrounded by one too many undesirables, was, in fact, the complete opposite. I met Patryk in the Black Ball as planned. When I walked down the stairs into the dimly lit pool hall, I spotted him pacing back and forth, skinning a roll-up cigarette and looking as impatient as ever. There wasn't a soul in sight. I handed Patryk the envelope with money inside and apologised for keeping him waiting. He opened it and took a look inside. 'G'wan,' he said and pointed towards the exit. I just kind of fumbled a thank you and didn't wait around. That was it. Done and dusted! Trust me when I write, that will be the last time I will (a) try to help the youth of today and (b) hoard a large sum of money for anybody. I don't care who they are!

My shirt is destroyed in kebab sauce! I suppose things could be worse... oh wait, I forgot I was about to have a child with a stranger.

Suzanne (Saturday, May 16th)

Dear Diary,

Mum and I went to 'The Greenhouse', one of Amsterdam's famous coffee shops. It didn't take much convincing for Mum to try a few joints. As she said herself, 'When in Rome.' Then she blazed half a joint to herself to kick off the proceedings. I said, 'Mum, we're not in the Vatican now.' Mum burst out laughing and after about a minute or so started laughing uncontrollably. Then I started to laugh at Mum. Before we knew it, we were both in absolute hysterics. Every time I looked at Mum wafting away on the joint, she was doing her best to blow smoke circles. She would make a little whistle sound each time, and every failed attempt made her giggle so much that tears were rolling down her face. I had to go outside as I thought I was going to get sick from laughing so much.

Stuart (Sunday, May 17th)

This morning I came back from the shops to find the female half of my French neighbours firing clothes and DVDs out of her apartment window. She was shouting uncontrollably and had become quite a spectacle. Her oaf boyfriend was nowhere to be seen but it looked like he fucked up big time as his shit was all over the road below. I felt bad for him. If Sue had done that with my records, I would not be happy!

Speaking of, I was on the phone to Sue for about half an hour tonight. She was well on it, as was her mother from the brief few minutes we spoke. Sue reckons Amsterdam is very relaxed. She also said that clothes shopping isn't stressful there. Did I hesitate to ask why?

Suzanne (Sunday, May 17th)

Dear Diary,

What a wonderful day we had. I have fallen head over heels in love with Amsterdam. The coffee shops are amazing, the weather is beautiful, the clothes shops have everything in my size, the health and beauty products are half the price of what we pay back home and the food… where do you begin? Everything from the street food to the hotel breakfast has been superb. I could happily stay here for another week, and while I do miss Stu, there's not much else I'm in a rush to go back home to.

Stuart (Monday, May 18th)

Trish seems happy to have me back at work. I could tell because she was chatty all day and that's unlike her. She was so chatty that I ended up confiding in her about the whole pregnancy situation with Zofia. Trish said she felt sorry for me but that I had a right to, at the very least, discuss some possible options about the future of the unborn child. Trish reckons that I could push for an abortion. I'm not sure if I have the balls to ask Zofia how she would feel about that. To be honest, I'm not so sure I would even want that. After all, this is my mess and I take full responsibility for my actions.

It would seem that I've become more in tune with the burdens of parenting. I stopped by Tesco after work and was prone to notice (1) a kid throwing the tantrum of all tantrums. Both parents were trying, but failing miserably to calm the kid down as passers-by looked on in disgust, (2) A father staring at his phone while his kid was rocking back and forth inside a pay-per-ride Bob the Builder truck and, (3) A father running out of the toy shop and up through one of the wings of the shopping centre in pursuit of his kid who looked to have done a runner with a toy monkey. I'm not sure if I'm cut out for this.

Suzanne (Monday, May 18th)

Dear Diary,

I am writing to you from 30,000 feet above the ground. I reckon I'll be too tired to make an entry once we get home.

Mum is out for the count about five rows up. She's stuck between two rugby players from what appears to be a full squad from back home. It's been a bit of a bumpy ride thus far. The captain said the weather was stormy in the UK, so I guess we're getting the brunt of it here.

I'm looking forward to seeing Stu. Even though it's only been a few days, I miss his goofy head. I wonder if he misses me. He better!!!

Stuart (Tuesday, May 19th)

Zofia phoned the store again. We ended up arguing over who was to blame for the pregnancy. Zofia said, 'You need to wear the glove, but no stupid Irish man, just think about next drink.' I guess she meant protection. I replied, 'Well, I assumed you were taking birth control and if you were that concerned there was always the morning-after pill.' I had to bite my tongue with all of this. No matter how understanding I was about the whole situation, even after offering my apologies for the mess we are in, Zofia still couldn't bring herself to take some responsibility for where we're at right now. I do know this, Zofia was very forward on the night we had sex and didn't stop to address any concerns at the time.

Sue texted to say they have landed safely. I'm contemplating telling her about Zofia and the pregnancy. I don't think I can hide it any longer.

Suzanne (Tuesday, May 19th)

Dear Diary,

I never want to smell the combination of fresh coffee and burning marijuana again. I think Mum would vouch for that, too.

Today was like a foggy hangover at work. I still felt like the world was going in slow motion and that my internal processor was taking in information sluggishly. To make matters worse, Fi was bawling her eyes out all day long. Fi said she left a party early Friday night and returned home to find Ugolino in bed with his workmate Fiachra. If that wasn't bad enough, Fi said that Ugolino was wearing one of her dresses as Fiachra was pounding him from behind with a strap-on. I tried but failed to stop myself from spewing the coffee from my mouth. Fi managed to laugh about it, albeit briefly. After that, it was back to the tears. The poor thing.

Speaking of poor things... Mr/Mrs Snuggles is not handling this pregnancy very well. He/she is refusing to eat his/her cat food and even went as far as to turn his/her nose up at his/her favourite pick-me-up, banana & strawberry flavoured Actimel (Diary, do forgive me). I still can't believe he is a she. It's going to be a long 2 months.

Stuart (Wednesday, May 20th)

The constant reminder that I'm going to be a father is everywhere. I can't escape it! From opening a box of Nirvana *Nevermind* LP reissues and seeing that iconic baby image on the cover to talking to customers with their kids to billboards with baby products on the walk home from work. Everywhere I look, it's babies and then more babies!

There's been a lot of noise coming from the French couple's flat. Not the usual groaning and hammering, but more the movement of furniture. The stairs seem to be pretty active with French people, too. I wonder if they're moving out. I know this might sound weird, but I hope they stay. Better the devil you know and all that.

On the bright side, I finally got to see Sue since she came back from Amsterdam. While I didn't ask if she partook in any recreational activity that might be associated with such a location, I did get a serious bang of weed from her pink jacket. And while I didn't mention it, I was happy to discover she wasn't a stiff.

Sue is exhausted and fell asleep about ten minutes into my post-sex conversation about safe sex. Though I've never raised the question, I felt obliged to ask Sue if she was on the pill. She said, 'No, but come on… you can be safe, right?' The only thing going through my head was visuals of Zofia bent over the sink with her arse in the air and then a mini Zofia (fringe and all) popping her head in the door of the bathroom while crying, 'Daddy, Daddy, I can't sleep. The monster is in my room!' I had to snap out of the fog, and quick. 'I can be safe,' I replied. Sue started laughing before responding, 'If you want me to go on the pill I will. You look worried.' To say I was relieved would be an understatement. The last thing I need is two kids from two different mothers. I mean how could I do it? What with the Deluxe 180grm Cocteau Twins album reissues and the Bomp Records box set out soon. I'd be broke! As I was thanking Sue for agreeing to go on the pill (I did go on a bit due to my current state of anxiety) she fell asleep. Hopefully, she remembers this conversation in the morning.

Suzanne (Wednesday, May 20th)

Dear Diary,

Work was treacherous today as a good percentage of my most hated clients were booked in one after another. I told both Fi and Siobhan not to let that happen again. My poor brain can't take the onslaught of wedding talk and baby talk. On top of that, I still feel super-groggy, maybe it's a combination of the past few days and sleeping in Stu's hard-as-a-rock bed.

I have a vague recollection of Stu discussing safe sex last night. Or then again, maybe it was one of my weird dreams (which I'm sure was made even weirder after my Amsterdam come down).

Grogginess aside, I managed to amass a maternity pack of sorts for Mr/Mrs Snuggles during lunch. The pack includes;

1 x Pregnancy pillow

1 x Super expandable collar (his/her fat ass has been choking over the past few days)

1 x month's supply of Meow Meow Mini Milks

1 x Heartbeat monitor (just so I can keep an eye on things)

Stuart (Thursday, May 21st)

I'm not sure how I'm going to approach Mam and Dad about Zofia and the baby. Maybe it's best to delay it for now. Who knows what kind of decisions will be thrown out there and agreed upon over the next few weeks? I'm not sure if arguing against abortion will do me any favours because at the end of the day it's Zofia's body and she can choose what she wants with it. Me, on the other hand? As messed up as this situation is, and as difficult as it would be to see the baby if it was raised in

Poland, I'd rather give it a chance at life and do everything in my power to support it than terminate it. Does that make me selfish? Or does that make me a man? I'm not quite sure?

Suzanne (Thursday, May 21st)

Dear Diary,

I called over to Mum's for dinner tonight. She cooked her famous hot pot, the same one Dad used to refer to like sex in a pot. Bless him!

During dinner, we listened to Mr Rocket's radio show live. Diary, I've never been so embarrassed. Mr Rocket didn't spare any detail when discussing his and Mum's sexual exploits with a live caller. Trust Mum to be thrilled to be mentioned on the radio. I couldn't even look at her I was so mortified, but she didn't care. Mum reckons she'll be the envy of every woman in Rockwood tomorrow. I couldn't bring myself to tell her that there are probably about 20 people listening to this show and most of em are coffin dodgers. Mum said, 'I'm going to need a new coat, just in case the paparazzi start following David and me.' I wonder how Mr Rocket puts up with her sometimes. Surely, he knows she can be as daft as a brush. Birds of a feather flock together and all that...

Stuart (Friday, May 22nd)

I am tanked so I'll keep it short as I take this long-overdue shit.

After work, I called up to the salon to collect Sue. From there we made our way towards The Barge as it was a gorgeous day and we wanted to make the most of the good weather as we were both hauled up at work all day.

Weirdly, I ended up sitting in the same seat where I met Sue for the first time. On top of that, Sue was the one who acknowledged it by saying, 'I was full sure you were paddling on the other side of the boat that night.' I asked her if it was The Queers t-shirt I was wearing. She admitted that she didn't see the band t-shirt, but it was more my frame and mannerisms. Talk about double standards. She wasn't moaning about that when her legs were wrapped around my head as she was yowling, 'Don't stop!' about ten minutes ago.

I've started looking at flights to Poland. I need to address this pregnancy situation with Zofia face to face. Arsing about and overthinking it is not going to get me anywhere.

Suzanne (Friday, May 22nd)

Dear Diary,

Mr/Mrs Snuggles had a case of morning sickness earlier. I did my best to console the poor thing, but the meowing was incessant for most of the morning.

I think I spotted the real Starman at the bar earlier tonight. Yes, Diary... Thee Starman, the one from the Love Quest dating site that I so badly burned in favour of not making a fuss. Then again it may not have been him. He was kind of looking over at me though... who knows?

Stu was in weird form tonight, certainly a lot quieter than his usual self. He only came to life after we got some post-pub takeaway... and when having sex just now.

I'm not sure what happened Zia. She had sent me several texts saying she would be at The Barge soon but never arrived. I tried to call her twice, but her phone rang out.

Stuart (Saturday, May 23rd)

God, it felt good to have a day off. Sue was working, so I had the entire day to myself. I felt sorry for Sue this morning. She looked a bit wobbly on her feet while getting dressed. She texted after lunch to say she was in a bad way.

I got up just after 1 pm and started the day with some Brian Eno and a fry fit for an army. After lunch, I sat in the sun out the back and compiled a list of things I want to ask Zofia when I get to Poland.

(1) Are you 100% sure I am the father?

(2) Do you want to keep the baby or were you thinking about having an abortion?

(2.5) How would you feel about calling the baby Polly Jean (after PJ Harvey) if it's a girl?

(3) What's your surname? (I only know Maggie's married name).

(4) How would you feel about calling the baby Iggy (after Iggy Pop) if it was a boy?

I'm staying over at Sue's tonight. Her house smells great!

Suzanne (Saturday, May 23rd)

I think I might need to hire a part-time hairdresser for the weekends, we seem to be getting busier and busier. I thought about asking the girls to take their day off during the week, but I think we all need a weekend break now and again.

I met Mum for lunch. She was sporting her new glasses from Spectacular. She seems to love them, but they look a tad oversized to me.

Mr Grimble from next door called to the house this evening. He said that my poor Snuggleflakes got caught in the cat flap. Mr Grimble asked, 'What in God's name are you feeding that cat?' I had to explain that Mr/Mrs Snuggles is expecting and to take it easy on him/her. Mr Grimble continued, 'Is it any wonder that she got knocked up, parading around from house to house. The last thing I need is for that thing to pop and then spend the day running around after the litter. Please, keep her indoors, dear.' I had to bite my tongue and apologise to Mr Grimble for the inconvenience.

Stu is here tonight. He made me watch some music documentary (that he swore I'd enjoy…) about some band that I've never heard of. Diary, it was shite! He fell asleep about an hour into it.

Stuart (Sunday, May 24th)

Sue and I spent the afternoon in the park making the most of the fine weather. We brought wine, grapes, some pastries and a deck of cards. Sue was shocked that I didn't know how to play poker, or most of the other games she suggested for that matter. Still, we had a good time playing snap and she enjoyed all three of my magic tricks (one of which I made up on the spot and managed to pull off). Sue was legitimately scratching her head wondering how I did it.

I was no sooner in the door of my apartment when I heard a brisk knock at the door. I answered to find the French girl from upstairs (looking smoking hot, it has to be said) standing at the door. 'Allo, sorry to be the bother. Just to let you know I am moving to a new place and my space is now empty. I forgot to give the spare key to the landlord, so he asked me to give it to you to pass on.' I wished her well and said I hope everything works out. She smiled. 'The slimeball is gone… so that is the first step,' she said. I didn't want to ask what happened, so I told her I was sorry to hear that (I wasn't sorry). Again, she smiled back, and I could tell she felt a bit lost in doing so. It was almost like she was looking for that familiar comfort she must have had. For about a millisecond I thought about inviting her in for a glass of wine. Then a quick flash of a Polish baby with bodybuilder-like muscles and a French baby holding a baguette raced through my mind. I thanked her for letting me know, before accepting the key, gently closing the front door and retreating to bed.

Suzanne (Sunday, May 24th)

Dear Diary,

I've got one of those awful wine headaches that just won't quit. I can only blame myself as Stu seemed content after two bottles of wine during our picnic. However, the devil was on my shoulder, nagging me to walk over to the supermarket to grab a 3rd bottle... and yes, Diary, we finished it. By late afternoon, not only was my face as red as a tomato from the sun, but my head was pounding. I asked Stu if I could, 'take the night off,' and go home to bed. In fairness to Stu, he did the gentlemanly thing and called us a taxi there and then. Poor Stu, he didn't even attempt to nurse me back to health. He simply walked me to the door and gave me the space I desired. He is a sweetheart. I hope to God this headache is gone by the morning.

Stuart (Monday, May 25th)

Trish was in one of her moods at work and didn't say much today. Not that she says much anyway. She sighed at a few customer requests, but that was about it.

I called over to Maggie at lunch to pick up a few steaks. I promised Sue I'd cook her something nice this evening. Maggie asked if I had been speaking with, 'The Vampire' (what a pleasant name for her sister) and whether I am going ahead with this paternity test. I've so much a lot on my plate right now that I can barely plan my dinner not to mind a paternity test in Poland. Maggie told me to get my shit together.

Sue seemed to enjoy my cooking. She's asleep in a food coma on the couch beside me.

Suzanne (Monday, May 25th)

No entry

Stuart (Tuesday, May 26th)

I stupidly agreed to have lunch with Maggie, knowing full well I'd be lectured for the hour. I wasn't wrong. Maggie started by giving me a list of options for paternity tests in Opole. Maggie said the flights to Poland are cheap at the moment and to, 'just fucking book it and get it sorted.' I do believe Maggie is still sour about me banging her one and only sister. Throw my new relationship with, 'that Jezebel,' (as Maggie refers to Sue) into the mix and suddenly I'm enemy number one.

After an endless tirade, Maggie eventually cooled the jets and kindly offered to accompany me to Poland if I go ahead with the paternity test. I told Maggie that I appreciated the offer and will make a decision tonight.

I still haven't made a decision.

Suzanne (Tuesday, May 26th)

Dear Diary,

Mrs Snuggles got trapped in the Grimbles' cat flap again. After some incessant knocking, I answered the door to find Mr Grimble holding Mrs Snuggles by her head. She looked petrified as her legs hung loose like she'd been hung out to dry. A lecture on the street being 'like a zoo' was the last thing I needed, but I did offer several apologies as Mr Grimble ranted on. I'll have to keep poor Snuggleflakes in the house until she pops.

Stuart (Wednesday, May 27th)

I'm not sure if it was a weird coincidence or if Trish was taking the piss, but much of today's work playlist was made up of songs with 'baby' in the title or lyrics;

The Ramones - Baby, I Love You

The Beach Boys - Good to my Baby

The Ronettes - Be My Baby

Big Star - When my Baby's Beside Me

The Supremes - Baby Love

I've arranged to meet Maggie for a few birthday pints tomorrow night. I have no idea what age she is as she still refuses to tell me.

Suzanne (Wednesday, May 27th)

Dear Diary,

I'm bloody exhausted! Work was hell, due to the faulty air conditioning and sweltering heat I had to deal with while working beside the window. Many of our clients went out of their way to harp on about it, knowing full well we had addressed it with them beforehand and offered them plenty of refreshments throughout their appointment.

Couple that with about 5 hours of sleep after the whole Mrs Grimble / Mrs Snuggles episode and you've got one cranky girl.

Zia texted tonight asking if I would like to meet for lunch. She said she's been, 'tied up' with a lad from the Rockwood Fire Brigade.

Stuart (Thursday, May 28th)

Maggie was in the store earlier this morning. She picked up a used copy of *Close to the Edge* by Yes. I didn't charge her as it was her birthday. Maggie rarely buys records, so I know she was up to no good. 'So, have you decided to go to Poland?' she asked. I hadn't, so instead of saying no I told Maggie I had a plan and would tell her about it later as I was under pressure at the time. The shop was empty, and she knew I was fobbing her off. She threw her eyes up to heaven and said, 'I'll see you later.'

Unfortunately, it looks like I'm Poland Bound. And yes, Maggie is 100% to blame! After work, we met up at the Slippery Duck. When I got there, Maggie had a white envelope on the table. I had assumed it was a birthday card from one of her co-workers in the butchers. I sat down and she slid the envelope towards me. 'For you,' she said. My first thought? Maggie was giving me an unwanted gift. My second thought? Shit! It's probably a letter from Zofia. It was neither. I opened the envelope to find 2 x return flight tickets to Poland. Maggie coughed nervously before questioning my earlier admission, 'You didn't have a plan, did you?' I shook my head to suggest a no. 'Friday week, book it off! We fly out at 6:10 am on Friday and fly back at 9:30 pm on Friday,' she said bluntly. What could I say but, 'Thanks?' Throughout the night, Maggie kept reminding me to tell Sue about the whole situation. Maggie reckons Sue will show her true colours (whatever she means by that) once I come clean about the pregnancy.

1:55 am

Fuck my life!!

Suzanne (Thursday, May 28th)

Dear Diary,

I met Zia briefly during lunch. She had gone to the fire station to drop a phone back to the guy she is seeing. She seemed flustered; her hair was a mess and she was panting profusely. When I asked how things were going with the fireman she admitted to, 'sliding down his pole' earlier. I can't take that girl seriously.

Stu's out with one of his friends to celebrate a birthday so I called over to Mum's for dinner. When I got there, Mr Rocket's radio show could be heard from the front gate; every window in the house was open. Mum swears that she is now a mini celebrity thanks to her involvement with Mr Rocket. And while she admitted to playing it down, she is convinced that a lot more women are smiling and saying hello to her when she's walking through Rockwood. I was reluctant to mention Mum's new glasses so just responded with, 'They'll be asking you for your autograph next.' Mum giggled like a little schoolgirl before responding, 'You're right darling, I better start practicing.'

Stuart (Friday, May 29th)

It looks like I have a new neighbour. Her name is Peggy and she's from Digglewood.

I spotted her struggling with some boxes by the elevator and asked her if she needed help. She seemed a bit startled at first but took me up on the offer. 'I'm Peggy, I just moved into apartment no.6 on the third floor,' she said. I introduced myself and told her that I lived in no.3 on the 2nd floor. Peggy smiled. 'PIL, good stuff,' she said, pointing towards a band t-shirt I've owned for about 15 years. I complimented Peggy on having a cool name and good taste in music. I admitted it was a refreshing change from the French neighbours who had just moved out. The elevator stopped. We both bent down to pick up the same box and ended up head-butting each other. 'I knew you were a punk,' Peggy quipped. 'Think of it as a welcoming gift,' I said. Peggy responded, 'As far as welcoming gifts go, a head-butt is certainly one I'll remember.' There was a bit of awkward silence as I helped her move the boxes into her apartment. I'm not sure if it's me or the lack of furniture or what, but apartment no.6 looks huge. It's spotless too, unlike my place. Once all the boxes were in, Peggy broke the silence, 'What do I owe you, Stu?' I suggested a random figure and told her to leave it in my postbox. She got the joke and said, 'See you again,' before closing the door.

1:45 am

I think I'm in love (again)

Suzanne (Friday, May 29th)

Dear Diary,

Stu texted during work to say he was going to relax at home on his own this evening. With no other plans in place, I took up Fi and Siobhan's invitation of post-work pints at The Barge.

The riverfront outside The Barge was thronged; a mix of office workers, students and the Mon to Friday club (Fi's name for a small group of unemployed band heads who sit and drink in the same spot every day).

At about 10 pm we ended up moving to a table that had a gas heater. As there were only three of us, there was plenty of space at the table and it wasn't long before a bunch of Scottish lads crashed in on top of us. They were a bit full-on with the innuendoes and lad banter at first, but once we showed them we were well able to give it back they settled down. Both Fi and Siobhan ended up with two of them. Fi went for a stroll down the riverfront with her fella and Siobhan, bless her lack of giving a shit, pulled her fella into one of the cubicles. Throughout the exploits, I was left saddled with the remaining lads; a retired council worker, his son (a fitter) and a lad who worked as a barman. They were all sweethearts and I enjoyed having a laugh and joke with them until close.

2:47 am

Diary, sometimes I wonder if my existence is as mundane as I imagine it to be. Tonight, was another reminder of this when talking to the Scottish lads. Even though they appeared as 'normal lads', all three had unique side stories, projects, ambitions and goals. The old lad, for example, he is in the process of setting up a water filter to eliminate fluoride from your kitchen sink. Then there was the fitter, he has spent the past three years buying up and renovating dilapidated houses and claimed he would be a millionaire before he hit 30. Then there was the barman who doubles as a theatre actor and whose only goal is to get a recurring role on *Coronation St.* As he said himself, 'Thay haven't git ony fuckin' Scots actors oan th' street 'n' a'm aff tae pat Blackburn oan th' map.' Is my life that shit? I don't even know what my ambitions are. A mother to a cat who is about to be a mother to many cats? Girlfriend to a record store worker? The life-long hairdresser who's spent the last 14 years alternating between, 'anything planned for the weekend?' and 'going anywhere nice for the holidays?' Diary, I need a serious reality check!!

Stuart (Saturday, May 30th)

I bumped into Patryk on the bus after work. He cheekily sat in beside me and acted like everything was cool. He claimed Maggie had informed him of my new relationship with Sue and questioned me by asking, 'What about my mudder? She'd do anything for you.' He was right. I told Patryk we were always just good friends who had each other's backs. Patryk responded, 'What about Aunty Zofia? My mudder said you knocked her up, no?' There was no bullshitting Patryk on this answer. I told him it was never meant to be. We were drunk, we had a bit of a kiss and then one thing led to another. I tried to put his mind at ease by saying it wasn't a big deal and we're going to look after it. Patryk replied, 'What d'ya mean?' Thankfully, we were just by my stop, so I was saved by the bell. 'I gotta bounce,' I said. 'Are you gonna murder the baby?' shouted Patryk as I waited for the doors to open at the front of the bus. I could feel the hot flush racing through my cheeks as everybody looked my way. 'I'm only on level 5,' I said, in an attempt to make it sound like we were talking video games. As the bus pulled out from the stop and I began walking towards my apartment, all I heard was,

'Murderer!' I looked up and found Patryk attempting to squeeze his mallet sized head through the bus's hinged window. He'll be the death of me, that young fella!

I was supposed to call over to Sue's this evening, but much like me last night, she said she was very hung-over. Instead, I opened a bottle of wine and dug out my Felt records.

Suzanne (Saturday, May 30th)

Dear Diary,

Shortly after noon, I woke up to the sound of Mum shouting through the letterbox. When I answered the door, both Mum and Mr Rocket were stood there dressed in their finest evening wear. 'Good morning, Suzanne,' said Mr Rocket enthusiastically. I told Mr Rocket that he looked dapper. He blushed and referring to his new suit explained, 'You can thank your mother, she picked this one.' He adjusted his tie and nudged it a little tighter. 'Darling, we said we'd stop by as it was on the way. I hope you don't mind?' asked Mum. What could I say? I asked Mum where they were going. Mr Rocket interjected, 'It's a gathering for the 'who's who' with the Mayor at the County Hall.' Mum chirped in, 'It's mainly for famous people from the town, you know, the captain of the rugby team, some of the sick children, that fella who runs the entertainment section of the local paper, some of the stars from the radio shows, people like that...'. It sounded like my idea of hell. I told them they got a great day for it weather-wise. As Mum and Mr Rocket made their way through two pots of tea, 16 quarter-sliced sandwiches and a handful of biscuits, I was subjected to Mr Rocket practicing his radio jingles. He asked me for feedback as I was, 'young and hip' and would know what the kids are into. I was reluctant to tell him it wasn't one of his regular Wham! singles for a start.

'Luuuuuuuurve... is in... the air, with me, your host, Dr David Rocket, only on 94.4, Flaaaaash FM. What do you think?' asked Mr Rocket as he introduced what sounded like the opening line of his show. I told him it wasn't bad. Mr Rocket rolled his eyes. I felt compelled to be honest with him. 'It's a tad dramatic... actually, it's very American sounding... and... a bit slow.' Mr Rocket looked somewhat miffed. 'It's the radio, dear. You have to be clear and concise so the listeners can understand you,' he replied. Mum butted in, 'I think it sounds very sexy.' 'See,' said Mr Rocket proudly.

'The luuuuuuurve line that connects hearts everywhere... you're listening to Love is in the Air with me, Dr Davey Rooooocket, only on 94.4, Flash FM. Well?' asked Mr Rocket again. 'That one makes me weak at the knees,' said Mum. Mr Rocket turned to me, 'What do you think, dear?' 'I didn't know you were a doctor?' I replied cheekily. 'A doctor of love,' said Mr Rocket as he adjusted his collar. 'Daviiiid,' said Mum looking rather embarrassed. If ever there were two people that were made for each other it is Mum and Mr Rocket. They are as bad as each other.

I spent the rest of the evening in a food coma/hung-over slumber on the couch. I told Stu to stay at home as I've got zero energy.

Stuart (Sunday, May 31st)

Sue invited me to her place for lunch. I think she felt guilty for drinking too much Friday and writing off yesterday. Sue made a beautiful risotto and we ended up sharing a bottle of red wine. Today, more than ever, I wanted to come clean about Zofia and the pregnancy. At one stage I came close and told Sue that I needed to tell her something. She looked worried and replied, 'This doesn't sound good.' I baulked on my admission and took off on a tangent about a world where The Beatles' *White* Album had preceded *Sgt Peppers*, and then *Sgt Peppers* was renamed the *Black Album*. I told Sue it would probably be considered the biggest album of all time. 'Ah, Jesus,' said Sue after leaving out a big sigh. She continued, 'I thought it was something important.' I explained that it would have been massively important. Sue stood up and excused herself to the shop to get more wine. Although the shop is straight across the street, she was gone for a good hour or so.

I made Sue watch *Spinal Tap* this evening. She didn't really get it or laugh all that much.

Suzanne (Sunday, May 31st)

Dear Diary,

I had a nice relaxing day with Stu. We started with some lunch and a couple of glasses of wine and by 6 pm we were too pissed to cook so we settled for some Chinese takeaway. Earlier I had an awkward encounter with a freezer door in the shop. My dress got stuck on a hinge and I couldn't quite retrieve it. Many customers stopped to help, as did the shop owner, but to no avail. In the end, a girl about my age managed to free me by closing the freezer door and threading the dress out. I was never so embarrassed. When I got home, Stu made me watch some awful band documentary about a heavy metal band. I struggled to stay awake.

Stuart (Monday, June 1st)

I arrived at work to find the words 'murdering cunt!' written, in what appeared to be dirt, across the shop window. It wouldn't take a brain surgeon to figure out who was responsible, but that didn't stop me from checking the cameras from the weekend. As I had suspected, Patryk was the culprit. At 2:35 am Saturday night, Patryk can be seen outside the shop eating a battered sausage while being hoisted up by a group of youths. Not one for giving a fuck, Patryk turns to the camera at 2:36 am, and with the battered sausage hanging from his mouth gives the camera the finger with both hands. From there, he pretends to eat the sausage suggestively while brushing back some make-believe long hair (no doubt imitating his aunty, Zofia), before he takes the sausage from his mouth and uses it to write the words 'murdering cunt' across the store window. For what it's worth, he finished eating the sausage.

Removing Patryk's damage was not an easy task. Actually, it was quite embarrassing, as I had to use several different window washes to clear it.

It has to be said, I don't know what Patryk's problem is? I have never mentioned abortion to him, nor does he know any of the facts. I suspect Maggie has been feeding him all sorts of propaganda about Zofia and me. I wonder if Maggie is jealous.

I finally found my passport after pulling the house apart for the best part of two hours. It had somehow ended up inside a box of 7" singles, the sleeve of my 10cc - The Things We Do for Love 7" to be exact.

Suzanne (Monday, June 1st)

Dear Diary,

I'm a little worried as I have yet to get my period. It's a couple of days late, which is a first for me and a little bit worrying. While I don't want to jump to conclusions, there is a chance, of course, that I might be pregnant! After work, I contemplated picking up a pregnancy test just to be sure but bailed when I got to the door. Instead, I did it the Irish way, I just ignored the problem.

How am I going to tell Stu if I really am pregnant? While I'm excited on the inside, I think most people can tell I'm pretty rattled on the outside.

Stuart (Tuesday, June 2nd)

I bumped into my new neighbour, Peggy in the elevator just now. She looked radiant with that long red hair, pale white skin and dressed in a skimpy summer dress. 'Stu, right?' asked Peggy. I replied, 'Good memory.' Peggy continued, 'How was your day then?' I did my best not to focus on her cleavage and told her today was going better than yesterday. Peggy smiled and said, 'And let's hope tomorrow is even better.' The elevator bell rang as we arrived on my floor. Before I had a chance to say goodnight or step out of the elevator, Peggy grabbed my arm playfully and said, 'You wanna see something cool?' I didn't know what to say or do as she caught me off guard, but I agreed to her invite. As we ascended to the 3rd floor there was silence in the elevator; Peggy was definitely ramping up the suspense. I did my best to distract my mind from flashes of gimp masks, a wardrobe full of dead arty types, and God only knows what else was racing through my head at the time. Ding! We arrived on the 3rd floor. Peggy led the way as I, again, struggled to subdue my imagination.

Inside the apartment, I couldn't help but be overwhelmed with the smell of cinnamon. It would seem most of the stuff I had carried up last day had been unboxed, as the previously empty shell of an apartment now resembled something out of Alice in Wonderland. 'A Drink?' Peggy suggested. I wasn't sure what kind of drink she was referring to so not to be rude I just said, 'Sure.' Peggy disappeared behind the alcove in the kitchen and returned with two straight whiskeys. 'One moment,' she said. As I sat there wondering where all of this was going, I became transfixed on a painting of Lou Reed on the wall. He was smoking a cigarette and looked like the baddest mother fucker on the planet. The signature on the painting appeared to read, 'Peggy O,' and just as I was about to stand up to investigate further, Peggy returned. She was hiding something behind her back. 'Check this out,' said Peggy. She handed me a copy of The Beatles' *Revolver* LP signed by every member of the band. 'My uncle passed away the year before last. The big C caught him,' said Peggy. I guess she was referring to cancer; as opposed to the sign from the Chicken Box takeaway that killed some bloke in the storm last Xmas. 'Ouch, sorry to hear that,' I replied. I waited for her to grab a tissue and wipe the tears from her eyes. I asked Peggy if she knew how much the record was worth? 'I never got around to pricing it, and anyway, it's not for sale,' said Peggy. 'If it was *For Sale,* you'd be lucky to get a fiver for it.' My reference to the *Beatles For Sale* LP went over her head. 'A fiver? Come on,' said Peggy.

What started as one drink ended up with Peggy and I making our way through two bottles of wine a couple of joints and an all-meat pizza. Sue has texted several times since, but I have yet to reply. I was very much engrossed in Peggy's stories about meeting Keith Richards in the women's bathroom of a Soho hotel, knocking a glass of wine over Kate Moss's dress and the time she had a one-night stand with that long-haired bloke from *The Mighty Boosh*. I'm not sure if Peggy was making this shit up on the spot, but she can definitely tell a story, that's for sure! With one slice of pizza, two empty wine bottles and two empty wine glasses on the coffee table, Peggy pulled down her ponytail, allowing her hair to fall over her shoulders. I got a quick flashback to the night I apparently knocked up Zofia. Then I remembered that bastard trip to Poland this Friday. Visions of men with bodybuilder physiques and girls with tight gym wear and even tighter bodies were suddenly interrupted, 'So, what now?' Peggy asked. I had to bite my lip. I told her I had a lot on tomorrow and that I should get going. 'You're only downstairs, it's not like you have far to go,' said Peggy. I was stumped. I genuinely didn't know how to respond. 'Ahhhh, girlfriend, right?' said Peggy. I took a deep breath and told her it was complicated. Peggy attempted to pour wine from the empty bottle. Upon realising it was empty, she replied, 'It always is.' She walked me to the door, kissed me on the cheek and said, 'It was fun. Goodnight.'

It's 2:25 am right now and my head is already pounding. Four hours of sleep isn't going to do me any favours for the morning.

Suzanne (Tuesday, June 2nd)

Dear Diary,

While I have yet to confirm my potential pregnancy, I can now relate to my poor Snuggleflakes. I see how she is having great difficulty when attempting to jump onto her usual spot on the couch. These days, she seems pretty content with the rug close to the TV. If I am indeed pregnant, I can see myself being one of those awkward pregnant women that become a burden to others at all times.

Still no reply from Stu. I must have texted him three times since yesterday afternoon. I even tried calling him after work, but his phone rang out.

11:17 pm

I woke to a text from Stu, it read:

"Phone is acting up, just seeing your messages and missed call now. Fancy a pint after work tomorrow?"

Even though he'll get my read receipt, I'll reply in the morning.

Stuart (Wednesday, June 3rd)

My head is too fucked to write anything tonight. Need time to think.

Suzanne (Wednesday, June 3rd)

Dear Diary,

Telling Stu that I might be pregnant might not have been the best of ideas after all. I did explain the missed period (again, a first for me) and that it was only a possibility and not definite as I have yet to take a pregnancy test, but Stu's reaction said it all. My poor baby ended up spewing a mouthful of Guinness all over the table, destroying some limited-edition record (copy #01 of only #100 copies pressed according to Stu). Poor Stu looked like he was crying as he did his best to clean the record sleeve. Then there were the words, 'Will you call me a taxi? I need to lay down.' It was the least I could do. I texted him this evening but heard nothing back. That dreaded silence once again!

Diary, I should probably take a pregnancy test. I'm after scaring the poor fella to death.

Stuart (Thursday, June 4th)

FML!

Suzanne (Thursday, June 4th)

Dear Diary,

I'm a bit worried about Stu. "Still laying down," isn't exactly the response I was looking for, but at least he texted me back. If he's still lying down, chances are he didn't go to work. I'm not quite sure what I should say or do?

It appears Mr Grimble's son, Royston is back living with his Mum and Dad for the summer. I spotted them unloading a lot of stuff from Mr Grimble's car tonight. I guess the college term must be over now.

4:17 am

I haven't slept a wink. I'm worried sick about being pregnant, not to mention Stu's current condition. I might have to call in sick tomorrow. My first sick day ever!

Stuart (Friday, June 5th)

I'm in a lot of trouble with a lot of people; namely Maggie (for not turning up at the airport this morning), Trish (for forgetting to tell her I was going to Poland today; albeit, I did inform her of my whereabouts and asked her bro to cover me at work) and Zofia (for skipping the paternity test).

I was scheduled to meet Maggie in the airport at 5:30 am, but instead of taking the bus from the station to the airport, I took the 307 to Talbot Road and then walked from there to Mam and Dad's place. I've been hiding out here with my phone on silent all day. Maggie has made 11 attempts at calling me and I haven't answered any of them. After Maggie's last attempt, she sent a message, "You're on your own now". It certainly hit home – my anxiety levels have been through the roof ever since.

Throughout the chaos, I did call Sue and apologised for giving her the cold shoulder over the past few days. She seemed relieved to hear my voice and assured me that we'll be OK. I thanked Sue for being so understanding and told her that I needed some time to digest the news. Sue said that was completely understandable and told me to take all the time I need. I told Sue I'd make my way back to Rockwood on Sunday night and reassured her, 'we'll be OK.'

Suzanne (Friday, June 5th)

Dear Diary,

I am pregnant!! I can't believe I just wrote those words but it's true!

I took two different pregnancy tests from two different brands and the results were the same. I've been lost for words all evening. At first, I broke down in tears, but after letting the news sink in, I'm kind of thrilled! Over the past few years, I became content knowing that it might never happen. I was fully prepared to be that lonely old cat lady who would inevitably die after choking on a ball of cat fur. I have yet to break the news to anyone, including Stu. Mum, God bless her, will be over the moon!!

Stuart (Saturday, June 6th)

I needed some time to process this pregnancy news, so I ended up popping down to visit Mam and Dad. I didn't open my mouth about the news, but I did join Dad for a few beers while helping him maintain the garden and changed two lightbulbs for Mam. Mam said Dad couldn't reach the bulbs and the last thing she wanted was him climbing ladders.

Later on, Mam made my favourite, cottage pie. She always makes this when I visit and accompanies it with a spiel about not eating enough. During dinner, Mam's upper denture got stuck on a carrot and fell on her plate. Dad, with more than enough drink in him at that stage, took out his top denture and replaced it with Mam's, before doing his best impersonation of her with a tea towel wrapped around his head.

Suzanne (Saturday, June 6th)

Dear Diary,

I told Mum the news about being pregnant and she fainted. Thankfully, she didn't hurt herself in the fall and came around shortly after. She was disoriented and asked what had happened. Again, I told her the news. Mum's eyes lit up. 'Ooooooh, darling!!! Finally!!! I thought you were going to share a house with the hairy-armpits girl (I guess she was talking about Zia) and buy more cats.' I was thrilled with her reaction; even if it was a little worrying. 'Wait, who's the father, the fella from the hospital?' Mum asked. She was referring to Stu but was always terrible with names. I confirmed that Stu was the father and that he was going to be a great one at that. I could hear Mr Rocket whistling as he came through the hall to the kitchen. 'My baby girl is having a baby girl,' shouted Mum. 'Who, Suzanne? Ah, now, we'll have to break out the champers,' replied Mr Rocket, before putting his arms around me and whispering into my ear. 'You're going to be a fantastic Mum.' I got a little overwhelmed, let it be said. I said thanks, kissed Mr Rocket on the cheek and then corrected Mum on the gender of my unborn child (I knew Mum was excited and all, but I told her not to assume it was a girl just yet). Mum smiled and said, 'I'm still in shock, I need a drink,' before popping the cork and drinking straight from the bottle. I'm beginning to wonder if the world needs a 3rd generation, Helen Conway.

Stuart (Sunday, June 7th)

I arrived back to Rockwood about 9:30 pm and was greeted by Peggy rolling a wheelchair into the elevator. We greeted each other and exchanged small talk about the weather. I contemplated asking her about the wheelchair, but because she didn't make any reference to it, I thought it best to say nothing. When the elevator stopped on my floor, she kept it simple and said, 'Have a nice night.' 'You too,' I replied. Man, she is hot!

Today was pretty good. I finished the garden with Dad, had a nice chicken dinner and had a good chat with some randomer on the bus home. The randomer worked for the electricity board and is about to dump his wife of 10 years. The more he spoke, the more I hoped she was still alive.

Back to reality tomorrow!!

Suzanne (Sunday, June 7th)

Dear Diary,

This might sound weird, but I'm super-excited about the baby. I can't wait to make it all official with Stu tomorrow, and now that he's had a few days to digest the news, I think he'll be just fine.

Mrs Snuggles and I spent the evening caressing each other on the couch; me with my hand and Snuggles with her head. I have a funny feeling she can sense that I'm pregnant. It's kind of like that extra sense dogs have for sick people, or so they say.

10:40 pm

I've made a shortlist of potential baby names;

Boys Names - Jack, Emmett, Elliott, Kyle

Girls Names - Penny, Lara, Louisa, Cara

Stuart (Monday, June 8th)

I did my best to track down Maggie during lunch as I wanted to apologise for bailing on her last Friday. When I called to the butchers, the heavy lad who doesn't like me said she had gone out for lunch. With a one-track mind, I spent the best part of an hour scouring through Maggie's favourite eateries in an attempt to find her and apologise. Unfortunately, she was nowhere to be seen.

After work, I met Sue in The Barge. Weirdly, we sat where we met for the first time. Although there were plenty of free seats outside and neither of us suggested the seats in question, both of us seemed to gravitate there naturally. I was about halfway through my pint when Sue took my hand and said, 'I took the test... twice. I'm officially pregnant.' I jolted, released her hand and knocked my pint all over my record bag –

destroying my new Captain Beefheart re-issue in the process. In a whirlwind of frustration, I ordered a few straight ones before excusing myself to the bathroom.

When I returned to Sue, she came around to console me. With her head on my shoulder and her arms wrapped around me, she said, 'It'll be OK, you'll be a great Dad.' I had to say something. I had to step up and take responsibility. I had to forget that I was also having a child with a Polish stranger. I told Sue this father thing might just be my calling. Sue said, 'Leave it to sit with you for a few days, I know I did, and I couldn't be happier.' I agreed. Sue smiled and looked straight into my eyes. She didn't say anything. I felt like she was looking for something more profound. Something that would assure her I would be a loving, caring and compassionate father. Something that would give her a sense of security. Something that would make her realise I actually give a shit about what we have. I began talking, 'Sue, from the first night I spoke to you I fell in love. I told the guys that I was going to make you my future wife no matter what it took. I regret not asking you for your number on that particular night, and no matter how hard I tried, I could not get you out of my head. It's tough to put it into words, but I guess it was just you. The full package. That smile, your blushes, the way you blink your eyes when you look nervous, your hair, your gorgeous good looks, your style, your walk, the way you move your hands to paint pictures when you talk, your stunning figure, I mean, you are faultless in every way. Imagine my luck when I realised you had picked up the wrong date! I'll never forget that moment. I'll never forget seeing you glow in the bright lights of the bar that night. And on top of that, now that I've gotten to know you, I don't think I've ever met such a soulful, joyful, real person, with such a truly amazing heart. I could search the world over to find the perfect mother and they wouldn't come close. Sue, I love you and trust me when I say that, together, we will raise and support the most wonderful child.'

Suzanne (Monday, June 8th)

Dear Diary,

It's been an emotional evening. My brain and body are tired so I'm going to keep this entry short. I told Stu that we are officially pregnant. After downing three straight whiskeys and tearing through 20 cigarettes, he seemed to come around. In fact, by the end of the night, he got emotional and said some beautiful words to me. I feel secure now. I feel like it's us against the world. Sue and Stu with a baby due.

Stuart (Tuesday, June 9th)

I'm sitting on the riverfront trying to process my life. I'm going to be a father! I have to say it allowed for it to sink in. I'm going to be a father!! I'm going to be a father!! I'm going to be a father... AGAIN!! As the water rushes by, I can't help but think of a new life overseas. Would anyone miss me if I jumped on the ferry never to be seen again?

Mam and Dad? They'd be sad, but not that sad.

Trish? She's half-dead anyway so it wouldn't make much of a difference.

Maggie? I would like to think so.

Sue? She would hate me for ending my life and not being around to raise our child.

Zofia? I'm surprised she hasn't flown back from Poland and done me in already.

The guy that listens to 'Some Might Say' by Oasis on the bus every morning? Fuck! I hope he can, 'find a brighter day.'

Suzanne (Tuesday, June 9th)

Dear Diary,

As much as I tried to keep quiet about my pregnancy, I let my guard down when Siobhan was talking about having put on weight. Siobhan said she was out for dinner on Sunday night, when the button of her jeans burst from its seam, flew through the air and landed on the plate of an adjacent customer. Siobhan's re-enactment of the event was hilarious and it's a good thing I'm only a few days into this pregnancy, otherwise, my water would have probably broken from laughing so much. When I told Siobhan, 'I'll be next,' she laughed it off unassumingly. Then I broke the news, 'I'll be next sooner than you think, I'm pregnant!' I blurted. Siobhan screamed in shock. 'Aggggggghhhhh! What the actual fuck? Already? Ye must be at it like rabbits.' Fi arrived in from the salon kitchen and screamed, 'Is it a rat?' Having misheard her words the first time, I replied, 'No, he's not a rat. He's different from all of my exes. He actually gives a shit.' Fi replied, 'What are you on about? Who was screaming? Did ye see a rat running through the salon?' 'Sue is pregnant!' proclaimed Siobhan, cutting to the chase. 'What the fuck! Already?' Fi said, echoing Siobhan's sentiments moments before. Fi came running over, wrapped her arms around me, and began swinging me around like a toddler. Once the commotion settled down, and every client in the salon had come over to hug me, all ongoing conversations moved from holidays and TV-soap scandals to babies, babies and more babies. Thankfully, I managed to get out of the building for an hour during lunch. I needed some time out from all the post-birth adjustment stories.

When I arrived back, Fi and Siobhan surprised me with flowers, Champagne and a giant-size congratulations card to celebrate the good news.

The card reads;

Dearest Sue,

Massive congratulations on the great news! We are so excited for you and can't wait to meet 'Mini Sue' (we hope it's a girl). You and yer man (sorry, we forgot his name) will make for great parents. Your mother will be so proud (totes emosh!!)

Lots of love,

Siobh, Fi and all the girls xxx

Stuart (Wednesday, June 10th)

Sue's advice to take some time for me over the past few days was a good call. I'm sitting in the back-garden listening to The Velvet Underground and drinking iced tea. I've tried but failed to get in touch with Maggie. She is refusing to answer calls and messages. I sent Patryk a text just now. It reads: "Tell your mother to give me a call. It's important."

In an unexpected meeting, I bumped into Effie in the supermarket. She came up behind me and whacked me on the neck with a karate chop, 'Hiiiiiiiiii yaaaaaaaa... doing, Stu?' She would do this all the time. It always hurts like hell. Effie was in good form and seemed genuinely happy to see me; even after our dramatic breakup. Effie began – 'I meet the guy from dating site again.' 'Oh good, how's that going?' I replied. 'Yap, not too bad. She is really nice.' It was clear Effie was still struggling with her English and her genders, but then she made it clear. 'She is the male model, very handsome.' I was afraid to ask if she had met a transgender. Then curiosity got the best of me, so I asked Effie to show me a picture. 'Yap,' Effie replied. She pulled out her phone and flicked through several images before she was satisfied. 'This one, here we go.' It was a bloke alright. He looked like something you'd see on a Michael Kors advertisement. 'She is called Scott, only 27, she from the Manchester.' It was nice to see Effie so content. I always felt it was a bit forced with me. In what might have been an act of goodwill, Effie strolled back to the shop with me, so I could let Trish take her lunch. Before we parted I wished Effie and her new partner the best. She smiled, kissed me on the cheeks and assured me I was a, 'scaring man,' I think she meant caring, or so I hope.

Suzanne (Wednesday, June 10th)

Dear Diary,

My poor Snuggleflakes has a bad dose of morning sickness. Diary, I can sympathise. I filled four bowls of milk and left every window in the house open before leaving for work. The house is just too warm for him/her and I'm paranoid about him/her having a miscarriage.

I texted Stu this morning and told him to take some more time for himself. It's been a crazy few days for both of us.

Zia arrived at the salon with a bunch of baby stuff this morning. She had met Mum on the street, and Mum, of course, didn't waste any time in bringing Zia up to date on my pregnancy. Zia was beaming with joy when she arrived. She was no longer in the door and she had already popped the bottle of Champagne she had brought. 'The party is over now,' said Zia jokingly, as the cork flew, and bubbly spilt all over her hands. I tried but failed to hold back the tears. In many ways, she wasn't wrong.

Stuart (Thursday, June 11th)

I should really disable my Love Quest account. I keep getting unsolicited messages from blokes. Check out this one from a bloke named bearinunderwear:

"Hey Sexy,

I see like you funk and disco. I really love 'La Bumba' ;) xxx"

I met Tony, Rodge and Charlie for lunch. It was Tony's birthday, so we shouted him to a few lunchtime cocktails. Charlie seemed surprised that Tony was getting stuck in. 'Jesus, you're a brave man. I'd be out the door if they caught me drinking on the job,' said Charlie. Tony replied, 'Most of the fuckers working for the council are half dead anyway, so I doubt any of em would know the difference. And truth be told, many of them come back from lunch half-cut.' As the lunchtime liquor-up continued (very much past the hour) I came clean about both pregnancies. Talk about a party-pooper, it was beyond lead balloon stuff. The banter and constant remarks about the waitress and her backside were replaced with an overtone of concern. The lads were shocked and genuinely concerned. 'What the fuck are you going to do now?' asked Rodge. 'Man, I'd be a goner. I'd be on the first plane to Timbuktu,' added Tony. 'You'll be alright, man. You've three babysitters here anyway. Three men and a little baby,' said Charlie. Rodge stepped in to correct him, 'Three men and two little babies.' An image of the three lads bringing my toddlers to Glastonbury flashed through my thoughts. I felt dizzy. I told the lads I had to go and made a break back to the shop. For the first time in ten years, I walked in behind the counter of Reality Records and felt lost. Everything I knew and everything I had become seemed like one big dream, like a materialistic cloud that I've spent most of my adult life floating in. The real reality was hitting home. It was harsh. It was unexpected. I was going to be a father to two children, from two different parents, at the same time. My thought process was interrupted by a customer waving a copy of Master of Puppets on vinyl and harping on about how it was faulty (it looked like he had his breakfast on the thing). He seemed to go on forever as I was still processing the conversation from lunch. In the end, I lost my patience. I took the record from the customer to inspect it. It was greasy as hell and smelled like fish and chips. I waved the record in his face and politely advised him, 'This isn't a plate.' God knows I have enough on mine!

Suzanne (Thursday, June 11th)

Dear Diary,

Stu is still making the most of his, 'time-out.' He texted me earlier to say he went for a few cocktails with the lads and was feeling banjaxed. I gave him the benefit of the doubt.

Fi texted, informing me that Mr Rocket announced my pregnancy to the world (well Rockwood and beyond) on his radio show this evening. Fi said Mr Rocket sounded emotional in congratulating his 'adopted daughter' and paid tribute to me by closing his show with 'Bye Bye Baby' by the Bay City Rollers. I'm going to kill him when I see him!!

Stuart (Friday, June 12th)

My morning routine was unexpectedly interrupted today. I was rolling up the shutters at the shop when I heard a voice behind me. 'Stu, we need to have a proper chat.' It was from Maggie. I was half asleep. 'It's Friday morning. I'm going to be flat out with new releases for at least two hours,' I replied. Maggie was persistent, 'Jesus Christ, can Trish not look after it?' I wasn't expecting such hostility. Like a bold child, stunned by a mother's sternness, I replied without thinking, 'Ahh, yeah, I guess she could.' Maggie was snappy, 'Leave Trish a note, she'll be fine. We can grab a coffee up the street.' She wasn't messing about. 'Sounds good,' I replied. I was full sure Maggie would have taken those well-grizzled butchers' hands to my head if I said otherwise.

The coffee shop was quiet. It was so early that the staff were still putting out the fresh array of pastries and buns along the countertop as the smell of fresh coffee filled the air. Maggie picked up the conversation, 'So, what the fuck is your problem? Are you a coward or something? Are you afraid to step up or are you going to be a man-child, holding on to your precious records for the rest of your life?' It was a low-blow and Maggie certainly hit a nerve. It was a bit of fun. Zofia is as much to blame as I am, and she knows it – and that's exactly what I told Maggie before she stormed off in a huff.

I'm over in Sue's place now with a serious dose of the shits. I've been on the toilet bowl for about 45 mins and my arse feels like I've given birth to a quintet of Cacti. Earlier tonight, I came very close to telling Sue about Zofia and how she is also pregnant. I guess I'm terrified of Sue's reaction and the possibility of losing her for good. What did I do instead? I ate Maltesers and browsed Discogs (I couldn't believe I stumbled upon a copy of Love's - Forever Changes (Mono) for £70) on my phone while I was supposed to be watching some God-awful rom-com with Sue.

Suzanne (Friday, June 12th)

Dear Diary,

Spending the evening cuddled up with Stu gave me a real sense of family and our future together. Most guys hate watching girly flicks but, in fairness to Stu, he seemed very into it. I could tell because I overheard him reacting to scenes in the movie under his breath, saying stuff like, 'no way' or 'wow' thinking that I couldn't hear him. It definitely bodes for a great future together.

Stuart (Saturday, June 13th)

What a beautiful day! Sue and I woke early and made a whopper of a breakfast; bacon, eggs, pudding, toast, croissants, fruit, coffee, the works. After breakfast, we lay out on the deck chairs and read the papers, although I couldn't stay long as I had promised Trish, I would cover her shift after lunch, as she and her brother are off to see Depeche Mode.

The shop was super-busy today, mainly Spanish students who were louder than the first Clash album I had been playing. The students spent a good hour or so loitering around the store, leaving Cornetto wrappers on the windowsill, sitting in the CD aisles and being a general nuisance.

I ended up losing my cool with them and shouted, 'Oi, scalimocho!' I have no idea if that's a word, but it was enough to get rid of em!

Suzanne (Saturday, June 13th)

Dear Diary,

I caught Mr & Mrs Grimble's kid, Royston filming me with his phone from his parents' bedroom. I had been enjoying my day off, sunning myself out the back, when I sat up to see this little Royston perv hanging out the bedroom window like a dog in heat. 'Are you enjoying yourself there?' I shouted. Royston didn't flinch and continued pointing his phone at me. 'I'm recording the birds,' Royston replied; his thick local accent was barely decipherable. 'I bet you are,' I replied sarcastically. Royston continued, 'I like to see birds in their natural habitat.' 'Oh, is that right?' I replied. 'Yeah, I have a massive erection,' said Royston, licking his lips and smiling like the little creep he is. 'I could have you done for harassment. Did you just tell me you have a massive erection?' I asked. Royston pocketed his phone and said, 'No, a massive collection. You need to get some cotton buds and clean your ears.' He closed the bedroom window and then had the cheek to close the blinds as if I had been bothering him. The little shit! He wouldn't have done it if Stu was there. I won't be long reporting him to Mr and Mrs Grimble.

Stuart (Sunday, June 14th)

I could have sworn I saw Peggy (from the apt upstairs) in a wheelchair this morning. I was on Summerville Road walking back from the shops when a head of bright red hair caught my eye on the opposite side of the road. She had been sitting outside Flava Coffee and appeared to be reading a book. I couldn't take my eyes off her, nor the wheelchair she was sitting in for that matter. As I passed by, I attempted to get her attention by looking directly at her. It worked... well, kind of. She looked up from her book, caught my eye and in a sense of panic lifted the book to cover her face. I didn't take my eyes off her the entire time. As I continued to stare, bemused at the appearance of this wheelchair, she retained her defensive posture. She did, however, peek out from behind the book to see if I was still looking. I raised my hand to wave, but Peggy didn't budge. I wonder if she's up to something or if she legitimately needs the wheelchair? Very strange indeed.

Suzanne (Sunday, June 14th)

Dear Diary,

Mum frustrates me at times! She has no patience when it comes to pricing stuff from different stores and trying to find the best value for money. Instead, she'll just agree to any price that is quoted to her, almost like that price is specifically tailored to her budget and her needs. Today was a prime example of this as she ended up spending an absolute fortune on paint. After spending almost two hours arguing with Mum about a specific shade of orange (she kept claiming that it was red) I had to call over a member of staff to take her off my hands. At this stage, my head was pounding so I told Mum I was going to sit in the car for a bit.

Almost an hour later, I woke up in the passenger seat to the sound of the young staff member loading tin after tin of paint into the boot of Mum's car. Mum said, 'I got a great deal, 5 gallons of red paint (it was orange) for 315 euro.' I told Mum she was crazy for paying so much.

Mum replied, 'The young man gave me a 10% discount. He said I'd pass as a student.'

Stuart (Monday, June 15th)

Fuck me, today was hot! Stupidly, I took the bus to work as I woke late. The bus was vile. There were people pressed against each other like sardines. There was a stench of man-sweat that would knock out an army, and as for the air con... I think the convicts from the movie 'Con Air' would be more fitting, given the heads on some of the passengers.

I can happily say I'm back on good terms with Maggie. Well, so I hope. I sent her a message after lunch;

2:13 pm - "Who'd win in a fight – Phillip Schofield or Michael Barrymore?"

It took her a bit, but Maggie replied with that expressionless face emoji:

4:55 pm - : | '

It's definitely a start!

Tonight, I had sex with a pregnant woman (Sue, that is) for the first time in my life. It didn't feel any different than normal. I guess she isn't showing much around the waistline just yet. I did, however, take it handily. I don't want to put a dent in the baby's head.

Suzanne (Monday, June 15th)

Dear Diary,

My poor Snuggleflakes can't walk because of all the weight she is carrying. I watched as my poor baby attempted to get up from her usual spot on the rug to go and get some milk. She made it to the edge of the rug and collapsed in a ball of fur. I felt terrible. The sooner she pops the better. I think her meowing has morphed into moaning as that's what I come home to every day, 'meeeoooaaaaan.'

Stu is in the bathroom taking his usual post-sex bathroom break. I'm not sure how I feel about having sex while pregnant. It's weird! I could tell Stu was being gentle as he's normally like a Duracell Bunny that's been let loose. During sex, Stu kept asking me if I was OK. I assured him I was fine, but he couldn't relax.

Stuart (Tuesday, June 16th)

I got a bit of a spook when I turned around and saw Peggy (from Apt no.6) in the shop today. She didn't have a wheelchair, but she was on crutches. 'I didn't know you worked in a record store,' she proclaimed. She looked superb in blue dungarees and a white t-shirt, with her long, red hair falling down over her chest. 'Yes, unfortunately. We get all sorts in here',' I replied. She smiled as if she fell into that category somehow. I asked Peggy what happened to her leg. 'It's a long story, don't worry about me,' replied Peggy, as she stood transfixed on the David Bowie hanging on the wall. Before I could dig a little deeper, Peggy swerved the conversation. '*Crooked Rain* or *Wowee Zowee*?' asked Peggy. She was asking what the better album by the band Pavement was. I told her it was a great question and explained that If she was new to Pavement, I'd go with *Crooked Rain* and if she had some of their other stuff, I'd go with *Wowee Zowee*. Peggy laughed and replied, 'I think I'll take both.' I took the CDs as she hobbled toward the counter. I was trying to keep my eyes off the slit in her dress as it was showing more leg than it probably should. I couldn't stop myself from passing her a compliment. 'You look fresh,' I said. I didn't mean it to come out like that. Peggy laughed and said, 'Fresh, nice! Is that what the cool kids say?' After a bit of flirty banter, she was on her way. I was none the wiser about her crutches, the wheelchair and her 'long story'.

Sue and I heard a hell of a racket just now. It sounded like two cats scrapping the shit out of each other. When I went out front to see what all the commotion was about, I found Sue's cat with its head stuck in the gate. That poor cat looks like someone stuck a bicycle pump up its arse and pumped it up like a tire. God help us when those kittens arrive! It'll be like a zoo here.

Suzanne (Tuesday, June 16th)

Dear Diary,

Mum has painted her bedroom black, white and orange (even though she thinks the orange is red). The walls are orange, the boards are white, and the floor and the curtains are black. Mr Rocket didn't seem too impressed when he returned from his golfing, 'Jesus, Helen, it looks like a whore house. What's with all the lights?' Mum barked back, 'Excuse me! I put a lot of time and effort into this. Anyway, how do you know what a whore house looks like?' Mr Rocket tutted and made his way downstairs. 'Honestly, sometimes I think I'm talking to the wall,' Mum confessed. In fairness to Mr Rocket, he was kind of right. Considering the decor of Mum's house, this room stands out like a sore thumb. I think Mum has been watching too many of these house shows during the afternoon.

My poor Snuggleflakes got her head stuck in the gate tonight. Stu suggested washing-up liquid to massage her head so that it might slide out easier. With nothing to lose, Stu held Mrs Snuggles by her wide arse, wiggling her from left to right with much effort. It took some time, but he finally got her out. Unfortunately for Stu, Mrs Snuggles let out an almighty fart in his face. Diary, you should have seen him.

Stuart (Wednesday, June 17th)

Patryk passed by the shop with a bunch of his no-good mates earlier. He wasted no time in giving me the finger as his mates laughed on. I was going to return the favour, but it probably wouldn't be good for business.

I had some quality time to myself tonight; including sitting on the couch in absolute silence for about two hours. It was great and long overdue. When I had enough of that, I decided to watch a bit of TV as I hadn't done so in ages. Gordon Ramsay was on with one of his cooking shows. He was chewing the head of some poor soul who was laughing his ass off about a typo on some ingredients. The poor fella was holding a bag of fish sauce that read "Creamy White Finishing Sauce" as opposed to "Creamy White Fish Sauce". Ramsey didn't look too impressed. All that meat chopping made me think of Maggie and where she's at. I remembered the emotionless emoji she replied with, so I texted her again.

The text read:

10:10 pm - "Who'd win in a fight... Prince Charles or Mr Bean?"

Maggie replied straight away;

10:10 pm - "Bean :)"

I might try popping into the butchers before 1 pm tomorrow. Maybe I can coax Maggie out for some lunch.

Suzanne (Wednesday, June 17th)

Dear Diary,

I caught Royston Grimble perving once again. I was on my way home from work when I spotted a young lad filming some poor girl's backside as she walked in front of him. When I crossed the road, I realised it was Royston. I marched right up behind him and grabbed the arm he was using to record. 'Hey, you can't be doing that,' I said angrily. He was wearing a grin that only a mother (poor Mrs Grimble, of course) could love. 'Get away from me. That's assault,' replied Royston, as he struggled to get out of the tight grip I had on his arm. I was furious! 'Do you want me to speak to your mother about this? Or how about your little *nature study* from the bedroom window last weekend? Would Mrs Grimble be happy to hear that her son was filming his neighbour sunbathing in a bikini?' I asked. Royston looked stumped. 'Well? Would she?' I persisted. Royston freed his arm and began running up Denmore Avenue back to his house. He's such a little shit!

Stuart (Thursday, June 18th)

There is peace in the valley of Rockwood today. Maggie and I are back on good terms.

We met up over lunch and apologised to each other for our over-the-top behaviour. Maggie admitted she was too involved and too pushy when attempting to get me to Poland for the maternity test. She felt she had to take the role of her mother, who had passed a couple of years ago. I accepted her apology wholeheartedly. I, in turn, offered my apologies for being a dick. I told Maggie that buying the tickets to Poland was very thoughtful of her and I understood her reasoning; because she cared for myself, Zofia and what we had created. Maggie assured me, 'It's OK.' I was relieved that she didn't give me a, 'What now?' question. Instead, she asked me what I had been listening to in the shop this week. To say I was surprised would be an understatement.

From there the conversation moved to Patryk. I asked Maggie what he had been up to and if he had any plans for the summer. Really, I was looking to see if he had ratted me out about losing his money. I'm not in his good books and I need him to be. Maggie said Patryk had asked her for some money to do a horticulture class in July. Maggie said that Patryk has become obsessed with harvesting and cultivating and has even purchased a few plants of his own.

I was over in Sue's mam's place for dinner this evening. Boy does she do a good homemade lasagne. Sue's mam is hilarious. She was well on it after her 2nd glass of wine and was in absolute hysterics at her partner, Mr Rocket's radio show that had been playing at a rather loud volume in the background. I got a piece of garlic bread stuck in my throat when Mr Rocket started advocating, 'strap on toys' for 'mummy and daddy time.' How this lad got on the radio is anyone's guess!

Suzanne (Thursday, June 18th)

Dear Diary,

Siobhan might be the youngest girl at work, but today she assured me that she'll always be there if I need pregnancy advice. I guess she is more than qualified after just giving birth to Arianna, her 6th child.

I'm not sure how I feel about attending the Hairs to You award show next month. While I'm thrilled that we're nominated for an award, the thoughts of parading about the place with a massive bump riddle me with anxiety. That said, I did find something that might work. It's a black slip dress that has a slight fold on the right waistline. It's a little loose around the waistline right now, but by the time the award ceremony rolls around, the sales assistant assured me it should fit just fine. I look pretty hot in it... even if I do say so myself.

Stu and I had dinner over in Mum's place tonight. Mum gave Stu a good grilling about how we should raise our child. I was doing my best not to laugh at Stu's face. Mum was straight up, 'That child needs sport, not music. Whatever came of those weirdos who listened to Marc Bolan or that Iggy Stardust fella? *There* was a lad that could have done with a plate of my lasagne and a good kick around with a ball.' I guess Mum was referring to either David Bowie or Iggy Pop. Either way, she wasn't holding back.

During dinner, we listened in to Mr Rocket's radio show. Mr Rocket paid tribute to, 'the love of his life,' by playing 'Straight down the middle' by Bing Crosby. Mum was ecstatic until she heard the lyrics and realised it was a song about golfing. When the song finished, Mr Rocket segued to a commercial by saying, 'You can't win em all.'

Stuart (Friday, June 19th)

I bumped into Effie, again! I was in the charity shop having a browse through the 2nd hand records when I saw her parading through the aisle modelling a fur coat. She was with another Asian girl who was in hysterics laughing at Effie's modelling poses. When Effie spotted me, she shouted my name and ran over to give me a hug. Effie asked what I thought of the fur coat. Of course, I agreed that it looked fantastic on her (and it did). I told her the coat didn't make her, but she made the coat. She seemed confused and reassured me that she didn't make the coat, she just picked it up in the shop. I wasn't arsed about trying to explain what I meant.

Tonight, Sue and I ended up going to the cinema to see this new rom-com, *Mothers, Daughters, Wives and Friends* that she's been harping on about. I fell asleep about 20 mins in as I had a skinful of pints with Charlie beforehand. Sue seemed to enjoy it and, from what I gather, was so engrossed that she didn't even realise I was asleep... thankfully!

When we got home, we found Sue's cat stuck between two of the balusters on Sue's staircase. It took about 20 mins and a lot of screeching and meowing to get it out. Sue spent the entire time crying and kept telling me to, 'watch the babies.' Once free, the cat hobbled down the stairs, collapsed in a heap and let out one of the loudest farts I've ever heard. Sue and I couldn't help but burst into hysterics, we had thought the cat had gone into epileptic shock as it hadn't moved for a bit.

Suzanne (Friday, June 19th)

Dear Diary,

The sooner my poor Snuggleflakes gives birth to those damn kittens the better. As much as I love her, she has become a real inconvenience over the past few weeks. Tonight, Stu and I arrived home to find her stuck between two of the poles in the staircase. The poor thing was traumatised and crying for her life. After some careful prodding, Stu managed to free her. I think I was crying more than the cat throughout the ordeal.

I finally got to check out, *Mothers, Daughters, Wives and Friends* at the cinema. It was hilarious! I don't know what I'd do if Mum and I got pregnant at the same time. As funny as it would be (and if the movie was anything to go by, very, very funny) I'd be mortified. Stu was out for the count for the duration of the movie. It's just as well as I wasn't looking forward to his usual barrage of actor-related enquiries, most of which are, 'What's her name?'

Stuart (Saturday, June 20th)

I just remembered something I spotted this morning; a female doctor (definitely a junior/trainee doctor) got on the bus wearing her doctor jacket and a stethoscope around her neck. Is it just me or is that a bit, 'hey everybody! Just in case you were wondering what I do for a living, here's a subtle hint?'

Work was bonkers and to make matters worse, Trish was in a foul mood all day. She didn't open her mouth to anyone. Not me, not the customers, not even Nick Cave Guy (or so we call him) who drives about 80 miles to our store every Saturday morning to (a) pick up his orders and (b) talk to Trish about goth bands from the 80s. Today, Trish's ritualistic Saturday morning flirting session (playing with her pigtails and batting her eyelids) was replaced by a sombre face too focused on the de-tagging of stock to reply. Nick Cave Guy looked sadder than usual.

I ended up enduring 30 minutes of non-stop crying from a baby on the bus home. Its mother was pretty useless and didn't do much to console it. I'm still not sure if I'm cut out for parenthood.

I ended up flying solo (Sue was too tired) to check out The Glitch Girls (post-punk band from Leeds) at The Plex. They were pretty enjoyable, if not a tad smug. One of their songs involved their lead singer smashing a gas heater (that had a mic placed in front of it and was fed through a fuzz pedal, no doubt) with a baseball bat and screaming something about pay rights, or it could have been playwrights; it was tough to tell with all the feedback. Thankfully, I had a nice (and peaceful) curry chip on the way home.

Suzanne (Saturday, June 20th)

Dear Diary,

It was great catching up with Zia today. She arrived over for lunch armed with a ton of baby-related gifts. We had to do three runs to the car to get it all in, including a bunch of clothes, a mini-stroller and some toys. Zia kept apologising about the stuff being 2nd hand (everything had been handed down from Zia's brother and his wife), which, of course, is fine. I thanked Zia for everything and told her the gesture meant a lot. I also promised to buy her brother and his wife a thank-you gift to show my appreciation.

10:45 pm

Diary, I'm feeling a little overwhelmed and Stu isn't here to console me. As I sit here looking around the living room, the realisation that I'm going to be a mother has just sunk in. Everything has happened so fast! I never envisioned us being at this stage so soon into our relationship. Weirdly, Stu is handling all of this pretty well, when I assumed it would be the other way around. Diary, I'm an emotional wreck. I think I need to talk to someone and fast. I can't go to Mum as she'll tell me everything is wonderful, the girls at work are too caught up in the latest series of *Love Island* and Zia, she's too independent to even begin to understand.

Stuart (Sunday, June 21st)

I'm always amazed to wake up and see a full diary entry that I have no recollection of writing (ala last night). And funnily enough, it's normally the next day that I either (a) make a short entry or (b) at times, write nothing at all. However, as I'm on death's door, having drunk enough Tequila to power Mexico's national grid, I have opted to create a to-do list. An important to-do list at that. I feel like this is a productive exercise given my current state.

To do…

1 - Tell Sue that I'm also having a child with Zofia.

2 - Tell Zofia that I'm also having a child with Sue.

3 - Tell Mam and Dad that I'm going to be a father to two children from two different mothers, from two different countries.

4 - Ask Peggy (from the flat upstairs) if she's willing to part ways with her copy of the Cocteau Twins - *Four Calendar Cafe* - LP I spotted on her floor.

Suzanne (Sunday, June 21st)

Dear Diary,

Royston Grimble has been arrested!

I was out in the back garden, sweating out that half bottle of gin from last night when suddenly I heard a clutter of commotion coming from the Grimble household. Over the back wall, I could see about 10 police officers closing in on Royston, who up until now had been painting the Grimbles' shed with his headphones on. I heard one of the officers ask, 'Royston Grimble?' Royston replied nervously, 'Yeah, why?' 'You're under arrest,' said the officer before elaborating on something to do with coordinating harm. As the officers swooped in on Royston, Mrs Grimble, dressed in her purple dressing gown, began roaring from her bedroom window, 'Hey, leave my son alone. He would never harm a soul.' Countless heads began popping over the adjacent yard fences. Royston, the weasel, put up a good struggle but was outdone by two burly officers who soon had him lying face down on the grass with their knees on his back. After a good ten minutes of wriggling and expletives, Royston settled down. With his hands cuffed behind his back, he was escorted to the front of the house by the officers on hand. Mrs Grimble, who was now in the back garden, walked with them, slapping the shit out of Royston's head with a cooking mitten along the way. Of course, I had to follow the action, so I made my way to the front of the house.

Between nosey neighbours and stopped traffic, the street was full. Most all were waiting for some insight as to what had happened. As Royston was being escorted into the back of the police van, he tilted his head back and roared, 'Do you think you can accuse me of this? It's not fair!! I'm going to do everything I can to put you all down! I did not abuse the internet... THE INTERNET ABUSED ME!'

God only knows what he's been up to.

Stuart (Monday, June 22nd)

I arrived at work to find Trish and two of her smarmy, games-night friends cackling like witches at the counter. Yup, she's still playing Gloom Heaven (right at home) or Gloomhaven, or whatever the fuck it's called. Trish said something like, 'Kettle lughormoHlu.' I replied, 'Who?' and when Trish repeated herself, I said, 'Never heard of em.' 'She's talking in Klingon,' said one of the gloom brigades. 'Klingon? I'm just about clinging on,' I replied, before excusing myself to the canteen for an extra hour's kip. As hard as I tried, I couldn't fall asleep on the canteen table as is normally the case. My mind was racing with worry. I haven't felt that anxious since PJ Harvey told me to, 'fuck off' after asking her for an autograph outside the Music of the Millennium Awards in '99. The hangover didn't help either!

I spoke to Sue just now, she said her neighbour's kid (name escapes me) got done for sharing dodgy videos on the dark web. Sounds gnarly!

Suzanne (Monday, June 22nd)

Dear Diary,

Apparently, Royston Grimble was arrested for sharing videos of children. What a disgusting little creep!! Word on the street is that Mr and Mrs Grimble are in a terrible way since finding out the reason for his arrest. In an attempt to take Mr and Mrs Grimble's mind off this horrible situation, I baked some scones and dropped them over to their house earlier. Mrs Grimble's sister answered the door and thanked me for the kind gesture. I didn't push for any updates, but I did tell Mrs Grimble's sister that I am here if they need me.

I picked up copies of *So... you're going to be a Mom* Volumes 1 and 2 during lunch. Why they didn't just condense it all into one book is anyone's guess. Here's the opening line of Vol 1:

"Babies are a lot like men, you're damned if you do and you're damned if you don't."

Stuart (Tuesday, June 23rd)

I helped Peggy carry some groceries up to her apartment. I could see she had purchased a chunk of records from Amazon as there were sliced boxes all over her kitchen table. Among the records was a copy of Shuggie Otis' - *Freedom Flight* - LP, which gave me a bit of a hard-on for Peggy.

Sue arrived over for dinner this evening. I prepared vegetable fajitas and mint mojitos, but Sue said she couldn't drink alcohol because of the pregnancy and, more importantly, the baby scan. She seems super-excited about planning. I tried my best to sound more excited than I was.

Maggie texted asking if I would meet her for lunch tomorrow. She sounded concerned.

12:22 am

Let it be said, for a pregnant lady, Sue put in a great effort in the bedroom just now. And while I'm fit for bed, I'd say she'd be up for a couple more rounds. Maybe those rumours about pregnant women and their hormones are true after all.

Suzanne (Tuesday, June 23rd)

Dear Diary,

I had an enjoyable evening dining over at Stu's, although his music taste is questionable.

I'll be arranging my first scan tomorrow, how exciting! Actually, it's very exciting!!! I hope Stu doesn't freak out if the scan shows twins. While I'm sure I'd be fine with it, I don't think Stu could hack two babies.

Stuart (Wednesday, June 24th)

Christ! I nearly dropped dead of a heart attack today. Maggie has cut her hair in the same style as Zofia. I was standing behind the counter repricing some stock when I turned around and spotted who I believed to be Zofia standing there staring at me. I was speechless at first, but quickly realised it was Maggie brandishing her new haircut. 'You look like you've seen a ghost,' said Maggie. I told her she was after scaring the shit out of me as I had assumed she was Zofia. We both started laughing. I think it was a mutual realisation of just how fucked I am right now.

During lunch, Maggie advised me to call Zofia. According to Maggie, Zofia has some mental health issues and could potentially do something stupid if nobody gives a shit about her.

Sue got the green light for our baby scan. It's very real now!

Suzanne (Wednesday, June 24th)

Dear Diary,

Our baby scan is booked for July 9th. The lady that booked the appointment was an absolute dote and was more than happy to answer any and all questions I had about the procedure. It all sounds pretty straightforward in fairness;

(1) Arrive with a full bladder.

(2) Don't be nervous.

(3) Try not to punch the assistant if the scan shows more than one child.

Stu didn't laugh at the third instruction. He can be very dry sometimes.

Stuart (Thursday, June 25th)

I called Zofia via video Skype. She still looks super-hot, but to say our conversation was awkward would be a serious understatement. Factor in Zofia's poor English skills and my attempt at asking some detailed questions about her wellbeing and you've got a recipe for disaster. Pretty much everything went over her head. I did, however, get clarification on the following;

(Me) 'Do you want to keep the baby?'

(Zofia) 'I want baby, not your baby.'

(Me) 'Have you seen a doctor?'

(Zofia) 'I wait for stupid Irish man.'

(Me) 'How do you feel about the names Donovan (boy) or Bjork (girl)?'

(Zofia) …………

(Me) 'What is the likelihood of booking a test to ensure I am the biological father?'

(Zofia) …………

Unfortunately, Zofia hung up at this point.

Suzanne (Thursday, June 25th)

Dear Diary,

Eating whatever I want, when I want, is the best part about being pregnant. No more calorie counting and no more 6 am planks (for now at least). Mum and I were invited to the official launch of Mr Rocket's radio show over in the studio. I wasn't sure what to expect, but the studio is actually a portacabin behind St Augustine's Church and is powered by a generator. The launch was attended by a scattering of people, including Fr Hartigan, a reporter from the local paper (who kept putting me in every photo), a stoner kid who apparently reads the news for the station, the station manager (a Scottish transsexual in her 50s) and some of the regular presenters. Mr Rocket was in his element as his show would be the first to be aired on their recently granted FM license. Mr Rocket even bought a new suit for the occasion and seemed to be in his element blasting out some dodgy dad rock; all the while delivering his ever-so-cheesy song introductions. I wanted Stu to come with me tonight, but he said he was too knackered after work. I think Stu would have enjoyed it.

Stuart (Friday, June 26th)

Trish seemed to be in great form at work. I'm guessing tomorrow's 'Dettol Black' in-store has a lot to do with it as Trish has played his album to death over the past few months. I quite like that, "pricks to the left of me, cunts to the right, here I am stuck in a riddle with you," song though.

Maggie called in just before 1 pm and offered to take me out for lunch. I told her about my short call to Zofia and the questions I had put forward. Much like her sister, Maggie didn't take to either Bjork or Donovan as suggested baby names. I was going to suggest calling my soon-to-be children, Mel and Kim (after the 80s pop-duo) but I guess they'd have to be twins or biological sisters at the very least. I kept my mouth shut. Maggie said that a guy asked her for her number in work. She claims he's part of a biker gang, or as she put it, 'The soft cuddly gang.' I'm intrigued!

Rodge and Tony's band, Satan's Arse have been asked to open for Slayer at the Culture & Arts Fest this weekend. Tony texted to say, "We're opening for Slayer on Sunday! WTF!! I'll put you down as road crew, we have 10 crew passes to use up \m/" I might take him up on that.

I met Sue and her Mother for a drink after work. Sue, again, wasn't drinking, but her Mam and I more than made up for her. Sue's mam reckons Ken would be a great name for a boy (she's obsessed with Ken Barlow from *Coronation St*) and is adamant Pauline would be a great name for a girl (a tribute to Sue's late grandmother). I nodded, smiled and didn't offer any comment on her suggestions.

At around 10 pm, I spotted Peggy from the apartment upstairs. She had come stumbling into the bar, laughing hysterically with an older gentleman. They were both tanked and when they got to the counter, spent a considerable amount of time deciding what to order. Peggy was very touchy-feely with this older gentleman as he stood scanning the top shelf and wobbling about trying to find his wallet. Fortunately, Peggy didn't see me, but I will admit, it was tough to take my eyes off her carry on. She's an intriguing girl.

By early morning, I could tell Sue had enough of her mam's drunken warbling and wanted to go home. On top of that, I'm almost sure Sue knew my focus was anywhere but the conversation at our table as I was trying to see what Peggy and this older gentleman were up to. After some gentle coaxing, Sue's mam and I reluctantly agreed to go home with Sue. All three of us sat in silence in the taxi home.

As I write, Sue is asleep upstairs and I'm down here in the kitchen making toasted sandwiches and listening to The Ruts (at a reasonable volume).

Suzanne (Friday, June 26th)

Diary,

I don't think I've ever felt as tired. And I'm sober!

Mum asked if Stu and I would like to go for a few drinks after work. Mum said she was, 'off the hook,' as Mr Rocket is away on one of his golfing trips.

Being sober and drinking with the closest people to you is frustrating; especially when they're playing, 'fuck, marry, kill' and downing tequila. I'm surprised at Mum and Stu – neither of them got sick; although, Mum's blatant disregard of the rules and willingness to shun both George Clooney and Pierce Brosnan for a 'fuck, marry and fuck him until he's dead' with Ken Barlow almost had me reaching for a paper bag. Fortunately, we're home now.

I tried to pick Mrs Snuggles up to cuddle on the bed, but between my pregnancy and the weight of my poor Snuggleflakes, I couldn't do it. I'm trying to stay awake to give Stu a kiss goodnight, but by the sound of the fury he is unleashing in the toilet bowl, I could be waiting.

Stuart (Saturday, June 27th)

I got a call from the landlord at 7:15 am saying the smoke alarm in my apartment was going off. I was fuming as I was still in Sue's and wanted to start our weekend off together in a relaxing manner. Reluctantly, I got out of Sue's bed and made my way home.

When I got to the apartment, the smoke alarm was making an awful racket, yet there was no smoke to be seen. I realised the battery must have been on its last legs, so I replaced it with a fresh one and it seemed to do the trick. With the crisis averted, I opted to get a taxi back to Sue's. On my way out of the apartment, I bumped into Peggy. It looked like she was just getting home after last night as she was still wearing the same clothes and looked a little worse for wear. Strangely, she was back on the crutches, even though I didn't see them last night. I attempted a stop n' chat but Peggy made a beeline for the elevator. 'Good morning,' I said sprightly, as I held the door and did my best not to be distracted by her low-cut top. Peggy responded, 'Heya,' kept her head down and hobbled straight to the elevator door. I was going to ask if she might be heading to the Slayer gig on Sunday but decided to let her go. As I walked out the front door, I wished Peggy a good day. I didn't hear any reply, but I could see Peggy stepping into the elevator and giving me a half-arsed wave through the glass.

Sue called over to mine for food and drink (well, a bottle of wine for me) this evening. Even though I was pretty buckled, I still managed to get it up for a good session on Sue's couch. I'll tell you what, Sue has got a hell of a lot of energy for a pregnant woman!! That said, I tried to take it handy enough as I don't want to damage our baby. God knows my old man probably wasn't as cautious back in the day.

The Slayer & Satan's Arse gig is tomorrow. I'm not so sure my body is ready.

Suzanne (Saturday, June 27th)

Dear Diary,

I'm exhausted! I woke up at 7:30 am. A call from Stu's landlord forced Stu out of bed to check the ringing smoke alarm at his apartment.

When I went to wake Mum, I found her passed out in the spare bedroom, still draped in last night's clothes. There was orange makeup all over the good bed sheets and from what I could gauge, the only thing she managed to remove was her bra (dangling from the Velux window) and her shoes (which were fired across the room as the heel of one had wedged itself in the chalkboard wall by the en suite. In her state, Mum ended up missing breakfast, lunch and dinner and had to be carried to Mr Rocket's car shortly before I left for Stu's.

The evening was very relaxed. Stu and I ordered some Chinese food from The Lucky Dragon and were more than content lying about in our own filth, watching the worst movie known to man (Transformers 2) and hammering back wine. Well... Stu was more content in that department. I had to settle for unfiltered tap water with ice. Oh, pregnancy...

Stuart (Sunday, June 28th)

I think I might have tinnitus after standing stage side for Satan's Arse support slot with Slayer. My roadie job for the evening included walking on stage and swapping over Rodge's guitars depending on the tuning of the song. Another friend of Tony and Rodge, Harry did the honours for Tony's bass guitars.

My God was it loud up there. The lads' drummer, Paul Whitehall is an absolute beast and hits harder than any other drummer I've seen (including Billy Cunt from The Pogo Stix). The 5,000 or so in attendance gave Satan's Arse a rapturous ovation and even broke into a crescendo of, 'One more tune! One more tune!' when the lads had finished their set and made their way backstage.

As Satan's Arse high fived each other and hugged their respective families and girlfriends after a killer show, Slayer's Kerry King popped over to say he enjoyed the set. The lads in Satan's Arse posed for a few pics with Kerry before they were interrupted by one of Slayer's crew members. The mood in our camp was ecstatic as playing with Slayer was like a dream come true for all of us. We had grown up on this shit, and Slayer, love 'em or hate 'em was the soundtrack to our youth. You only had to look at our crew during the Slayer set. From the set opener, 'Angel of Death', to set-closer, 'War Ensemble', our variety of heads – brandishing everything from arse-length hair to receding, almost monk-like locks – jolted back and forth like we were 13 again. Despite potential tinnitus and a neck stiffer than an 80 quid bottle of scotch, it was still worth it.

Once Slayer had wrapped up, we made our way to the backstage area to make the most of the free booze on offer. We were no sooner seated when Slayer's Tom Araya and Paul Bostaph came over to our table brandishing a bottle of Jameson Whiskey. Alright!' said Tom Araya, before handing Rodge the bottle. 'You guys were fucking vicious. Heavy as fuck!' elaborated Tom; referencing the ear fucking onslaught unleashed by Satan's Arse earlier in the evening. 'Nice one!' said Tony, as Tom accepted Tony's offer of a handshake.

The banter continued for a good thirty minutes before Slayer's crew put out a call that they would be leaving for the hotel soon. Before everyone departed, members of Slayer and Satan's Arse posed for pics together. A very drunk Rodge, removed the rosary beads his grandmother had given him and placed them over Kerry King's bald head. Rodge was teary-eyed as he kissed Kerry on the top of his head and proclaimed, 'Yer a fucking hero, man! Really! I mean it. You're a fucking legend!' Kerry looked a bit perplexed but was kind enough to show his gratitude by dipping the rosary beads into a beer glass, kissing and blessing them with his hands, and placing them back over Rodge's head. 'Now, from one legend to another, and blessed by Slayer. These beads are more valuable to you than they'll ever be to me,' said Kerry, as everyone looked on in awe. With Slayer long gone, and a handful of security guards kicking out the remaining VIP-area stragglers, we ordered three cabs and went back to a house party in Tony's place. I'm here now in Tony's garden, smoking the arse end of a joint and recording this entry with the voice recorder. I think tonight will go down in one of the many Rockwood, 'D'ya remember the night...' stories.

Suzanne (Sunday, June 28th)

Dear Diary,

It was nice to have some 'me time' today. God knows it's been a while.

Mum was up early as she was picking up Mr Rocket from the airport. She was praying that he had bought her some expensive jewelry; unlike the mantlepiece miniature golf bag, he got her last time 'round (no pun intended).

Stu was off gallivanting with his friends at a metal concert for the day. For the life of me, I can't remember the name of the band.

All of this left me with plenty of time to put my feet up and read a book, until the itch to do some baking got the better of me. Come lunchtime, I had two apple tarts and a tray of scones good to go. In an effort of goodwill, I popped 'round to Mrs Grimble and gave her and Mr Grimble one of the apple tarts. She was delighted, as was Mr Grimble, who fawned over the fresh smell of pastry and hot apple. They're both good people suffering family upheaval, so I asked if they were OK. Mrs Grimble replied, 'We are distraught, my dear. Our whole world has been turned upside down.' Mr Grimble chirped in, 'I blame these movies, a bunch of maniacs the whole lot of em. Whatever happened *The Quiet Man* eh? Tis far from fucking quiet we have now.' The veins on Mr Grimble's neck were throbbing as he spoke. Mrs Grimble advised him to sit down, 'Conny, you're going to give yourself a heart attack. Have a slice of apple tart and take a seat.' Mrs Grimble wasn't wrong. With his hand slightly below his left breast as if he was preventing some form of heart spasm, Mr Grimble pulled over his footstool, slipped in between the coffee table and his armchair and dumped himself into the seat like a bag of bricks. The armchair springs, no doubt on their last legs, cranked as he did so. I made sure the Grimbles were OK and said my goodbyes, telling them not to think twice about popping into me if they needed anything. I could tell they were grateful.

Back over in my house, it was just Mrs Snuggles and me for the remainder of the evening. We watched several episodes of *Your House, Your Home* and a rerun of *The Lion King* (poor Snuggleflakes was glued) before I passed out. I'm still half asleep!

I only received one text from Stu;

"Satan's Arse ripped Rockwood a new one \m/"

I have no idea what he's on about??

Stuart (Monday, June 29th)

Before opening the store, I smoked half a joint with my morning coffee. It's nothing something I'd normally do, but I had run out of smokes and the shops had yet to open. Unfortunately, the weed knocked me for six and I ended up falling asleep on the canteen table, thus missing our usual 9 am opening. Fortunately, Trish was on today and woke me shortly after she arrived at 10 am. 'Phone call for ya,' she said as she handed me the wireless phone from the office. I was still half asleep and pretty pissed off that someone had interrupted my dream (dancing with the chick from The Bangles in the local indie club). I gave a half-arsed, hello, only to be greeted with, 'It's Maggie's sister, Zofia'. I wasn't long waking up! 'I come to you for test on Monday. I arrive at weekend and will stay with my sister,' said Zofia bluntly. Zofia hung up the phone before I had a chance to reply.

Suzanne (Monday, June 29th)

Dear Diary,

Only eleven days to go until the baby scan. I don't think I can contain my excitement! Imagine, Stu and I are sitting there, and the screen displays octuplets. Hahaha! I think Stu would have a heart attack there and then. My God, the thought of it! It's funny, we've been gifted so many baby clothes at this stage we could comfortably dress 8 kids every day of the week and still have spares.

I have it on good authority that Royston Grimble was arrested for distributing crude images of children. Poor Mr and Mrs Grimble – they don't deserve that level of hardship. No parent does.

Not surprisingly, Mum was also alert to this information about Royston Grimble. She called over after work and couldn't wait to get the gossip off her chest. 'That dirty little ferret. Pulling his little willy and drooling all over the place,' said Mum. She was referring to Royston Grimble of course. 'He'll get what he deserves inside that prison – two black fellas with big Willys. They'll be sword fighting over the fresh meat,' Mum elaborated. She was never one for holding back her thoughts.

Stuart (Tuesday, June 30th)

I had a mini panic attack at work and asked Trish if she would mind covering me for the afternoon. Trish was lost in a haze of Tangerine Dream, pumping through the stores' speakers at the time and gave a half-nod as if to say, 'go ahead.' That I did.

On the way home I texted sue to cancel our cinema plans. Sue was delighted as she was knackered.

I have packed a gym bag full of clothes, to jump on a ferry and do a runner first thing in the morning. I can't do this! Again, how can I tell Sue about the baby with Zofia? How can I tell Zofia about the baby with Sue? Or more importantly, how the fuck can I explain all of this shit to my parents? They're going to think I'm some sort of pornstar wannabe. I hope everyone can forgive me, including poor Trish, whom I'm sure will do a great job of managing the store until I figure out what the hell I'm doing with my life.

11 pm

I ended up making a call to Patryk to (a) apologise for messing up his money and (b) score some more weed to calm my nerves. Patryk, unsurprisingly, was cool about it. He admitted his most recent behaviour was just him busting my balls for being a prick to Zofia. He was fully aware that I got her knocked up, but as I was now, 'part of the family' he wanted to make peace. In doing so, Patryk offered me two bags of weed for the price of one. Of course, I took him up on the offer. Patryk arranged for some young fella to drop over the gear, which saved me a shit ton of hassle.

1:10 am

I have no food in the apartment, so I ended up mucking into Sue's beloved Special K cereal. She keeps a box here for any time she stays over, After I devoured five bowls of this stuff, I now understand why it's the best-selling cereal on the market.

Suzanne (Tuesday, June 30th)

Dear Diary,

Work was horrible today. I had a few odd customers in the morning, but nothing came close to the absolute wagon we had to deal with this afternoon. The client had been treated by Siobhan, who confirmed the requested shade of blonde with the client several times before starting the process. Unfortunately, the client wasn't too happy with the result and said, 'I look like a bloody stripper!' She also called Siobhan, 'utterly useless,' and referred to her appointment as, '150 notes down the drain... LITERALLY!!' The client was so ignorant that I felt like saying it was her fault for signing off on the colour and not doing her research; particularly on the samples and how they can, at times, appear brighter or sometimes darker, depending. Instead, I offered to fix the colour free of charge and asked the client if she would like a coffee while she was waiting. The client stood up and said, 'Do you think I'm going to let you two bozos sabotage my hair a 2nd time? You must be joking.' She grabbed her bag and walked straight out the door, slamming it hard as she went. Nobody said a word. As silence filled the air, a client who was waiting to be seen to, gave her two cents, 'She looked like a stripper before she came in.'

Stuart (Wednesday, July 1st)

No entry

Suzanne (Wednesday, July 1st)

Diary,

I can't stop crying! My whole world has been turned upside down by a man I thought I could trust. A man that was always honest, a man who I opened up to on so many levels, a man I trusted to be part of my life, my home, my family, a man who I could see myself spending the rest of my life with, and a man who I was sure I could trust to raise a child. Boy, was I wrong!

It's funny, I have left for work at 7:15 am every day since I started working in the salon. If I happen to be running late, I would still leave my place at 7:40 am at the very latest. This morning, however, I woke at 7:55 am in a panic. When I'm late I become scatty; I'm knocking over teacups, putting the wrong key in the keyhole and I always end up forgetting my reading glasses or my keys.

Standing in the kitchen, amid this morning's kerfuffle, I spotted an envelope dropping through the letterbox. I assumed the mail schedule had changed as my mail normally arrives between 11 am and 12 am. I walked to the door and picked it up. It wasn't stamped but bore the word 'Sue' (written with a giant S and a barely legible U and E). Of course, I opened the door. What I didn't expect to see was Stu closing the garden gate from the outside. He was carrying a rather large gear bag which I'd never seen before. He hadn't copped that I'd seen him. I opened the patio door and shouted after him, 'Baby, what's this? Are you trying to surprise me with gifts? You are too sweet. Come in for a coffee and we can get a taxi to work.' Stu froze. He closed the gate, walked back in through the front gate, and gave me a half-hug/awkward kiss on the way.

Seated at the kitchen table, I asked, 'What's up with the bag?' Stu sighed and said nothing. Again, I asked if everything was OK? Stu didn't reply, instead, his head fell into his hands and he took a deep breath. I told him to take his time as I prepared some coffee, thinking that something had happened to his parents or maybe even the record store. As the coffee boiled, I realised I was still holding the letter Stu had dropped through the letterbox. I decided to open it. I was amped with excitement and questioned Stu as to what it might be. Again, Stu didn't budge. Inside the envelope was a letter that was dated at the top (I'm still holding it now). I began to read it aloud;

June 30th

'Dear Sue,

I want to apologise in advance for being a cop-out and a fuck up! You do deserve better.

Several months ago, I had an encounter with my best friend's sister, Zofia. It was brief – a one-night stand of sorts that never went further. Dispiritedly, I soon discovered that Zofia was pregnant, and according to Zofia, I was the father. I didn't know how to tell you. I discovered all of this shortly after we met, and trust me when I say that (1) I fell in love with you from the day we met, (2) the last thing I wanted to do was upset you and, (3) I blocked Zofia and her pregnancy out of my mind as a coping mechanism of sorts.

Sue, I didn't know how to tell you. You would have had my head on a plate there and then. I am sorry, and I do mean that when I say it, I am sorry for putting you through all of this. I know some guys might be able to handle this, but I'm not that guy. I've decided to pack my bags and leave. I don't know where I'm going and I don't know if I'll ever be back, but I will send you money for the baby. I believe that is the least I can do for now.

I am sorry for all of this. I love you with all my heart, but you deserve better. You deserve a real man.

Stu x'

I stood still; I couldn't find the words to relate my feelings. In an act of frustration and sheer anger, I turned to Stu and told him to sling his hook. Stu didn't budge. I screamed, 'Go!' Stu slid the chair back and bounced to his feet like a jack in the box. His eyes were red and tearful as began to speak, 'Can we talk about this like adults?' I laughed before replying, 'Adults? Ha, you must be laughing.' I told Stu to take his bag and get out of my house. Stu made his way to the hall, where he stood with his head hanging in shame. He opened the door, took a deep breath and then turned around to me and said, 'I'm sorry, Sue. What else can I say?' I shook my head as there were no words. Stu gave up. He closed the door gently and there was silence. I stood in shock for several minutes before calling the salon and telling Siobhan that I wasn't feeling well. After that, I must have sat at the table for about three hours as the only thing that startled me was the mail dropping through the letterbox.

Diary, what now? I'm heartbroken and poor Mum is going to be devastated.

Stuart (Thursday, July 2nd)

Between the glitch on my Spotify (it's preventing me from listening to anything but Radiohead playlists) and being MIA due to this fucked-up situation with both Zofia and Sue, I'm thinking about pulling a Richey Manic. I guess poor Richey must have been in the same boat. Life, I'm sure, was getting the better of him so he up and left in a mysterious disappearing act of sorts (possible suicide) where he hasn't been seen to this day. I'm not advocating suicide, but I do like the idea of landing in Mongolia or Alaska and starting a new life where I can forget my past. For now, however, I'm back to square one, Mam and Dad's place. I'm not sure why I backed out of getting the ferry yesterday. To be honest, my head was all over the place and the last thing I needed was several hours rocking back and forth on the Irish Sea.

I didn't have the balls to go face-to-face with Sue and tell her about Zofia's pregnancy. Instead, I arrived at Sue's with a note I had written and was fully packed and ready to leave the country on the ferry. Sue caught me on and, considering the many ways in which this confession could have transpired, her reading aloud the contents of my letter had to be the absolute worst. With a gaze that would burn a hole through your soul, Sue asked me to leave. I tried to explain my side of the story, but Sue flipped and screamed at me. Before I left, she took another jab at me, saying something like I wasn't a real adult; whatever that means??

7:45 pm

I'm still in Mam and Dad's place, watching reruns of *SpongeBob SquarePants* on Nickelodeon. According to SpongeBob's Bikini Bottom driver license, SpongeBob will celebrate his 32nd birthday this year; I always knew we had a lot in common. I haven't heard a peep from anyone, not Sue, not Zofia, not Maggie, not Trish. I guess I'll lay low here for another day or two before checking the temperature back home.

Suzanne (Thursday, July 2nd)

Dear Diary,

I called the salon early this morning and asked Fi if her and the girls would be OK without me. Without asking questions, as best friends do, Fi assured me they'd be fine. After that, I called Mum and told her I wasn't feeling well. I asked if she had any plans and if not, would she be willing to nurse me back to life over in her house for the day. Mum, being Mum, was only too happy to drop everything and come to pick Mrs Snuggles and I up.

When we got to Mum's we had a nice brunch and I told her and Mr Rocket about this supposed claim that Stu is the father of this Zofia's baby. Mum called Stu every name under the sun (including Bone Head). By the time Mum finished her never-ending rant where she repeated herself on multiple occasions it was dinner time. I had wondered why Mr Rocket was so quiet but then realised he had been preparing some delicious chicken fajitas and spicy rice all this time. Nobody said a word over dinner. I'm not sure if they were processing the Stu/Zofia situation or just salivating over the food. After some small talk about the soaps, Mum did her best to put my mind at ease. 'You have us, you'll be OK.' Mum nodded and made a heart shape with her hands. She must have seen someone do that on TV. I didn't know what to say, so I just hugged and thanked them both, served some leftovers to Mrs Snuggles and went home.

11:56 pm

Diary, I'm not sure how I feel about all of this, but what I can tell you is this... I love Stu. I do. Yes, I'm angry with him. Very, very angry, but I still love him. The worst part about all of this is the fear of losing him to this Zofia girl. Who knows? Stu could end up prioritising one parent and child over the other; I've read stories about this in the magazines at work. It's called spouse favouritism and it's a real thing! Maybe this Zofia girl's baby will be more beautiful than mine. Maybe Stu is in love with her and I don't know? Maybe there are a whole bunch of girls that Stu's managed to knock up. Diary, right now, I feel like I don't know anything.

Stuart (Friday, July 3rd)

I was up at 5:30 am to take the bus from Mam and Dad's back to work. When I arrived at the store, Trish was hard at it, mopping the floor. Her hair was down over her face and she was listening to The Smiths at an unreasonable volume. She reminded me of the Nirvana kids who would 'wash the floor with their hair' in the Alternative Arcade club we used to frequent back in the day. Addressing Trish, I said, 'Good morning.' She looked up from the floor and gave a gentle nod. She never was the morning type.

After making coffee in the canteen, I returned to the floor to open the store and put together a playlist for the morning. Trish wasn't long making her presence felt and informed me Zofia had phoned twice. Zofia told Trish to write down what she had to say and pass it on to me. The note was stuck to the till and read;

"She will arrive on Saturday, July 4th. She said she will not be celebrating Independence Day. She is staying with her sister, Maggie. She said you better be about for the test on Monday. She will stay for as long as need be. She asked if we had a copy of Talking Heads - The Best Of, *and if so, how much did it cost and could she maybe pass herself off for a student discount, or even better again, a staff discount."*

Just when I thought things were cooling down. And the cheek of her. There should be an international ban on discounting anything Talking Heads related. You pay for quality, and that's that!

How am I going to co-exist with Sue and Zofia in the same vicinity during this difficult time? Maybe Richey Manic was right, maybe it's time to get my ass out of here once and for all!

Suzanne (Friday, July 3rd)

Dear Diary,

I am struggling to pull myself from this slumber and get back to work. Again, I was up early and called the salon to say I wouldn't be in. I do know Fi was fine with that, but I could hear Siobhan swearing in the background. In fairness, Siobhan has every right to swear as some of my clients are a handful. I texted Siobhan to apologise, and although she ignored me all day, I did get a reply saying, "It's OK," later this evening.

Speaking of, Zia was here tonight. I had asked her to pop over as I needed to talk to someone other than Mum. I also felt it would be good to get an outside perspective on all of this madness! Unfortunately, the tears haven't stopped. Having discussed everything with Zia, I think my biggest fear is losing Stu as both a partner and a parent because I know he can be great at both. Zia reckons Stu deserves a lot of slack for not telling me about the other girl, that aside, Zia also reckons Stu deserves another chance. I'm not so sure if I can be as forgiving.

Stuart (Saturday, July 4th)

I'm a bit 2 drnk to write now, but Inhave realisd he thing in my pants is th lproblem. I'? Cheerd!!;

Suzanne (Saturday, July 4th)

Dear Diary,

Reluctantly, I returned to work today, but for the life of me, I couldn't concentrate on anything. The only thing racing through my head was Stu. Should I be worried about him? Even when I factored in all the grief he has caused me over the past few days, I couldn't help but have that worried feeling in my stomach. And why wouldn't I? He hasn't texted me or called me. I have absolutely no idea if he has been at work. For all I know he could be passed out somewhere after going on some sort of self-destructive bender.

If today wasn't difficult enough, we had a visit from Eric and Mark Reeves. Eric's nose had certainly healed well; I thought I might have damaged it for life a few months back. The brothers were wondering if we were interested in some cheap hair products from China. Eric said his mate who owns Hair Today, Gone Tomorrow in Digglewood swears by them. It sounded sus, but when Mark Reeves showed us a quote our jaws dropped. Fi reckons we could up our wages quite a bit if we were to try the Chinese product, and after doing the math, she wasn't wrong. I told the Reeves brothers we'd start with a small order to see how it goes. They seemed chuffed and were happy to do business.

7:40 pm

It feels weird sitting lonely on a Saturday night. Normally, Stu shares the couch with me; even if I'm subject to band documentaries and *Match of the Day*. Even Mrs Snuggles is ignoring me. Although the couch has become quite the challenge considering the size of my poor Snuggleflakes. I must do some more research on cat birth as I think it could get pretty messy here.

Stuart (Sunday, July 5th)

4:25 pm

My head is pounding! I'm not sure how much I had to drink yesterday but I do know it was a lot as (a) I found yesterday's wet clothes in the oven and (b) the toilet bowl is covered in vomit!

As promised, Zofia arrived yesterday. I had been dreading this over the past few days as I wanted Sue to forgive me. The last thing I needed was this Polish prick-teaser floating about the place.

Yesterday morning was quiet; the usual horde of Saturday morning regulars and post-market wanderers. Shortly after 11 am, I was bent down behind the counter when I heard that voice. 'Is he magician now? Maybe he want to make baby disappear.' It was Zofia. She was no sooner in the door than she was already throwing jabs. In an attempt to play her at her own game, I stood up from behind the counter and said, 'Ta-da!' (as if I had re-appeared from a cloud of smoke). 'Not funny,' replied Zofia. Trish, bemused by this interaction, gave a shy nod and made herself scarce. Zofia looked hot in fairness, kind of 1972 era Mariska Veres with the hair, face and makeup, complete with Lily Allen style dress sense. With the Sue situation up in the air, I thought maybe Zofia and I could work; I was very much hoodwinked by her appearance as I later found out. 'We will meet at this bar when you finish the work. We talk the business then,' said Zofia; she was pointing to The Round Inn on her phone (a notorious stomping ground (in every sense) for local drug dealers and ex-cons). Not to rock the boat, I told her that sounded great and I'd be there just after 6 pm. Zofia gave me one of her trademark smiles where her whole face scrunches up in an attempt to look happy before returning to her default bitch face.

When I arrived at The Round Inn Zofia was standing outside smoking a cigarette, chatting to two burly Polish lads. I walked up and tried to butt in with some talk about the weather. Zofia nodded her head towards the bar as if to say, 'keep walking,' so that I did. 'I follow you,' she shouted after me.

As it was early, the bar was pretty quiet and populated for the most part by old men reading their papers and drinking their pints. Nobody seemed to bat an eyelid. I walked up to the bar and was greeted by a young girl with her hair tied in a bun. She looked me up and down before asking, 'What can I getcha?' I was scanning the taps to see what was familiar and stupidly made the mistake of asking, 'What's good?' The young girl said, 'We have a few bottles of wine and a few bottles of gin.' She was already pigeonholing me. In an attempt to nip the awkwardness, I ordered a pint of cider with ice. The young girl looked more shocked than she should have.

I took a seat and waited for a good twenty minutes before Zofia came in from outside. In the meantime, several young mothers and about 15 kids had taken a seat around me. They were all extremely noisy, but very nice and chatty at the same time.

Before Zofia finally took a seat, she ordered a pint of Guinness and two packets of bacon fries (she ate both packets without offering me any). Zofia began, 'Monday, we take test. We find if you are father of baby and if so, what is plan for future. I have test booked for 11 am so please, do not be late.' What could I say, I knew this day would eventually come, and to be honest, I wanted to know the truth? I was sick of all the *what if...* scenarios. Without hesitation, I told her all of that sounded great. Zofia said she had a lot of different plans depending on the outcome, but she will address them once we get the results. She then placed the ball in my hands, 'So, what about you? What do you think is the plan? It's OK, yes?' I think Zofia was asking me if my plan was good. I was unsure about what to say, and the last thing I wanted to do was rock the boat, so I took her approach. I told her it would all depend on the results and how it would be easier to put a plan in place from there. I tried to sound as confident as she did. Zofia looked surprised, 'Wow! I'm impressed. Maybe you are real man.' There was a long, awkward silence. Somehow, I thought this would be the perfect opportunity to bring Zofia up to speed on the happenings here. I began, 'Before we go ahead with the test, there's something you should know.' But I struggled to find the right opening line. Zofia interrupted my thinking and in a teacher-like tone said, 'Are you waiting for bus? Spit it out.' A chill went up through my spine. I began my admission (the second in under a week). I told Zofia that Sue is pregnant, and I am the father. Zofia's face widened, almost like it was going to combust there and then. She stood up and slapped me with all her might. It stung like hell. Now, every one of the punters had stopped what they were doing and were looking our way. Zofia picked up her untouched pint of Guinness and poured it over my head. Zofia began her tirade of abuse, 'You fucking stupid. You just think of you and fuck all the girls. Not think of future! Not think of baby and baby's future. Fuck you!' She grabbed my pint and downed it in one go. As she made her way towards the door, the entire pub started whistling and hollering in her favour. When she left, everyone was shaking their heads and looking at me in disgust. I sat tight and waited for the commotion to calm down. 'Monday, 11 am, be there!!!' Zofia had stuck her head in the door and screamed her instructions across the bar before disappearing again. I didn't think twice about waiting around. As I made my way to the door, I was blasted with abuse, 'Fuck off!' 'Never come back!' 'Casa-fucking-nova, get out of here!'

I wasn't sure what kind of reaction to expect from Zofia, but I certainly didn't expect that. I feel hurt and, as unmanly as that sounds, I think it's justified. I didn't plan this pregnancy with Sue, it just happened. It wasn't like I wanted revenge on Zofia, it wasn't like there was a master plan to create another life so that I wouldn't have to deal with being the father of Zofia's child and everything that goes with it. I pawed at my soaked hair and shirt and began an uncomfortable walk home.

When I got back to the apartment, I needed to unwind so I poured myself a hot bath. And of course, no hot bath is complete without a couple of glasses of scotch and some decent music (not in my abode anyway). Turning the volume down on The Stooges - *Raw Power* is sacrilegious, but I had no choice as the neighbours were banging the shit out of the wall and shouting, 'Turn that shit off!' Their pounding ultimately crashed my bourbon brimmed bath blowout. With the alcohol buzz in full effect and all my worries in the back of my mind, I decided to take a taxi to The Hanger Club for some cheap booze and a bit of a boogie.

The Hanger was jammed. Most of the punters seemed to have been at the Floyd & The Gingerbread Men gig over at The Plex earlier that night. After an hour or so I spotted Peggy (from the flat upstairs) on her own on the dance floor. She looked legless and was doing her best to hold herself up as New Order's - Blue Monday played through the club's speakers. I didn't think twice about going over and tapping her on the shoulder. 'Stu! Oh my God! I'm so happy to see you. I don't know anybody here,' said Peggy. I told Peggy she looked great and asked her if she had been there long. Peggy grabbed my hand and accompanied me off the dance floor, past the bar and over to the cloakroom where we took a seat.

'One second,' said Peggy. I thought she needed to catch her breath as she looked shattered. Peggy began fooling about with her handbag. She was trying to find something. I was well on it at this stage and had become distracted by a Katy Perry lookalike over at the cigarette machine. A couple of minutes later, Peggy brought me back to Earth. 'There we go,' said Peggy. I turned my head to find Peggy legless, literally!! I had no idea she had artificial legs. Peggy slid across the couch and placed her legs beside her. 'Ah, sorry about this, but, is there any chance you could put my legs in the cloakroom?' For the first time in my life, I completely stumped... is that a bad choice of words? I blurted a reply, 'I had no idea!' 'How would you?' asked Peggy.

I picked up the artificial legs and walked over to the girl in the cloakroom. I was mortified! I didn't know what to say. 'Just these please.' I'm sure the colour of my face said it all as I handed over the artificial legs. The cloakroom girl leaned over and helped me get the two legs through the cloakroom hatch. 'Two euro, please,' said the cloakroom girl. I was shocked that she had charged me, but who was I to know any better? I handed her a fiver and she handed me back my change with a numbered ticket, which I passed to Peggy. 'No.11 again, coincidence can be an evil bitch,' proclaimed Peggy. I had to bite my lip. 'Can you carry me to the bar? My wheelchair is by the exit door.' Again, I didn't think twice. I picked Peggy up and threw her over my shoulder.

As we made our way to the bar, Peggy said, 'I had enough of the dancing, the legs were getting too heavy.' I sobered up pretty fast and assured Peggy that she was in safe hands for the rest of the evening. With Peggy comfortably seated in her wheelchair, we decided to hit the smoking area for some 'fresh air'. Here, Peggy told me about the motorcycle accident that led to both of her legs being amputated. It sounded gnarly as fuck and she is lucky to be alive. I told Peggy that I was going through a tough time and I needed a night to escape from my worries. We ended up talking for what must have been three hours before the bouncers started to clear the place.

When we went back to the cloakroom, I took the ticket and handed it back to the cloakroom girl. She seemed to be taking forever down the back of the cloakroom, before she finally returned, holding only one of Peggy's legs. 'I'm very sorry, I can only find one of her legs.' I looked at Peggy as if to say, 'Is this cloakroom girl for real?' Peggy threw her eyes up to heaven. I turned back to the cloakroom girl and said, 'You are kidding, right?' Worryingly, the girl explained, 'You can come in and look for yourself. I looked everywhere. The other leg is nowhere to be seen.' I turned back to Peggy and said, 'I'm so sorry about this, give me a few minutes and I'll find it.' Unfortunately, I didn't find it. Nor did any of the bouncers who spent a good hour scouring the club. 'We'll let you know if it turns up.' Those were the parting words from the head bouncer as I wheeled a half-cut, one-legged Peggy up the wheelchair ramp and out of the club. We took a short detour to get some takeaway before availing of a wheelchair-friendly taxi at the taxi rank. Peggy didn't have any qualms about telling the missing leg story to the taxi driver and, in a strange turn of events, just as Peggy was coming to the end of the story, the taxi driver interrupted her, 'There it is! The little bastards!'

Further up the street, I spotted three young lads, who were no doubt students considering their dress sense and the area. One of the students was holding Peggy's missing leg and swinging it in an attempt to hit the other two lads. The taxi driver sped up. 'Those little shits!' he said out loud. Peggy followed suit, 'The little shits.' The taxi driver pulled in beside the kids. Both he and I jumped out of the taxi. 'Oi!' the driver screamed, at the top of his voice. The three lads began to run as the driver, and I gave chase. The kids were fast, let it be said. I was tired and pretty pissed off at this stage and roared, 'Put down the fucking leg.' The student holding the leg yelled back, 'Did you break your sex doll? You fucking creep!' as all three continued to run. Both the taxi driver and I chased the students until we both collapsed in a heap and the students got away.

When we got back to the taxi, poor Peggy was still strapped into her wheelchair in the back but was now in the company of two cops. They had come to check up on her after two cars were dispatched for Peggy's 999 calls.

Back at Peggy's, we got soaked going from the taxi to the front door of the apartment. Fortunately, Peggy had some XL t-shirts and pants for lounging about and was happy to let me change into them as long as I helped her to dry off and fetch her pyjamas.

After necking a bottle of wine on the couch Peggy and I ended up having sex. I didn't plan on having sex with Peggy, it just kind of happened. It was a natural end to a pretty unnatural night. As we lay on

Peggy's bed in the afterglow of our exploits, Peggy broke into an a capella version of Neil Young's - Don't Let It Bring You Down. It was probably the most beautiful thing that I've ever heard, and I struggled to fight back the tears. I guess my only complaint from the night is that my arms are killing me from holding Peggy up during sex.

Suzanne (Sunday, July 5th)

Dear Diary,

I came close to buying a cot that was on sale in Mother's Way, but Mum talked me out of it. She asked, 'What if you end up having twins? It'll be a tight squeeze in that thing.' She was right. I agreed that it was best to wait for the results of the scan on Friday.

When we got back to my place, we bumped into Mrs Grimble, who looked very upset while attempting to trim the hedges in her garden. Mum stopped to ask her if she was OK. Mrs Grimble admitted that she hadn't been well and was worried sick about Royston and how he will be treated by his fellow offenders. Mum, for better or worse, used one of her go-to responses that I've also picked up over the years, 'Birds of a feather flock together.' Mrs Grimble responded 'You're right. They're all as bad as each other and they'll pay the price when they have to answer to God in the end.' I didn't know where to look, but the brief encounter seemed to do wonders for Mrs Grimble as she smiled and thanked Mum for asking how she was.

11:15 pm

I texted Stu just now...

"All OK?"

Stuart (Monday, July 6th)

There has been some contact with Sue! All is not lost just yet. She texted late last night. I told her where I'm at but didn't get too soppy or try to apologise just yet. I think she needs some more time to cool down.

I'm happy to admit that the paternity test was a piece of cake! I'm not sure why I was dreading it so much. We were in and out in under 30 minutes. The nurse who took my blood samples was a bit of a looker, and I will admit getting semi-hard when she used her latex covered hand to take a swab sample from my mouth. Zofia, in fairness to her, made it all the more comfortable by not being a complete bitch and keeping her mouth shut for the morning. The nurse reckons we'll have the results Friday as we have paid for the high-end test. I gave Zofia 250 of the 500 quid I owed to pay for the test and promised the rest on Friday.

With the test done and the rest of the day off, I contemplated asking Zofia if we should get to know each other a bit. Just as I was about to suggest some quality bonding, Zofia declared, 'I go now!' and walked away, applying lipstick with her handheld mirror as she went. As awkward as I sounded, I wished her a safe trip home. I kind of wished she wasn't so cold all the time. Then again, it's a bit of a turn-on, what can you do?

Suzanne (Monday, July 6th)

Dear Diary,

I woke up to a text from Stu, it read -

"Heya, I'm OK, thanks! How have you been? I went for the paternity test with Maggie's sister. It normally takes a few days for the results to come through, but I'll let you know how it pans out."

I'm not sure how I would react to the result of Stu and this girl's paternity test, but I have a funny feeling a positive result will devastate me.

Mum has agreed to some nude modelling for the art college after answering an advert in the paper. As much as that grosses me out, she has wanted to do this type of modelling for years; and in fairness to her, her body is holding up quite well for her age. Mr Rocket, on the other hand, threw a wobbly when Mum told him her plans. Mr Rocket said, 'Come on... it's not like you're a page 3 model. You'll scar those poor kids for life.' Mum seemed unphased by his comments and instead of getting upset, she begged Mr Rocket to join her in an 'act of love' (as Mum put it). 'She'll be doing bloody porn next, wait 'til you see,' said Mr Rocket. He was talking to no one in particular, but he made sure his point was heard.

Stuart (Tuesday, July 7th)

I just remembered that Peggy and I didn't use any form of contraception on Saturday night. I'm not even going to entertain the thoughts of Peggy getting pregnant. It's bad enough that she texted saying they found her leg, albeit missing a few toes. Still, imagine it, instead of the movie *Three Men and a Baby* I'd be starring in my very own, *Three Babies and a Man*. Although, *three babies and a Complete Fuck-Up* might be closer to the truth.

Sue has replied to my text:

"I'm still angry, but I do hope to see you at the scan on Friday."

Suzanne (Tuesday, July 7th)

Dear Diary,

I think I might be attending the scan on my own as Stu hasn't bothered to reply. That alone says it all for me. After everything we've been through, he still doesn't have the balls to turn up and do what a real man would do regardless of the outcome. I have asked Mum if she will accompany me instead. Mum accepted, saying that she wouldn't miss it for the world. Mr Rocket offered to pop along, too, but Mum, who was still irate after Mr Rocket questioned her desire to do some nude modelling advised him to stay at home.

Stuart (Wednesday, July 8th)

All of this waiting is killing me. Between the results of the paternity test with Zofia and the baby scan with Sue, I'm not sure if I can handle all of this pressure. To make matters worse, I couldn't concentrate at work, I haven't eaten all day and now I'm at home lying on my bed and thinking of doing a Richey Manic disappearing act once and for all.

Suzanne (Wednesday, July 8th)

Dear Diary,

I have yet to get a reply from Stu, which means he doesn't give a shit about me or our baby and is more concerned with his Polish girl and the baby they are having together. Diary, it's tough not to be upset about all of this. I've been so distraught over the last bit that I'm afraid it might have a bad effect on our baby; or should I say *my* baby at this stage?

Mum is contemplating whether or not she should go au naturel as she is or do a bit of housekeeping on her lady bits before posing for the art class. She was here earlier tonight and spent a good hour Googling vagina hair variation. Mr Rocket had been pottering in and out of the back garden doing a bit of gardening when Mum stopped him in his tracks and asked, 'What about the landing strip?' Mum pointed to her crotch and illustrated the design with her finger. 'Come on, love... I'd say something if you were a Brazilian model,' replied Mr Rocket. Mum didn't miss a beat, 'Oh wait, I spotted the Brazilian style... what was it again?' Mum asked, as she frantically tapped the back button of her phone. 'I'll be out mowing the lawn,' said Mr Rocket, as he made a break for the back garden. 'I'll be upstairs doing the same,' replied Mum.

Stuart (Thursday, July 9th)

The Manic Street Preachers – *Holy Bible* album probably wasn't the best of choices at work today. All I could think about was shutting up shop and doing my Richey Manic disappearing act. Thankfully, towards the latter part of the afternoon, common sense prevailed, and I didn't go through with it. How could I leave two babies behind? I could never live with myself.

Suzanne (Thursday, July 9th)

Dear Diary,

I'm super-nervous about tomorrow. I had hoped Stu would be by my side, but unfortunately, that is looking more and more doubtful. In preparation for the scan, I have prepared some bottles of water so I will have an adequately full bladder. After that, there's nothing else I can do but wait until the nurse gives me some insight into the baby's health and progress thus far. God! I'm shaking here and I still have a full day to go.

Oh yeah, I almost forgot. The girls at work gave me a good luck card and a voucher to get my nails done. Each of them wrote a little message.

Fi – "Best of luck tomorrow, hun! Don't be worrying, you'll be fine xxx"

Siobhan - "I'm sooooo excited I think I'm going to pee!! I promise it won't be like the morning after the Xmas party... soz again!! :)"

Nicole - "To my favourite person in the world! I still can't believe you're going to be a mum! We're all so proud of you, and we just know you are going to be the best mum ever!! PS - thanks for giving me the weekend off for Avril's bday. Luv U."

Stuart (Friday, July 10th)

10:40 pm

Sue is passed out on the couch beside me after a long day of baby scans and doctors. I almost missed the whole affair as I got stuck talking to one of our regular hoarder customers on the way to the hospital. He had picked up a test press of Abba's - *Survival* LP for a fiver. The jammy fucker!

When I got to the hospital I realised that I stunk and looked like I hadn't slept in days. Before I had a chance to open my mouth the girl at reception asked, 'Would you like to see a doctor?' I did contemplate it but put my priorities in place. I asked the girl where the baby scan department was. The receptionist pointed towards the elevator and told me to get out on the third floor. God, hospitals are odd places. I hate

STEPHEN PURCELL

seeing people walking about with tubes hanging out of them. It makes
me wonder if I'll end up like that someday (probably sooner rather than
later the way things are going).

After taking a seat outside the baby scan department (or Foetal
Medicine Unit as I read on the door), I could hear Sue's Mam making a
fuss inside the room. 'Sue, are you sure your bladder is full? Sue replied,
'For the fifth time, yes, it's full. If you give me any more water, I'm
going to end up peeing the bed.' Picking the right time to enter the
room was tough as I could overhear Sue's mam complaining about
everything from the ultrasound screen being too dark (apparently it was
turned off) to the smell of eggs in the room. She then joked, 'Sue, you
must be pretty fertile. The smell of eggs is overbearing.' This was my
chance...

That's eggs-actly what I was thinking,' I said, as both Sue and her
Mam looked on in shock as I entered the room. Sue spoke first, 'That
was a terrible pun, but... OH MY GOD!!! I can't believe you're here!
Thank you so much for making the effort.' The comment made me feel
a million miles away from Sue and more specifically our relationship.
Sue looked delighted, as did her Mam, who hugged me before
whispering a hushed, 'Thanks.' in my ear. In an attempt to break the
awkward silence that followed, I asked, 'Are we having twins or
quadruplets?' Thankfully, a nurse overheard me as she entered the room
and answered my icebreaker. 'Well, let's get this process started so we
can find out.' There was a sense of excitement, anticipation and anxiety
in the room, as the nurse rummaged around gathering everything she
needed. 'Right then, lift this for me,' the nurse requested, as she helped

Sue lift her shirt to her chest. 'So, how many trips to the loo did we have this morning then?' asked the nurse. Sue replied, 'I lost count.' Sue's mam butted in, 'She's been like a racehorse.' The nurse couldn't help but laugh. 'Great! Now, let's get some of this gel on you and we can begin the scan.'

As the nurse applied the gel, I caught Sue looking at me. It was a look of love. A look I hadn't seen for many years. It was only then that it hit home. I was madly in love with Sue, and even if I had done a Richey Manic disappearing act, the 'Motorcycle Emptiness' in me would have come running back to Sue for a refill. 'Now, that should do the trick', said the nurse, as she finished applied the gel to Sue's stomach. Sue put her hand out for me to hold. I gave a little squeeze and a smile before holding her hand tightly. 'All of that lube reminds me of a man I dated after your father passed,' Sue's mam confessed. Sue cut her off, 'Mum! Not now, please!'

I will admit, this experience, my first and hopefully last, was a bit nerve-racking. Sue and her Mam were nervous too. Christ! Even the nurse was a bit jittery as she hit a few wrong buttons on the monitor of the scanner. 'OK, sit back slowly for me,' asked the nurse, as she glided the scanner over Sue's stomach. Everyone looked very tense, so I decided to break the ice. 'Beep! Beep! Unexpected item in the bagging area!' I said. Everyone shook their head and frowned. After a few minutes of scanning and silence, Sue interrupted the nurse, 'How's it looking?' she asked. The nurse replied, 'Hmm'. 'Is that a good hmm or bad hmm?' asked Sue's mam. The nurse responded, worryingly, 'Well, I can't see anything.' Sue gripped my hand tightly. 'There's no sign of the sac, it might be too early, or it could be entropic,' the nurse explained. 'Oh my!' replied Sue, as her eyes welled up with tears and started to cry. Thankfully, Sue's mam did a good job of calming Sue down. 'It's OK, dear. This stuff happens all the time. It's probably too early.' I kissed Sue on the forehead and told her everything would be fine. In truth, I was in as much shock, as I had no idea what entropic meant.

With Sue being consoled by her mam, I excused myself to the bathroom to Google entropic. It took a minute or two to regain my composure after doing so and I returned to the room. When I got back, the nurse asked Sue if she had been to a doctor before coming for the scan. Sue said, 'No, I just booked the scan over the phone.' 'Oh? OK, then,' said the nurse, as she stared at the now-blank monitor and held the scanner in her hand. 'So, no blood tests then?' asked the Nurse. 'No, I haven't had any blood tests,' replied Sue. The nurse replied, 'OK, then, I'm going to send you to your GP for blood tests asap. We can book you in for a more detailed scan if need be.' With that, the nurse excused herself momentarily. Sue's mam was pacing back and forth inside the room. Suddenly, she stopped and asked, 'What's an egg tropic, then?' Sue and I started laughing. 'You've eggs on the brain, Mum? Did you not have any breakfast?' asked Sue. 'Entropic pregnancies happen all the time. In this case, the baby is growing outside the uterus,' I said; trying to sound like I knew what I was talking about. Sue's mam replied, 'Oh my god! That's terrible! The poor baby swimming about in no-mans-land.' At this point, Sue was visibly shaken and doing her best to fight back tears. She asked, 'What now?' Stupidly, I forgot to read about Entropic procedures and their repercussions so I played it cool and said,

'The nurse will know where things are at.' 'That poor baby could be swimming around in your arse and you wouldn't even know. What if you sat on it?' said Sue's mam worryingly. Just as Sue was about to raise her voice to her mam, the nurse returned and said, 'Now, we're in luck. I spoke to your GP and he had a cancellation at 2 pm today if that suits you? He said he always looks after the Conway family and has done so for three generations.' 'Awww, Dr Higgins, bless his heart,' replied Sue's mam. Sue followed, 'Wow! That was fast. Thank you so much for all your help.' The nurse replied, 'You'll be just fine, and just in case you need anything, there is a range of services available at the natal clinic.' Everyone shook the nurse's hand and thanked her for her time and effort.

With two hours to spare, Sue's mam drove us back to her place for sandwiches. Sue didn't eat much and spent most of the time doing stuff upstairs. At around 1:30 pm, Sue reappeared downstairs and asked if I would be going to the doctor with them. 'Of course,' I said. Sue threw her arms around me and said, 'I don't want to lose you. You mean the world to me and I know we'll get through all of this.' I told Sue I was there now and both she and the baby were my no.1 priority. Sue smiled and we kissed intensely. 'Come on lovebirds,' said Sue's mam as the sound of the car alarm deactivating became our calling card.

Dr Higgins' waiting room was thronged with all sorts: junkies, people coughing their lungs up and sneezing uncontrollably, kids running riot, you name it. The sooner we were in and out of there the better. I imagined Dr Higgins was thinking the same when he stuck his head in the doorway of the waiting room. 'Ah, Suzanne Conway, please.'

said the doc, doing his absolute best not to look like he needed a break from the madness. Sue, her mam and I stood up and followed the doc towards his office. 'You must be the father then? Please, take a seat,' said the doc as we entered the office. 'Yes, sir,' I replied, before shaking the doc's hand. 'And how about this lady, eh? How does one stay so beautiful?' asked the doc. He put his arm around Sue's mam, who was blushing heavily. 'Oh stop,' said Sue's mam, no doubt flattered by Dr Higgins' smooth talk. 'I can have you out of here in five minutes,' said the doc, as he dialled up Sue's info on the computer. The Doc continued, 'Sit up here for me. Just a quick jab and we're done.' Sue didn't seem bothered by the needle, but she did ask the doc, 'Is it possible we could have an ectopic pregnancy?' The doc replied, 'Anything is possible with a pregnancy, but let's take it one step at a time.' Sue's facial muscles relaxed, and the worry seemed to wash away before she hopped down from the examination table and hugged her mam. It was good to have Sue's mam with us there and then. 'Right, I can have the results of these tests turned around by the end of the day. I'd only do this for a select few, just so you know. If ye weren't Conway's you'd be waiting 'til Monday,' explained the doc. 'Really? That would be great,' said Sue, as her attempt to hug the doc turned into an awkward handshake. 'Would you like me to call you? Or will you be staying around the town?' asked the doc. Sue replied, 'We have no reason to be home, so yeah, I guess we could grab a bite to eat and de-stress for a few hours.' Sue's mam chirped in, 'I'm starving anyway.' The Doc replied, 'Great! Pop into me at 5:30 pm, that'll give me enough time to get the results.' We thanked the doc and made our way towards The Barge for some food.

Sitting at The Barge in the company of Sue, I was engulfed by many emotions. Nostalgia, empathy, love – a smorgasbord of everything we had been through and everything we were about to go through. I could tell Sue was nervous. I think Sue could tell I was nervous, too, but didn't let on. Sue's mam did a good job of keeping things positive. She talked us through every item she had sampled on the menu, giving a detailed review as she went. Everybody chose soup and sandwiches as the weather was a tad blustery and wintery. Once finished, Sue, her mam and I sat playing with our phones until it was time to go back to Dr Higgins. I doubt I would be wrong in assuming all three of us were reading up on ectopic pregnancies.

As the clock struck 5:30 pm, Sue, her mam and I were back in Dr Higgins' waiting room as advised. There was one other patient in the waiting room, who informed us she was waiting for a prescription. A few minutes later Dr Higgins appeared. He handed the prescription to the waiting patient, wished her well and invited us back into his office.

The doc continued, 'Ten minutes max. You're supposed to check the result after ten minutes Why did you wait so long?' he asked. Sue replied, 'Really? But I thought you had to let it settle to be sure, no?' Sue's mam interrupted the conversation, 'You're not cooking a chicken, love.' I didn't know where to look. 'So, tell me what you discovered after taking the pregnancy tests?' asked the doc. Sue replied, 'Both tests came back positive. I can show you. I kept both of the tests just in case.'

Sue began rooting through her bag. 'Here we go,' she said, producing two pregnancy kits from her bag. She handed the kits to the doc. 'OK, right, I see,' said the Doc. Sue's mam butted in, 'What do you see Dr Higgins?' Dr Higgins took a deep breath, walked over to his chair and sat down. 'You may not like what I'm about to tell you,' he said. Sue's mam blurted, 'Oh, Jesus! The baby's dead!' before bursting into a flood of tears. Sue, in shock at what her mam had said, followed suit. At this stage, I couldn't help but be overcome with emotion as my eyes filled up with water. I did my best to hold them back. 'You're not pregnant, Suzanne,' said the doc. 'You never were.' Sue looked startled. We were all startled. 'Are you positive?' asked Sue's mam. 'I am positive, unlike the results of your blood test and these pregnancy tests,' explained the doc. 'I don't understand!? Both tests said I was pregnant. What about my period and the pains I've been experiencing in my breasts?' Sue asked. She was crying in a bout of frustration and confusion. I tried to console her by rubbing her head and telling her, 'It'll be OK.' The doc replied, 'If you checked the results of the pregnancy test after the recommended time has passed, the results might look like a positive test result. The thing is, in most instances, this is not a positive result, but an evaporation line left by the urine after the recommended time for reading the test. Sometimes it can be a different colour to the line that will appear as a positive result, hence all this confusion.' 'I bloody knew she was colour blind,' said Sue's mam. 'I've been telling her this for years and she won't listen to me.' Sue shook her head and asked the doc, 'Does that go for both tests?' The doc gave a gentle nod. My heart sunk. I felt relieved but gutted. All I could think about was making things work with Sue, but the burden of Zofia, and having a child with her, were wreaking havoc on my mind. I looked at Sue, she was speechless. I looked at Sue's mam and for the first time in her life, she was speechless, too. Sue turned to the doc and said, 'So, you are 100% confident that I'm not pregnant?' The doc replied, 'Well when you went for the scan, there was no sign of a gestational sac. This would be identifiable after so many weeks unless it was entropic. Now that we have the results of the blood tests, coupled with the knowledge that you surpassed the expected wait time for the pregnancy kit results, which in this case resulted in the discoloured evaporation lines, it is safe to say, with 100% confidence, you are not pregnant.' Sue turned around to face me. She looked like a deer in the headlights; shocked, scared, lost, frozen. 'I'm sorry,' said the doc as Sue fell into my arms and held me tightly. I could feel her shaking and hear her crying gently. I rubbed her back and told her everything was going to be OK. Sue's mam took over from me. She told Sue that it might be best to go home and have an early night. Sue, bless her, looked exhausted and agreed.

When we got back to Sue's place, I filled Sue a hot bath and poured her a glass of wine. While Sue spent a considerable amount of time in the tub, she didn't touch the wine or say a single word for that matter. She's passed out on the couch at the moment and snoring ever so gently. It's been a tough day, and to make matters worse, I now have to tell Zofia that Sue is not, nor ever was pregnant. Can I text that? Or is it in the phone call tier? Fuck! I'll leave it 'til the morning.

Suzanne (Friday, July 10th)

No entry

Stuart (Saturday, July 11th)

I texted Zofia about Sue first thing. I wrote: "Heya, just to let you know that Suzanne is not pregnant. The doc confirmed it with blood tests and said Sue read the pregnancy test wrong."

It took Zofia eight minutes to reply:

"Good!!"

Sue was dead quiet most of the day, responding only with a few words or grunts bar telling her mam, 'I feel like such an idiot,' before bursting into tears over breakfast this morning. I feel so sorry for Sue, she is heartbroken. I guess most people would be the same if they got accustomed to being pregnant.

After breakfast, I popped back to my place to grab some fresh clothes as I had been wearing the same smelly-ass shirt for about three days. It smelled like a combination of weed, stale sweat and alcohol. Back at the apartment lobby, I stumbled upon Peggy and a bloke who looked like Jean Paul Gaultier hiding behind the tenant mailboxes. Peggy spotted me and made an 'Shhh' sound while pressing her finger against her lip. She waved her hand as if to guide me towards the elevator as quickly as she could. I had no idea what Peggy and her Eurotrash-looking friend were up to, so I gave a quick nod and made a break for the elevator. 'Oi, you two, get the fuck out here!' shouted some random bloke with an English accent. The bloke began banging on the lobby door while pointing at Peggy and her friend. 'That cunt kicked my car! Police!! Police!! That cunt in there kicked my car,' screamed the English bloke. I looked at Peggy's friend, he looked pretty chilled. He stood up from behind the mailboxes and began shrugging his shoulders.

'Non, no,' said Peggy's friend innocently. 'Come out you fawking cuuuunnnntttt,' shouted the bloke outside. Peggy stood up from behind the mailboxes. She must have been reunited with her stolen leg, or at least got a replacement as she had two legs again. Peggy said, 'Don't look, just keep walking.' I asked her what was going on? Peggy replied, 'We were on the zebra crossing and that guy outside nearly knocked us down. Sebastian, frustrated, gave a light kick to the wheel of that guy's car and now he looks like he wants to strangle us.' 'Oi, Vidal Sassoon, get your fawking arse out here now you cuuuuuuuunnnntttt, screamed the bloke outside. I had enough on my plate, so I took Peggy's advice and made my way up to my apartment. In the interest of safety, I took it upon myself to call the police. The last thing Peggy needed was some maniac attacking her.

After grabbing a quick shower and some fresh clothes, I headed back to Sue's place. She was fast asleep in her bed as an episode of *Friends* played out on her iPad. She slept through the entire evening and is still conked now. I'm here with a bottle of wine watching 70s *Top of the Pops* reruns on BBC. I'm worried about Sue; it's going to take some time to get over all of this.

Suzanne (Saturday, July 11th)

No entry

Stuart (Sunday, July 12th)

It looks like I'm back in the bad books with Sue. After what I can only describe as a magnificent breakfast, I told Sue to rest upon the sun lounger out the back. In the meantime, I'd hit the shops to fetch her the Sunday papers.

When I got back from the shops, I found Sue boxing up all the baby clothes we had been gifted over the past few weeks. I asked Sue what she was doing with the clothes and she said she was getting rid of them. Without thinking, I blurted out, 'I might need those.' Sue looked at me like she wanted to drive a knife through my heart. She shook her head in disgust and said, 'Unbelievable.' I made a quick attempt to apologise, but it was too late. I had mentioned the war in a time of what some might call mourning. 'Go, please...' said Sue. She walked up the stairs with her head down. I didn't know what to do or say, so I left Sue's house and went home.

I don't think I was being inconsiderate when I mentioned keeping the clothes for the second potential baby in my life. If anything, I thought I was being resourceful. Unfortunately, Sue didn't see it that way.

8:22 pm

I texted Sue to apologise about asking for the baby clothes. She has yet to reply.

I will admit, I am nervous about the paternity test tomorrow. I felt super-anxious even talking about it, not to mind going ahead with it.

Zofia sent on a reminder about an hour ago. It read:

"Don't forget test tomorrow. Remember, if you don't go... we won't know."

Zofia must think I'm a right fucking idiot at times.

Suzanne (Sunday, July 12th)

Dear Diary,

I haven't been myself over the past few days, hence the lack of diary entries. I can honestly say I've never felt so down. Imagine thinking you were pregnant all this time, only to find out that you're a colour-blind moron who mistook evaporation lines for a positive pregnancy test result and a complete idiot who thought a missed period means you're pregnant and that's that. If that wasn't bad enough, imagine waiting all this time to go through with a baby scan; and if the outcome wasn't bad enough, then taking a blood test, just to put a nail in the coffin.

I kind of feel like I'm living in the afterlife. Everything is in slow-motion, my thought process, the words and sounds I hear, the way I process those sounds. I feel like I've died and come back to life, but now life serves no purpose. I feel empty, sick, nauseous, tired, upset, emotional... I could on and on... Both Mum and Stu (until today) have been wonderful in supporting me and assuring me that everything will be OK. I'm not so sure if it will. It feels like I've lost something – something special. But the truth is, there was nothing there to lose, there never was. So, here I am asking myself, why am I so upset? Is it because a baby is something, I didn't even know I wanted? Is it the realisation that having a baby might make my life complete? Is it because I got accustomed to the idea of raising a baby and everything that goes with it? Is it because I thought I was making that final jump into adulthood; albeit being oblivious to the fact I was seeking it in the first place? Or, am I upset knowing all of this is still a possibility for Stu but not for me? Maybe I'm jealous of Stu and the fact that he is having a child that I will have nothing to do with? Diary, I don't have the answers. I don't. To add fuel to the fire, I spent the last hour boxing up the baby clothes that Stu and I were given as presents only for Stu to return from the shops and say, 'I might need them.' I mean, really?

Diary, I think I need to speak to someone. I'm having thoughts that I've never had before and they're not good.

Stuart (Monday, July 13th)

The paternity test is done and dusted! Now we just have to wait for the results. Zofia, strangely, was in good form today and even cracked a smile, albeit an evil one, when getting her blood test done. The doc said, 'Just a small prick.' Zofia replied, 'I'm used to them, don't worry,' and fired a devilish grin my way. The doc was super-nice but just hard to understand due to his thick accent. I kept having to ask him to repeat what he said until it became so awkward that I just replied with 'Great!' to everything. Unfortunately, that didn't go down too well when the doc said, 'There is a possibility that you are not the father of this child.' If it wasn't for Zofia shouting, 'Stupid man! Have the respect!' at me and then repeating what the doc said, it would have gone over my head. The doc reckons it'll take a couple of days for the results to come back. In the meantime, he advised me to prepare myself for both outcomes (father, not father, yadda yadda.) and to watch my mental health. Zofia threw her eyes up to heaven and said, 'I wish he had to push baby out of his ass and feel the real pain.'

I walked Zofia from the doc's office up as far as the taxi rank. Neither of us said a word. When we got to the rank, she held my hand softly, kissed me on the cheek and said, 'I appreciate.' She smiled (genuinely), climbed into the back seat of the taxi and gave a gentle wave as it pulled out and they headed back to Maggie's house.

I'm not so sure I'm prepared for the result of this paternity test. If it's yes, and I am indeed the father, things are going to get very complicated. If it's a no, and I am not the father of Zofia's baby, I'm not so sure how I'd feel, to be honest. I don't think I've processed this situation enough as I got so wrapped up in Sue's pregnancy.

I called Sue several times, but she didn't answer. Instead, I opted to text her with an update on the paternity test. I wrote:

"Hey, babe, the paternity test to determine if I'm the father of my friend's sister's baby went well. The doc said we should have the results in a few days. Unfortunately, my friend's sister is not colour blind. A real baby is living inside her.

PS - Can you set the DVR to record the Punk documentary on BBC4, it starts at 10 pm xxx"

1:17 am

Still no reply from Sue

Suzanne (Monday, July 13th)

Dear Diary,

Sometimes I wonder if Stuart Jackson is from this planet or some distant galaxy where emotions, feelings and common sense are not common traits of the inhabitants. Stu texted me last night and had to cheek to tell me that he is grateful the girl he supposedly knocked up has a real baby inside her and unfortunately, she is not colour blind. I mean, really?? Is he that stupid? Or, is this Stu being the goof that he is? Is it his way of joking about in an attempt to cheer me up? Either way, I do believe it's too soon for this type of carrying on as it was a bit too close to the bone, joke or not.

I didn't bother going to work or tell the girls that I'm not pregnant for that matter. I sent Fi a text and told her I was feeling ill and might be out for a few days. Fi replied with, "OK, hun xxx"

Stuart (Tuesday, July 14th)

Still no word from Sue. I called twice this morning and even passed by her salon after work; one of her workmates said Sue was feeling ill and was at home resting. I contemplated calling up to Sue's place but decided against it considering she might not be in the best of form.

Being back at work is pretty weird. I could tell Trish wanted to ask why I've been MIA over the last bit, but she decided to respect my privacy and didn't ask. According to the figures, Trish and her brother have been running a tight ship while I was gone. Sales are up 18% week on week; that's the first time we've been out of the red all year. I thanked Trish and her brother for holding the fort and gave Trish an extra day off as she more than deserved it.

Zofia texted this evening. The text read:

"I hear nothing from doctor. We wait some more days."

Suzanne (Tuesday, July 14th)

Dear Diary,

I have decided to return to work tomorrow. I think I'm going to crack up if I have to spend another day coiled up inside these four walls. And besides, I'm feeling a bit better now!

I've been doing a lot of thinking over the past few days and I have come to realise that I do love Stuart. Yes, he can be a bit aloof, and he does have a habit of saying the wrong thing at the wrong time, but underneath it all, I truly believe his idiosyncrasies are his way of dealing with awkward situations. I know things are going to get pretty difficult once Stu and that girl have their baby, but I am willing to put all of that aside as I believe Stu is worth it and does care about me.

10:15 pm

I sent Stu a text just now. I had to break the ice. Knowing that my outburst about the baby clothes might have been the last straw for us, I needed to confirm that we still had a chance. My text read:

"Let's meet up on Friday. I'm not angry with you, I just needed some time to process all of this. We can make it work if you want to?"

11:47 pm

No reply from Stu.

Stuart (Wednesday, July 15th)

I woke to a text message from Sue. She said she was sorry for snapping at me the last day and wanted to know if we could meet up on Friday and attempt to make a go of things. I accepted and said I would be happy to meet up.

I've been enjoying a bunch of new Ace Records reissues at work. I spent most of the morning filtering through the five or so discs at full volume.

I had another text from Zofia. It read:

"Still no result from doctor. Hopefully tomorrow."

As work was quiet, I ended up making a list of baby names. Here's what I have so far:

Iggy, John, Paul, George, Ringo, Donovan, Pete, Roger, Ray, Dave, Dylan, Neil, Mick, Keith, Leonard and Prince. That's about all I've got for boys' names.

Ronnie, Dusty, Carole, Donna, Tina, Nina, Jonie and Billie. The girls' names are tough.

I hope Zofia will be happy with at least one of the above.

Suzanne (Wednesday, July 15th)

Dear Diary,

Stu has accepted my invitation to meet up on Friday. Although I couldn't quite gauge where he was at. All he said in the text was, "Yeah, sounds good."

It feels good to be back at work. When I arrived at the salon, I sat the girls down and came clean about the pregnancy situation. I will admit, it wasn't the easiest thing I've done and while there were a few laughs and many 'Oh, Sue…' comments, ultimately, the girls didn't take the piss. In fact, they were great and weren't in any way shy about consoling me and making sure I was OK.

Regardless of what happens with Stu and me as we go forward, I have decided to give him and the girl he got pregnant the baby clothes. I think Dad would be proud of me for not being stubborn about the situation and doing what is best. God, I wish he was here to hug me. He always had the best advice, especially when I needed it.

Dad, I miss you every day and love you more than you will ever know. RIP.

Stuart (Thursday, July 16th)

I met with Maggie during lunch. Her first words were, 'Hey, stranger!' Unexpectedly, she was sitting with her new biker boyfriend, Jeb. He didn't bother to introduce himself or shake my hand for that matter and instead excused himself to the bathroom as I took a seat. 'Things are moving fast then?' I asked. 'Stu, I haven't seen you in about three weeks. We're moving along nicely. I wouldn't say fast.' Maggie got up and walked to the counter to order a coffee. In the meantime, Jeb had returned and taken his seat. He pulled the paper he had been reading up over his face and ignored me. When Maggie returned, she rubbed Jeb's hair playfully and took a seat. He put his hand on her leg and began rubbing the inside of her thigh while continuing to read his paper. It made me jealous, I will admit. Maggie asked if I was excited about the results of the paternity test. I told her the sooner we know the better and that all of this waiting around was driving me crazy. It was a politician-style answer that avoided Maggie's question, but it worked.

Maggie claimed Zofia had been moping about the house for the past couple of days but changed her tune once she found out Sue wasn't pregnant. I was shocked that Zofia had told her and I made it clear. I told Maggie that I wanted to take this time to give her the full story. Maggie admitted it wasn't her fault that she knew and said, 'Of course Zofia was going to tell me. She's been living with me for the past few days. Zofia needed someone to talk to and who better to talk to than your flesh and blood?' Maggie was right, of course. Regardless, Maggie made me recall the entire story of Sue and her false pregnancy. She wasn't shy about laughing out loud either and muttered, 'That Jezebel...'

several times as I relayed the story. Each time Maggie laughed Jeb would laugh with her. What the fuck? He doesn't even know Sue, and his laughing made her sound like a complete moron. My blood was boiling at this stage.

As I sat staring a hole through Jeb's newspaper, Maggie got serious and informed me that Zofia has been coming out with some very random stuff as of late. Maggie reckons Zofia is on some sort of medication for anxiety… or something of that nature! Zofia had asked Maggie, 'Would you prefer expensive car with shit engine or shit car with expensive engine?' Maggie said that some of Zofia's ramblings have been very child-like and when she speaks to her, she can identify regressive behaviour. I told Maggie that Zofia has a lot on her plate at the moment. First, she found out she was pregnant. Then she realised I, her one-night stand, could be the father. If that wasn't bad enough, Zofia second-guessed herself and asked me to take a paternity test – which of course could only mean one thing, I might not be the father. To add fuel to the fire, I tell Zofia that I am expecting a baby with Sue. Then, several days before we take the paternity test, I turn around and tell Zofia that Sue was never pregnant. Maggie agreed that it was a lot to digest and said she'd monitor Zofia's behaviour during this delicate time. When it was time to leave Maggie assured me it was great to catch up. Jeb, on the other hand, coughed up a gobbet of phlegm and spat it out right in front of me. What a disgusting pig. I don't know what Maggie sees in him.

6:03 pm

Text from Zofia:

"Fuck the doctor!! Slow as the snail."

I guess that means no result just yet.

Suzanne (Thursday, July 16th)

Dear Diary,

I'd be lost without my girls, really, I would. When I got back to the salon after lunch, they had left a bunch of flowers, a sorry card and a gift bag full of shampoo and body lotions.

The card read:

"To Sue, our favourite boss. We were gutted to hear that you will not be having a baby this time. We told you many times just how great a mother you will be, and we look forward to the day when that statement becomes a reality. Now, get back to work with Stu and make some real fucking babies!! Love you, hun, Siobhan, Fi & Nicole xxx"

If that didn't make me shed a tear, the girls closed the salon early so they could make me, 'even more beautiful' for my meet-up with Stu tomorrow. I do look pretty fantastic even if I do say so myself. I just hope all this effort is worth it.

Stuart (Friday, July 17th)

12:42 am

In the words of Sir Billy Corgan (officially ordained by me at a house party back in the day) -

'Today is the greatest day I've ever known.'

I am not the father of Zofia's baby!!! I repeat, I, Stuart James Jackson am NOT that father of Zofia's baby!! I'm in the bathroom of The Barge with Sue, after downing many, many pints. Hopefully, this recording comes out clear as I'm not used to making diary entries with the record button. If it does, I want this to be archived in the Jackson family history book as a historic moment for every Jackson walking God's green earth.

3:17 am

Settling for a voice record again. Too lazy to type. What a glorious day! I'm pissed drunk now, but I can't stress how relieved I am. I'm here in Sue's bed, feeling like the luckiest man alive. Never, will I take things for granted again.

I found out the result of the paternity test on my lunch. I had been sitting in the canteen when Trish called me to say that Zofia was downstairs. When I got down to the ground floor, both Maggie and Zofia were standing by the counter. I could see Zofia looked upset. I thought, 'Oh shit, here we go again.' I walked over to the counter, collected my thoughts and asked, 'Everything OK?' Zofia replied, 'I got result, you are free. You are not father of my baby. I am very sorry to put you through all the pain. I hope you can forgive me.' I froze. I didn't know what to say. 'It's OK, please don't feel sad. You will be better on your own. You don't need to put up with the shit from me,' said Zofia. I was gathering my thoughts but managed to muster a reply, 'Thank you for telling me in person. I do hope you are OK and if you need anything, please don't hesitate to ask. I might not be the father, but I do have a heart... somewhere.' Both Maggie and Zofia broke their icy stance and laughed. I know the, 'If you need anything...' line is one of those things you say when a friend gets dumped or when you need to console someone mourning a death, but it was better than nothing. Then curiosity got the better of me. I was curious to know if I wasn't the father, who was? Did Zofia know? Just as I was about to ask, Zofia said, 'OK, I waste enough of your time. It was nice to meet you and thank you for the patience.' Zofia hugged me and then began ushering Maggie out of the store. I could tell Maggie felt awkward as she turned and whispered, 'Will catch ya Monday,' before Zofia yanked her arm and pulled her out the door.

When the sisters left, I ran back up to the canteen and shouted the loudest, 'FUCKING, YES!!!!' I've ever shouted in my life. From there I walked straight to the stockroom to grab an overstock copy of Kool & The Gang's - *Best Of* to 'celebrate good times'. I sat on my own with a shit-eating grin downing a bottle of Champagne Trish and I won in some random Stores of the Street raffle a few years back. After downing two glasses of Champagne, I called Trish downstairs and told her to close up shop and join me in my celebration. Trish asked me if I had won the lotto? I replied, 'No, but I did avoid two pregnancies in one week, so that's close enough.' Trish claimed she had a few bits to do and said she would join me for one (she didn't) before going home. I wasn't too fussed about Trish doing a runner as I had plans to meet Sue for dinner at 7 pm.

By the time I got to the restaurant, I had downed the entire bottle of Champagne and had a sneaky one-skin joint. When I arrived, Sue was standing outside looking radiant. Her hair was styled differently, too. Instead of her usual middle parting, she was now sporting a rather 60s looking fringe with heavy bangs, a vintage-looking orange dress with flowers and some knee-length black boots. She looked like Brigitte

Bardot. As I walked towards her, I could hear my heart beating. I was falling in love all over again. I could hear the music in my head, it was Dusty Springfield's 'I Only Want to Be with You,' the 3rd greatest pop song ever written and an apt choice from my internal jukebox. When I reached Sue, we embraced each other with a hug. I said, 'You look amazing!!' Sue blushed and replied, 'Thanks, how many have you had?' She doesn't miss a beat that girl. I replied, 'I had one, just to wet the whistle.' I didn't mention it was one bottle of Champagne as opposed to one beer as she might have assumed. My answer tied her over. 'Let's go in, I'm bloody starving,' said Sue as she led me down the stairs and into the restaurant.

With our orders placed and our glasses full of wine, I didn't waste any time updating Sue on the results of the paternity test. I began, 'Good news! I am not the father of Zofia's baby.' Sue looked me dead in the eyes as her face lit up. 'No fucking way!!' she said. 'Yes, fucking way!!' I replied. Sue jumped to her feet, reached over the table and nearly made me retch she hugged me so hard. Sue sat back down, swamped the glass of wine in one go and said, 'Oh my God, I thought I was going to lose you to her forever. I can't believe it. I'm over the moon!!' I don't think I've ever seen Sue so happy. 'So, what happened?' she asked. I told her the whole thing was one big anti-climax that had me smothered in fear for many weeks. I knew I was getting emotional when speaking about all of this as the bottle of champagne had me wankered. Not only that, but I could tell Sue was reacting to my emotions by getting emotional herself. 'Here, don't cry,' I said as I handed Sue some tissues to dry her eyes. She asked me if I was sad? I didn't even stop to think about it and replied, 'I'm a little tipsy and I'm a little emotional, but more importantly, I'm the happiest man in the world and I will do anything to make sure you are the happiest woman in the world.' 'Aww, that's the sweetest thing that anybody has ever said to me,' said Sue before continuing, 'I'm sorry honey, but I gotta call Mum and tell her the good news. Will be back in five.'

After dinner, Sue and I floated from the restaurant to the place where I first laid my eyes on her, The Barge. We danced, we laughed, we fell over each other, we fell over others, I got sick in the taxi home and Sue passed out on the kitchen table while eating a curry chip.

Sue and I may not be swimming in money, and we may not have many plans for the future, but right now, living in this moment is the happiest I've ever been. And who knows? Maybe we'll have a baby someday. But for now, at least, it's us against the world and I wouldn't want it any other way.

Suzanne (Friday, July 17th)

Dear Diary,

I can't believe it! Stu is not the father of his friend's sister's baby!!! The paternity results confirmed this earlier today. I just called Mum to tell her the news; even though she didn't seem phased in any way. I have to keep this short and sweet as I'm in The French Cafe having dinner with Stu. Diary, I still can't believe it. I'm over the moon!!! Wait until I tell the girls... lol.

4:05 am

Diary, I've spent the past 20 minutes puking my guts up. Thankfully I'm off tomorrow so I can suffer in the comfort of my own home. My head is pounding, but I wouldn't change tonight for anybody. Tonight, there was a connection between Stu and I that I've never felt before. I'd go as far as to say a connection that I've never felt with anybody. It was love, it was energy, it was genuine, it was understanding and for the duration of the night, it was unspoken. I could feel it! I could tell Stu felt it, too. We were back to our old selves, the two brazen school kids tearing up the town when they should know better. Who knows how it will all pan out? I reckon we can forget about birth, pregnancies and minding little ones for a bit. I'm just happy that we can start afresh and make a go of things. Sorry, Diary, I need to vomit again…

Stuart (Saturday, July 18th)

No entry

Suzanne (Saturday, July 18th)

8:22 am

Dear Diary,

Arrggghhhh. It's official! I'm a mother… to 10 kittens, nonetheless. My poor Snuggleflakes gave birth about an hour ago!!!

There I was, dreaming of holidaying on the Beckhams' private Island when suddenly I was overwhelmed by this incessant screeching. Being half awake and half asleep while also being well over the alcohol limit must wreak havoc with your dreams… or so one might think. The truth was, the screeching noise wasn't coming from my dream it was coming from my kitchen. It was my poor Snuggleflakes and she was giving birth!! I had no idea how to handle this, so I woke Stu from his slumber. Unfortunately, Stu didn't know what to do either, so we both sat at the table as Stu did his best drunken Blue Planet commentary over the proceedings. When the last kitten popped, I attempted to pick it up to wipe it down only for Mrs Snuggles to hiss and attempt to claw me for doing so.

10:30 pm

Good God, Diary! It's like an animal hospital here. Mum, Mr Rocket and Stu are all on the ground rolling about with the cats as I sit here typing today's entry. We have named all the cats bar two. The first cat is the strangest of the pack and makes a weird meowing sound that kind of resembles a hyena. The other one is the heftiest of the litter and has an actual cat's lick. Stu suggested that each of us (himself, Mum, Mr Rocket and I) should name two cats each and we could play paper, rock, scissors to decide who gets to name the last two. For now, at least, I've insisted all of the cats are regarded as gender-neutral. Nobody batted an eyelid. These were the names we settled on -

Mr Rocket - Romeo, Juliet

Mum - Ken (after her beloved Ken Barlow) and Barbie (blame Mr Rocket for starting a couples trend).

Stu - Ray, Dave (I thought these were dreadful names for a cat, but Stu insisted on paying tribute to some band... The Klinks or The Cooks, or some name like that...)

Me - Adele and Zane (the cat with the streak through her hair looks like a streak of misery and seems rather sad so I named her Adele. Zane is a tribute to my secret crush, Zane from One Direction... Diary, you didn't hear that from me.

So, with two cats left to name, we took Stu's advice and played paper, rock, scissors to see who would name the remaining cats. Stu said the winner would have the first choice and the runner-up could name the remaining cat. We all agreed that sounded fair.

First up, it was Mum vs. Stu. Mum won with her rock over Stu's scissors. Next up, Mr Rocket and I. Sadly, Mr Rocket beat me scissors over the paper. Finally, it was Mum vs. Mr Rocket, with the winner having the first choice over the remaining cats. After a few mistimed attempts, Mum overcame the odds to beat Mr Rocket with rock over scissors.

Mum was thrilled, 'Haha, in your face!!' Mum began dancing around the kitchen with joy. She said, 'Right, we have eight out of ten cats named, so I'm gonna call this little fella Jimmy because he sounds like that fool on TV.' We assumed Mum was talking about Jimmy Carr but didn't ask. Mr Rocket named the fat cat Elvis and said, 'Well, Elvis was the coolest cat around, so this little fella gets to pay tribute to The King.' Mr Rocket attempted to pat Elvis on the head, but Mrs Snuggles nearly took Mr Rocket's hand off with her claws. Stu then suggested we should try and keep the litter warm with the unused baby clothes we had been gifted over the past few weeks. Thankfully, everyone pretended like they didn't hear Stu's suggestion and continued petting the cats and calling them by the wrong name.

Stuart (Sunday, July 19th)

Sue's crazy cat gave birth to 10 kittens this morning. At least the cat and I have something in common; the cat with her proverbial nine lives and me with my ability to dodge bullet after bullet. I think I'll keep the head down for a bit, I don't want to end up clawing myself out of another catatonic state. After all, dealing with two pussies over the last bit nearly killed me, now I've got almost a dozen pussies to deal with – Sue has asked me to move into hers.

www.ingramcontent.com/pod-product-compliance
Lightning Source LLC
Chambersburg PA
CBHW060129130626
46556CB00006B/2285